ACCLAIM FOR CATE HOLAHAN

HER THREE LIVES

"The stuff of which blockbuster movies are made."
—*Midwest Book Review*

"Starts with a bang and never lets up. If you think you've got this one figured out—think again."
—Liv Constantine, international bestselling author of *The Last Mrs. Parrish*

"Slick and twisty. A high-tech spin on the domestic thriller that's packed with secrets, lies, and suspicion."
—Riley Sager, *New York Times* bestselling author of *Home Before Dark*

ONE LITTLE SECRET

"A psychological thriller that will keep you up all night . . . Get ready."
—*Good Morning America*

"Well-drawn characters . . . [an] absorbing page-turner."
—*Booklist*

"A great beach read for those with a penchant for scandalous secrets and gossipy suspenseful mysteries."

—Library Journal

LIES SHE TOLD

"A suffocating double nightmare."

—Kirkus (starred review)

"Recommended for anyone who enjoys Paula Hawkins or Gillian Flynn, primarily because it's better."

—Library Journal

"Engrossing...Holahan keeps the suspense high...until the surprising denouement." *—Publishers Weekly*

THE WIDOWER'S WIFE

"One of those rare thrillers that really will keep you reading all night, especially if you pack it to take on your next Caribbean cruise." *—Kirkus* (starred review)

"In this chilling cat-and-mouse tale...Holahan keeps the action going." *—Publishers Weekly*

"Ingenious and engrossing. *The Widower's Wife* is a twisting, *Gone Girl*–esque thriller full of lies and secrets that kept me

delightfully off balance right to the end. Cate Holahan is a star on the rise." —Brad Parks, award-winning author
of *Unthinkable*

DARK TURNS

"*Dark Turns* provides a master class in murder."
—Jan Coffey, *USA Today* bestselling author of *Trust Me Once*

"[*Dark Turns*] has a dark, sinister atmosphere that will suck you in completely, and you won't be sure who you can trust as the story races through twists and turns." —BookRiot

"Holahan's debut will appeal to fans of precocious teen conspiracies like Sara Shepard's Pretty Little Liars series, as well as to fans of grown-up, plucky-heroine-must-fight-for-herself thrillers." —*Booklist*

ALSO BY CATE HOLAHAN

Her Three Lives

THE DARKNESS OF OTHERS

CATE HOLAHAN

GRAND CENTRAL
PUBLISHING

NEW YORK   BOSTON

Copyright © 2022 by Cate Holahan
Cover design by Adrienne Krogh. Cover image by Getty Images. Cover copyright © 2022 by Hachette Book Group, Inc.

Grand Central Publishing
Hachette Book Group
1290 Avenue of the Americas, New York, NY 10104
grandcentralpublishing.com
twitter.com/grandcentralpub

First Edition: August 2022

Grand Central Publishing is a division of Hachette Book Group, Inc. The Grand Central Publishing name and logo is a trademark of Hachette Book Group, Inc.

The publisher is not responsible for websites (or their content) that are not owned by the publisher.

The Hachette Speakers Bureau provides a wide range of authors for speaking events. To find out more, go to www.hachettespeakersbureau.com or call (866) 376-6591.

Library of Congress Cataloging-in-Publication Data

Names: Holahan, Cate, author.
Title: The darkness of others / Cate Holahan.
Description: First Edition. | New York : Grand Central Publishing, 2022. | Summary: "Psychiatrist Imani Banks and her restaurateur husband Philip are living the New York City dream. They own a posh townhouse in Brooklyn Heights, their two children are standouts at their private school, and they are well-liked in their affluent community. Tonya Sayre is living the NYC nightmare. After moving to Manhattan with dreams of becoming a Broadway star, she has found herself stuck in a waitressing job and struggling to support her teenage daughter, Layla. She also fears Layla's father, Rick, who is back in their life. When Philip's restaurant closes due to the lockdown, they decide to take on a renter and let the extra rooms to Tonya and Layla. As Tonya begins skipping payments, the tension with Imani grows. She becomes convinced that Tonya is a professional grifter who preys upon the sympathies of men to live rent free. She even thinks Tonya might have been involved in the shocking murders of the Walkers, a neighboring family. But evicting someone during a pandemic is no easy feat. Imani soon finds herself stuck with a woman whom she believes to be a killer" — Provided by publisher.
Identifiers: LCCN 2021053702 | ISBN 9781538709184 (trade paperback) | ISBN 9781538709191 (ebook)
Subjects: GSAFD: Suspense fiction.
Classification: LCC PS3608.O482864 D38 2022 | DDC 813/.6--dc23
LC record available at https://lccn.loc.gov/2021053702

ISBNs: 9781538709184 (trade pbk.), 9781538709191 (ebook)

Printed in the United States of America

LSC-C

Printing 1, 2022

For Madaline Holahan and Gloria Fidee
Thank you for the Love, Support,
and Enduring Example

"Knowing your own darkness is the best mehod for dealing with the darknesses of other people."

—Carl Jung, psychiatrist and founder of analytical psychology, letter to Kendig B. Cully, September 25, 1937

THE
DARKNESS
OF OTHERS

PART ONE

CHAPTER ONE

OKSANA

The Walkers were hiding. Oksana tried not to take it personally as she hauled her vacuum down a narrow staircase to their finished basement. Clients liked to pretend she was invisible. They avoided eye contact with the jowly blonde whom no one would believe was only forty if they'd asked, treating her like a product that disappeared toilet rings and eliminated carpet stains rather than a person who scrubbed and wiped and hauled, who'd escaped a military invasion and mortar shells to start her own American business. Life's unfairness was less embarrassing that way, she figured.

Celebrities were frequently the worst, often refusing to remain in the same room once she appeared. But the Walkers had always been different, acknowledging her biweekly presence with warm smiles and casual inquiries about her health and family. Oksana knew that they didn't expect her to answer too honestly or at any length. Even so, the effort at polite conversation had been something, providing tidbits with which to regale starstruck friends or, once or twice, sell to gossip rags. *Melissa Walker Bathes Skin in Snail Mucus. Nate Walker's New Gig: Stay-at-Home Dad.*

Oksana stepped off the wooden stair onto the white marble floor. She carted the unwieldy vacuum another several feet to a patchwork cowhide carpet, which was surprisingly easy to care for despite its undoubtedly exorbitant price tag. A single pass with the Dyson typically did the trick, as long as there weren't any real stains.

The vacuum's various attachments clattered as she set it down. Oksana unwound the cord and began dragging it toward the socket tucked beneath the open staircase, wondering which floor the family was holing up on. It was the pandemic making everyone extra cautious, she told herself. If the Walkers had suspected her of leaking that headline about Mr. Walker's lack of employment, they would have fired her already.

Then again, maybe not. The pandemic had made people desperate to retain their small circle of previously vetted people, even when it became clear those relationships weren't working out. Maybe she'd simply been grandfathered in.

Oksana crouched to the outlet. A merlot-colored mark shone on the tile in front of her. She dropped the vacuum cord and crawled toward it, pulling a wet wipe packet from her back pocket. Red wine stained everything, even seemingly hard surfaces, and the basement floor was honed, making it more porous than the shiny stone version. To prevent a permanent mark, she'd probably have needed to treat the marble yesterday.

Still, maybe there was a chance.

As she reached the stain, Oksana saw that it had company.

Red dots led a jagged path to the den. Somebody had gotten tipsy and then sloshed his or her way to the stairs, she decided. A damp tissue wouldn't clean this mess. She'd need a paper towel at a minimum. The mop most likely.

Oksana straightened, pressing one hand to the floor and the other to her bad knee. She followed the spots to the open den door, muttering about the importance of holding one's liquor. If there were spills on the carpet or, worse, vomit, she would need to rent a steam cleaner and give them a quote. And she wouldn't be able to offer any guarantees. Red wine, puke, blood, and pet piss were the four horsemen in her business. Removing such fluids from carpet or fabric furniture was nearly impossible.

As she entered the den, she immediately noticed more splashes on the suede wallpaper behind Mr. Walker's large, wooden desk. A scotch glass sat on the top with a ring of gold liquid in the bottom. She spied the bottle in a bin beside the door, trashed despite the liquor still inside. Scotch and wine. She'd cleaned up the family's dishes long enough to know that Mr. Walker rarely drank alone, especially not hard liquor. He'd been entertaining. First time since the shutdown, probably. No wonder someone had gotten sloppy drunk.

Oksana approached the wallpaper. The largest spot had hardened into a crust, less like wine and more like ketchup. She scratched at it. It didn't flake off, but particles slipped beneath her nail.

Oksana stepped back, considering the gunk on her finger. She heard the wet squish before registering the sensation beneath her shoes. The sides of her gray sneakers were coated in dark, brick-colored goo. She whirled around, looking for the source of this new stain.

On the floor, behind the desk, lay a near-headless body. Oksana couldn't immediately tell whether she was looking at the figure's front or back. The face was nearly gone. Brain, identifiable only by its whitish color amid all the red, had dribbled and dried over the places where the eyes and nose had been. The arms were splayed out as if the victim had fallen backward. A black handgun lay in his palm.

Most people would have screamed. However, most people hadn't learned to sleep through shelling and wake at the rumble of tanks rolling past their home. They hadn't grabbed blankets off beds to cover bodies or scrubbed blood from cobblestone hearths.

As there was nothing to save, calling the police could wait. Oksana reached for the garbage and then her phone. She withdrew her cell and clicked on the camera app. She stepped back until what was left of director Nate Walker fit in the frame. Then she placed her finger squarely over the screen and tapped its big red dot.

CHAPTER TWO

MELISSA

"I'll get out of here!"

Melissa shouted the words, though she knew no one was listening. It was too late. Too dead. The city that never sleeps had finally found its bedtime. COVID o'clock. Everyone was indoors, waiting for the cold weather and coronavirus to pass, venturing out only to take in packages. She'd been one of them. Cautious. Careful. Relegating friendships to phone calls, shrinking her social sphere to shared genes. Some good it had done. She'd never get sick in here. She'd die first.

"I'll get out of here." She repeated her intention, quieter this time. Saving her voice could be important. Still, she needed to hear the echo, to prove to herself that she was alive in this darkness. What surrounded her was an indescribable black, not so much color as void. There was nothing for her eyes to adjust to, no shades of gray with which to orient herself. She was trapped in a starless universe. Only the hard floor beneath her palms and feet assured her that there was an up and down, that she was still gravity-tethered to Earth, subject to the laws of space and time. And biology.

She wasn't hungry or thirsty yet, but she would be. The last thing she'd consumed was a green juice intended to "cleanse" away the quarantine fifteen. Silly, the things she'd once considered crucial. Waist size. Boob size. Butt shape. Who the hell really cared?

Hollywood, she conceded. Her husband.

She pictured Nate as she'd last seen him, roguish face shredded by the bullet's impact, brilliant brain splattered on the wall. He'd deserved it. She wondered whether the world would ever know that. Violent deaths had a tendency to turn men into martyrs. Even if the news ultimately leaked, the media might refrain from publishing it, afraid of slandering a sacred cow whose work had suddenly become "important" now that its auteur was incapable of producing more of it.

Nate didn't deserve more accolades. But, as he was too dead to enjoy them, Melissa preferred praise to the alternative. Better for their daughter to think Nate a talent taken too soon than to live under his real legacy.

She imagined Ava asleep in her bed, dreaming to the sound of soft rain. The memory morphed into others. Instead of her own life flashing before her eyes, Melissa saw her daughter as a swaddled baby, lips stretched into a smile from passed gas. She pictured her as a grinning toddler, feet racing to keep up with the forward momentum of an oversized blond head, and, later, as a hammy elementary schooler sing-shouting her heart out in the school production.

Melissa recalled her kid more recently, Ava's face melding into some version of her own, though with a fierceness and confidence that Melissa had never possessed. She pictured that beautiful visage morphing into openmouthed terror when she saw her father's body.

Melissa considered herself an atheist, but the adage was true. Nonbelievers didn't exist in foxholes—or in the dark. She prayed to the God of her childhood, unsure whether her eyes were closed or open. "Please don't let Ava go downstairs," she whispered. "Please let someone else find him. Please let her go to school without seeing."

Beyond that, Melissa didn't know what to ask for. A doorway? Light? It didn't seem possible that God could grant such requests. If he could, then why was she in here? What punishment was she serving, and for which crime?

Would those sins be visited upon her child?

Imani would pick Ava up, Melissa realized. In her mind, she could see her friend striding into St. Catherine's, gathering Ava in her arms, pretending to have it all together. Imani had been getting better at that. Pretending.

She'd taught Imani to play a part too well. What role would she take with her daughter?

CHAPTER THREE

IMANI

They were already arguing. From her curled position on the couch, Imani could hear her two o'clock warming up for their weekly verbal wrestling match. The strip of drywall separating her office from the hallway couldn't muffle the condescension in the husband's tone or the hysterical notes in the wife's as each attempted to force the other into apologetic submission.

"But you don't know," the woman snapped. "Why do you always assume to *know* everything?"

"It's a logical conclusion that any thinking person would come to," the man responded.

Imani pulled up the surgical mask cupping her chin. She hated how face coverings complicated reading patients' expressions. However, she appreciated that the fabric would cover her own downturned lips.

Had it not been for the pandemic, she might not have accepted Mr. and Mrs. Halstead's business. The couple didn't want to fix their marriage. Not really. They wanted to rage about who hadn't done the dishes or helped with homework until they could agree that they'd tried but simply weren't happy. She was the witness to their failed attempt, the person whom they'd point to later as evidence of their efforts and say, hey, we paid thousands to save our relationship, but it wasn't salvageable.

Imani couldn't turn down thousands at the moment.

"I *think* she had nothing to do with it," Mrs. Halstead shouted outside the door.

Imani tugged the hem of her sweater so that it rested a little lower over her backside. She'd caught Mr. Halstead checking out her rear during their last session and didn't want to tempt him into doing it again.

"Guilty people run off," the husband countered. "People with nothing to hide stay and—"

The door's creak cut him off. Mr. Halstead was dressed for work in a well-tailored wool coat, suit pants, and KN95, which was a stark contrast to his wife's snakeskin-patterned leggings, blinding white ski jacket, and floral face covering. Imani silently wished that the woman had dressed more business casual. Mr. Halstead was already dismissive of his spouse's financial contributions. Looking like the whole day could be spent on a yoga mat wouldn't help the woman's argument that her work was of equal importance.

Imani sat on the edge of her Eames lounge chair, positioned kitty-corner to the long couch at a nonconfrontational angle that still made clear she was part of the conversation. As she waited for the couple to sit down, she remembered looking up at the cement sky earlier that morning. Gray was the most prominent color in New York City between December and March. There was nothing particularly depressing about that fact. It was just the way the year started, a blank slate, which was what Imani needed her face to be.

Years earlier, her best friend had taught her the trick to controlling her micro-expressions. "You're an open book," Melissa had said, too many glasses of pinot grigio rendering her assessments brutal. "When you anticipate something bad, your brow scrunches and your nose flares like you've caught a whiff of day-old diaper. You need to keep a neutral face. There was this one film financier who had a reputation as being a misogynistic bully. Before he came in to talk to me, I pictured a wall so that my affect would be completely flat."

"And was he as awful as everyone said?" Imani had asked.

"Worse," Melissa had quipped. "By the end of our conversation, I was imagining that bastard buried in that wall."

A smile crept behind Imani's mask at the memory. "So, how are you both this week?" she asked the couple.

"Fine," the husband said. "Things are picking up at work, so that's a bit stressful."

"And I'm juggling clients and the kids." The wife glared at him.

"You both have demanding careers and a lot on your plates, which makes it difficult to carve out space for one another. How has that—"

A buzz from Imani's pocket interrupted her. She reached inside and, without looking, sent the call to voice mail. "Were you two able to have any focused time together this week?"

"I tried the other night," the husband said. "I brought up drinks to the bedroom."

"You brought scotch for yourself."

"I brought the bottle. You could have had one."

"I don't drink liquor before bed."

Imani cleared her throat and directed her attention to the husband. "So, you wanted to initiate some intimacy and feel your signals didn't register with—"

"Oh, you knew what I wanted. You were just busy reading."

"I offered to watch something."

"You only like that true crime stuff where everyone kills their spouses."

"That's not true."

"She's obsessed. Even during the cab ride over here she was talking about a murder that's on the news."

It took a beat for Imani to realize that the husband was now addressing her rather than volleying another barbed comment at his wife. "Well, we all have interests," she said. "Our partners don't need to share every one of them. Perhaps if true crime doesn't appeal to both of you, you two could—"

"I thought you'd be into it." The wife was back in the game. "You were all googly-eyed for that actress when we met. You saw all her movies."

"That doesn't mean I want to know all the gory details of how she killed her husband." The guy pointed at Imani. A smile glinted in his eyes. "Put it on record, my wife has a penchant for mariticide. If I end up with a bullet in the brain, and there's some suspicious note..."

Imani knew her patient didn't fear his wife. He was trying to curry favor by flirting while diminishing his partner's interests. Imani shifted her knees so that they pointed in

Mrs. Halstead's direction. "True crime is very popular right now. What are some topics that you believe would interest both of you?"

A beep emitted from Imani's pocket, signaling a new voice mail. She wondered if Melissa had called. The prior night, her friend had texted and, surprisingly, asked to meet up— ASAP. Imani hadn't yet replied because she still couldn't fathom where they would go. A polar vortex had slammed the brakes on outdoor socializing, and Melissa had previously made clear that she was too nervous to see anyone indoors—especially not possible vectors like Imani, who still saw in-person patients and was married to a man who spent six days a week in a restaurant kitchen. Melissa hadn't worked since Broadway's close, and Nate's latest project had been on hold for two years. Imani wasn't sure if the Walkers had left their house since October.

"Finance!" Mrs. Halstead threw up a hand. "Money and the markets are the only things that interest him anymore. He finds stock more compelling than a famous director being shot dead in his twelve-million-dollar brownstone."

Imani realized that the wife was doing the same thing as her husband, trying to win over the therapist by painting her spouse as myopic. If Imani had been at a bar and not mid-session, she might have asked about the case. It wasn't every day that a wealthy celebrity was murdered. But she couldn't let the wife score a point for the same competitive behavior that she'd pointedly ignored from the woman's spouse.

"Let's think about subjects that interest both of you." She clapped, trying to focus them on the task at hand. "When you first got married, what were some of the things that you talked about?"

A buzz from her cell interrupted the silence that followed. Imani hesitated but ultimately reached into her pocket. The restaurant was filled with sharp knives and dangerous machinery, and Philip had been doing more of the food preparation since laying off 15 percent of his staff. Whoever had left a message could be alerting her to an emergency.

"Excuse me one moment." Imani withdrew her phone. The school's number shone on screen.

Imani pictured her kids quarantined in the school's gymnasium. A rash of psychosomatic symptoms followed. Sore throat. Shortness of breath. "I'm sorry," she said, forcing the words through her empathy-inflamed larynx. "I have to take this. It's my children's school."

Her office was only the one room. Two hundred square feet packed with a couch, a chair, two bookcases, and a secretary desk. It was no place to take a private call. She turned her head toward the wall as the husband muttered something about cost per minute. "Hello. Imani Banks."

"Hello, Mrs. Banks, this is the office at St. Catherine's. We need you to come right away."

Imani fought the urge to cough. "What's wrong? Are my kids all right?"

"Yes. Your children are fine. We need you to pick up Ava."

Ava was not her daughter's name. Her kids were Vivienne and Jay. Had the school made a mistake? "Do you mean Melissa and Nate Walker's daughter?"

"You're listed as one of Miss Walker's emergency contacts."

"Is Ava okay?"

"Yes. But it would be best if you picked her up."

She's caught it, Imani thought. What other reason could the school have for wanting Ava immediately removed from its premises?

Imani unconsciously touched her neck. As an athletic fifteen-year-old, Ava would probably be fine. But Imani was forty-two. She maintained a healthy body weight, which was in her favor, but she also suffered from mild asthma and, since the pandemic's start, enjoyed a nightly glass or two of red wine. Statistically, she was far more likely than Ava to get very sick. And if she fell ill, who would take care of her own kids?

"Have you tried Melissa's cell? She's usually home at this hour."

A sharp intake of air answered. Silence followed, as if the person on the other end had muted herself. Imani waited a beat before saying, "Hello?"

"Mrs. Banks, Ava's parents are unavailable. It's truly imperative that you come and collect her. This isn't about COVID."

Imani wanted to ask what it could be about. But something about the tone of the woman's voice, an undercurrent of panic that pushed her words together, drowned out additional questions. Imani promised to be right there, hung up, and then returned her attention to her patients. "I am terribly sorry to do this, but I need to reschedule. There's been an emergency."

The husband nodded as if he understood but then flashed a hard look at his wife. Imani sensed that he hadn't wanted to attend their session. Her abrupt departure would become ammunition in a later argument to cease therapy altogether.

"I will, of course, comp today and the next visit. We can even do this virtually, if that would be easier." Imani grabbed her coat off a hook and then opened the door wide. "I am terribly sorry."

The wife's eyes crinkled with sympathy as she rose from the couch. "Kids come first."

"Thank you for understanding."

As Mrs. Halstead gathered her jacket, her husband strode to the door. Imani realized that he'd never removed his coat. Perhaps he hadn't planned on ever getting comfortable. He exited with a gruff "good luck" and continued down the hallway, not waiting for his spouse.

Beneath her mask, Imani's frown deepened. She felt terrible for the conversation that her female patient would soon face about the "pointlessness of therapy." She felt even worse that, in this particular case, the husband was probably right.

"I'm sorry to have overheard." Mrs. Halstead's brow was tightly knitted above her mask. "But did you mention Nate Walker?"

Imani's stomach tightened. She tried not to share any personal information in her sessions. Therapists all had stories of clients romanticizing the shrink listening to all their problems. She struggled to recover her gray-sky expression. "I should probably go," she said.

Mrs. Halstead leaned forward, shortening the not-quite-six-feet of space between them. "I only ask because he's the director who was found dead this afternoon, and his wife is still missing."

CHAPTER FOUR

TONYA

Abrupt temperature changes made people sick. Where did that knowledge nugget come from? Her mother, Tonya was sure. All mothers said it. She'd repeated it herself that morning when nagging Layla to don an extra layer beneath her coat. But had she been parroting an old wives' tale like viruses were caught from chilly weather, or did the immune system actually struggle to adapt from hot to cold?

Tonya prayed she'd been spouting nonsense as she emerged from the restaurant's equatorial kitchen into the barren tundra of the dining room before heading to the outdoor dining "igloos" with only an apron over her uniform. Her shivers vibrated the platter balanced atop her right palm, forcing her to steady it with her left hand like a newbie. She was still trembling as she reached the clear plastic wall shielding her guests from the wind.

"How are we this afternoon?"

Muted grunts answered her question. The diners wore sheepskin parkas with thick, fur-trimmed hoods covering their heads, as if they'd agreed on Inuit costumes for a themed dining experience. Such heavy clothing wouldn't have been required in a real igloo, according to Layla. Her bookish kid had brought up an article the other day explaining that traditional ice houses used snow as an insulator, enabling body heat alone to toast their insides to an eminently tolerable fifty degrees.

City health regulations prevented the restaurant's bubble tents from building up such warmth. Two sides had to be vented at all times to allow microbe-dispersing air circulation. Even with space heaters operating full blast, diners were lucky if the "indoor" temperature remained above freezing. Tonya certainly couldn't detect any difference as she began placing plates in front of her four patrons.

The four patrons, she realized. Summer's uptick had almost convinced her that New York City's hospitality industry had survived the harsh spring and emerged on the other side. But the months from June to November had been the eye of the storm. Winter had barreled in like a nor'easter, dumping on new challenges that even the novelty of dining street-side in clear domes, yurt villages, or tiny greenhouses couldn't counteract. People were scared. They were cold. They'd become resigned to hibernation.

As Tonya set down the meals, she watched the diners' faces for reactions. Some of the brave souls who ventured out demanded the full restaurant experience complete with their server's mask-muffled explanation of the spice rub coating the steak. Others wanted her to leave as soon as the last dish touched the table.

Judging from her patrons' averted eyes, Tonya decided

that this group belonged to the latter category. She thanked them for braving the weather and then backed out into it, hoping they could detect her smile from the corners of her exposed eyes. Her best chance at earning a decent tip was this table. No line waited to be seated in the empty huts.

"Miss." One of the female diners called out from an opening in the plastic. "Could we get four hot toddies and two slices of chocolate cake to share?"

They were already ordering dessert so as to not wait an extra second in the cold. That meant they wouldn't want another bottle of wine, which meant her tip wouldn't reflect the usual alcohol bonus of two bottles to four guests. Tonya felt her smile fade as she responded with a bright "of course" before retreating into the restaurant.

Banque Gauche's dining room was more pleasant than its igloos, though far too opulent to feel cozy. That was by design, Tonya figured. The vast space had catered to business clientele during the day and the theater crowd at night. It had made money by churning out Michelin-starred small plates and turning over tables, not encouraging diners to loiter.

In its prime, the restaurant had operated with the efficiency of the bank it had once been, the essence of which remained in the decor. Glass fireplaces stretched inside sleek marble walls that had once borne the logo of a savings and loan. Velvet curtains flanked massive arched windows. The space's designers had even preserved the long mahogany bank teller's desk, transforming it via gold inlays into a bar worthy of Versailles. They'd repurposed the security grates as hip room dividers separating the kitchen from the dining area.

All those details still shone, advertising the money that

Banque Gauche had once minted and the million-dollar refresh that the space had undergone three years earlier. The
only visual cues that the restaurant had fallen on hard times
were the lack of fresh linens atop wooden tables and the
metal wall at the room's far end.

Ten months earlier, a massive circular hole had punctured
the riveted steel expanse, revealing the opening to Coffre,
a swanky supper club located in the bank's former vault. It
had opened in November 2019 with a long, lacquered bar,
glass shelves stocked with glittering, golden whiskeys, and
a menu serving up gourmet bistro fare long after most NYC
kitchens closed. The "new hotness," as it had been dubbed
by none other than *New York* magazine, was among the
pandemic's first casualties. The tight space lacked windows,
preventing business from resuming even after indoor dining
had temporarily reopened in the fall. The vault had closed
at the end of March, just four months after its launch. It had
stayed shut.

As Tonya approached the kitchen, she got a strong
whiff of fish, a sign of less-than-fresh catch. More pungent
aromas presented themselves as she drew closer to the
refurbished security grates: black pepper, cumin, frying oil,
tomato sauce. Such smells were new. A small army had
once made sure that the odors of the various ingredients
never escaped the kitchen.

She shouted through the metal grates. "Two slice chocolate cake."

Samuel, the garde-manger in charge of the pantry and
cold first courses, made eye contact and dropped his chin.
He'd added the dessert station to his duties after the pastry

chef had been let go. The takeout orders that had become the majority of the restaurant's business tended not to include decadent sweets. It had been easier for the kitchen to cut the dessert menu to three inexpensive options prepared by the neighboring patisserie.

Order conveyed, Tonya jogged over to the bar and the handsome man behind it. Mike looked like the movie star that he one day hoped to become with a diamond jaw, piercing eyes, and a height several inches shy of six feet. Of all his features, Tonya might have appreciated Mike's size most of all. Had he been tall, his youth would have been wasted on starstruck, immature girls, shaping him into an insufferable womanizer lacking in wit or real talent. As it was, Mike had developed a charming, flirty personality, a fun sense of humor, and an ability to play piano. He might make it in the movies, Tonya thought. Topping thirty wasn't the career ender for actors that it was for actresses yet to hit the big time.

"Four hot toddies, please," she said.

"That's a sick person's drink. They're not hacking up lungs, are they?"

"Just cold, I think."

"Well, keep your distance as you deliver it."

Tonya's smile was genuine this time, though her mask still covered it. "You're always looking out."

The corners of Mike's eyes crinkled. "It's such a nice view."

Tonya injected a little swagger into her walk as she headed back to her patrons. The rule of waitressing was to check on your table within "two bites, two sips, and two minutes." If something was wrong with the food, the patrons would want to complain after a couple forkfuls. Let them stew about their unsalted potatoes or overcooked pasta too long, and they might decide to say nothing and take out their dissatisfaction on the gratuity.

"Hey, Tonya." Mike's baritone rang out over tinkling glasses. "It looks like I don't have cinnamon sticks."

"I'll ask the kitchen."

Tonya headed back to the grates. Samuel's curly hair and yellow-brown skin was nowhere to be seen. Perhaps he'd run next door for more chocolate cake slices.

Tonya scanned to see who might be manning the pantry. Chefs chopped vegetables, seasoned meat, and tossed pans over flames so high that they would trigger most sprinkler systems.

To anyone who hadn't known Banque's kitchen before the pandemic, it might appear a well-oiled machine with no missing—or spare—parts. But Tonya had worked there for over a decade. The absences stuck out like missing teeth. Where was Jason, the eyebrow-pierced saucier who had dribbled rich ragùs atop medium-rare cuts of meat? Or why was Seon-mi, the pink-haired abouyer, head down at the grill and fry stations rather than shouting for dishes to ensure that each table's entrées all emerged at the same time? Why was there no culinary student from whom she could demand more cinnamon sticks?

Everyone was busy cooking save for one man in the corner—the most important one. Owner and executive chef Philip Banks paced at the end of a long cord appended to a relic of a wall phone. His free hand raked through his graying hair, spiking it with whatever fats and oils coated his long, calloused fingers. Over and over, he brushed the few remaining strands off his broad forehead, revealing the trenches that had dug in during the past year.

"Yes, it's terrible, honey. And I get you want support, but I can't..."

Tonya stepped closer to the metal slats, straining to hear what was terrible. Did Philip intend another round of layoffs?

"I'll tell you what's more important—I'm running a fucking restaurant."

Philip ran his hand through his hair again and then let it fall toward his eyes. The irises of each were blue gas flames that seemed to flare as he spoke. "Okay. I know. I'm sorry. But you know I'm understaffed."

A tongue, one that probably possessed more taste buds than the average human's, pulled in his bottom lip and then spat it back out above the mask cupping his chin. "Nate was a friend."

Philip wasn't discussing the restaurant, Tonya realized. He was talking about Nate Walker. She felt her body go rigid, as it always did at the mention of Nate's name. Images flashed in her mind. A glowing cigar cherry. Bleached teeth glinting in dim light. A gold ring tapping a glass tabletop. The same pictures always played when Tonya thought of the renowned director, celebrated family man, philanthropist, and pathological liar. She refused to picture his face.

"Of course I care that he's dead," Philip said.

A rush of endorphins shot through her stiff torso. She had the sudden, involuntary urge to laugh or maybe shout. Nate Walker. Dead.

"I'll do my best." Philip pressed his fingers into his closed eyes before running them over his head again. "Well, it will have to be. I'll see you soon."

He placed the receiver back in its cradle and then stared at it. "Cake's up."

Samuel was back. He marched over to the security grates and slid the plated orders through a deliberately widened space. Tonya blinked at them. Chocolate cake slices did not fit the scenes running through her mind.

Philip noticed her, finally. His eyes were turned to maximum heat. He knew she'd been listening.

Tonya collected the plates. "Do you have cinnamon sticks?" She directed the question to Samuel but said it loud enough for Philip to hear in an attempt to excuse her loitering. "The table asked for hot toddies, and there aren't any at the bar."

A vein pulsed above Philip's thick brows. "Hot toddies aren't on the drinks menu."

Tonya's gaze retreated to her cakes. "I think they wanted something warm."

Samuel rotated to the pantry. "We have them, I think. One minute."

Tonya kept her eyes on the desserts' mirrored chocolate glazes as Samuel slipped into the back. She didn't want Philip to see the emotion on her face. The glint in her pupils that she could almost see reflected in the dark cocoa ganache.

Though she wasn't looking at him, Tonya still felt her boss's critical stare. Chefs prided themselves on tracking everyone in the kitchen, knowing who was distracted and likely to mess up a service, who was hungover and therefore not to be trusted with the heavy machinery—who could get someone killed.

A glass bottle slid across the opening to Tonya. "Cinnamon sticks," Samuel crowed.

Tonya shoved the ingredient into her apron. Seconds later, she plopped it on the bar along with her cakes and instructions for Mike to watch them for a second. Before he could respond, she was out the front door with a tray in hand.

"How's it going?"

Her voice sounded like grass in a strong wind, too breathy to be intelligible. Still, the igloo patrons looked up. Two had nearly finished their meals. The other two, both women, had left about a third on their plates.

"Was everything to your liking?" she asked, hating the need for past tense. She'd made them wait too long.

One of the men offered a pained smile. The others were too cold to bother with politeness. "All done, and we'll take the cakes and toddies to go," the man said, gesturing to the women. "It's more frigid than we thought."

"Totally understand. No problem." Tonya began loading the tray, placing the heavier items in the center and on the side nearest her neck. She balanced it on her right hand, bracing it on her shoulder as she opened the restaurant door.

What are you willing to do?

The question resounded in her head as if Nate Walker were standing right behind her. She whirled around, ready to confront the taunting ghost. The tray wobbled atop her palm and then tilted toward the floor like an abruptly abandoned seesaw.

Tonya wrenched her body in the other direction, but it was too late. Glasses and plates smashed against the stained concrete floor. *Crash. Bang. Ping.* A contemporary classical symphony begging for an operatic *opa!*

"Shit." Philip emerged from the kitchen, muttering worse curses. The neck visible above his chef's jacket was lobster red. His face bore the expression of a fish about to be gutted.

"I'm so sorry, Chef." Tonya dropped to her knees and began placing shards on her tray, ignoring the needles stabbing through the fabric of her pants. "You can take it out of my tip."

Saying it sounded ridiculous. The worth of several wineglasses and plates would be far more than her gratuity.

"I'm sorry. I—"

Footsteps cut off her apologies. Out of the corner of her eye, Tonya saw Mike emerge from behind the bar. Juan, one of the dishwashers, was also en route.

I'll do anything.

Tonya heard herself mutter the words, though they didn't emerge from her mouth. After speaking them once, she'd promised herself never to say them again. She hadn't really meant them the first time.

Whatever you need. The memory of her words overwhelmed her murmured apologies. In the distance, someone told her to get up. Someone said that her foot was bleeding.

Anything, her phantom voice echoed. *Absolutely anything.*

CHAPTER FIVE

IMANI

The murder was so fresh that the press had yet to get creative with headlines. *Nate Walker, Acclaimed Director, Dead from Gunshot*, was the lead story on the *Times*'s website. The *Post* had allowed itself more alliteration and assumption: *Nate Walker, Moviemaker, Maybe Murdered in Mansion*. But none of the news outlets or blogs were playing with puns involving Nate's many films, some of which had been crime thrillers.

As Imani stormed down the sidewalk, she scanned articles on her cell for any mention of Melissa's last known whereabouts, trusting her fellow New Yorkers to dive out of her distracted way. As far as she could tell, the papers didn't have any info. The articles only said that police were "actively looking" for Mrs. Walker. No one in law enforcement had been quoted expressing concern for Melissa's safety.

Imani considered the implications of that as she crossed the street to St. Catherine's gleaming limestone facade. Everyone in the area knew the beaux arts building. The school was something of a beacon for bourgeoisie Brooklynites seeking a straight path for their kids from nursery school to America's top universities. She'd lobbied hard for Vivienne's and Jay's acceptance, pledging to volunteer for committees in lieu of providing donations that she couldn't afford.

Imani jogged up the steps to the iron double doors, hit the buzzer, and then faced the screen above it, identifying herself. A sharp click announced that she'd been recognized. As she entered the lobby, an unseen conversation, punctuated with laughter, bounced off the ionic columns and double-height ceilings. Its youthful pitch raised the baby hairs on Imani's neck. Children's voices didn't seem to belong in St. Catherine's operatic vestibule. Of course, that had likely been the reason for the school designing such an entrance. St. Catherine's wanted its students to grow accustomed to adult spaces so that they'd be able to hold court in them later.

The main office sprawled behind glass walls. Ava was visible through them. She sat in front of a long mahogany desk, facing someone out of view. Seeing her was to look at a youth-filtered version of her mother. The teen possessed the same wide-set eyes and, above her mask, the beginnings of the same snub nose. Her blunt-cut bob had been styled by her mom's hairdresser. Ava's age softened the photogenic angles so prominent on Melissa's face, but it would only be a matter of years before the girl's full cheeks and round chin pinched to her mother's heart shape.

Imani's vision blurred. She loved Ava as she did her own nieces and nephews, which was to say that she wanted the girl's life brimming with joy and success. But that love—real as it may be—did not make Imani family. Some messages should only be delivered by blood.

Melissa had chosen her in the event of an emergency, however. Imani took pride in that, the same way she'd always felt a kind of puffed-up satisfaction in her status as Melissa Walker's closest confidant. That pride, perhaps more than her love, enabled her to pull back the door, despite the stabbing pain in her chest. It propelled her across the room, prepared for whatever fight would be required to protect Melissa's daughter.

Imani's presence wrested Ava's attention from the adults beside her. One was a woman of fifty or so with dark hair pulled into a severe bun and a string of pearls topping a black turtleneck leading up to a thick black mask. The ensemble seemed a costume to Imani. Ruth Bader Ginsburg feminist assassin, or something. The older man beside Ava with a *Spread Kindness* mask over his mouth was Headmaster Steve Goodman.

"Is my dad okay?"

The squeaky hope in Ava's question nearly made Imani lose it. Tears bubbled behind Imani's eyes, hot bile threatening to spew forth. She forced them back, imagining a cement dam dug deep into the ground, its foundation bolted to New York City's bedrock. Ava would eventually want loved ones who could share in her grief. Right now, she needed adults to assure her of safety.

"As we explained to Ava, we haven't been able to contact her mother." Ninja Ginsburg leaned forward over her thighs, changing Imani's assessment. The body language screamed school therapist. "Not since Mr. Walker suffered his serious accident."

The last few words answered Imani's earlier questions. The school had clearly been informed but had chosen to keep the news secret from Ava. Telling her would be Imani's job.

"We've told Ava that we're here and available in any way to help her," Goodman said, rubbing his right thumb over his left. Imani had never observed the nervous tic in him before. As headmaster, Goodman was both educator and marketer, a telegenic evangelist for the school's project-heavy curriculum. Imani was accustomed to him standing behind a podium, delivering chummy speeches to auditoriums packed with the city's rich and powerful. It was disconcerting to see him hunched over, looking up from beneath thick gray brows, worrying his knuckles.

"And that she shouldn't be concerned about missing any classes," the woman added. "The most important thing is her wellness."

The last word solidified Imani's assessment of the stranger. She was definitely the school counselor.

"They took my cell." Ava stood as she spoke. Both her reedy voice and slight teenage body trembled. "I can't look up what happened. I don't understand why my mom isn't here. Is she with my dad in the hospital? Is she home?"

Ava gestured to the school therapist. "She keeps saying that she doesn't know anything. But there must be something online or else they'd let me have my phone back. Just tell me. Why won't anyone tell me anything?"

Imani remembered asking something similar at Ava's

age. When Imani was in high school, her mom had been diagnosed with metastatic colon cancer. Unfortunately, both her parents had kept that news from her until nearly the end, each blaming any bouts of weakness on sleeping difficulties. The misguided effort to preserve her childhood had unintentionally eradicated most of the joy from her teenage memories. Imani couldn't think back on some high school party where she'd kissed a crush or a sleepover with her best friends without viewing it as time squandered on people who would never matter as much as her dying mom. Lies, even well-meaning ones, were so rarely a kindness.

"Sweetheart." She grasped Ava's hands, holding them between both of her own. The girl reacted to the touch as if it alone had announced the seriousness of the situation. Veins throbbed in her neck. Her eyes watered.

"Your father was shot," Imani said. "He died. I'm so sorry."

Ava made a sound like a tire screeching to a halt. Her thin mask invaded her mouth, stretching over the opening like shrink wrap. Imani brushed the girl's blond hair away from her tears, unlooping the PPE from her ears in the process. School policy be damned. The child needed to breathe.

"And Mom?" The question gurgled from Ava's throat.

"Everyone is looking for her."

Imani guided Ava's head to her chest and belted her arms around her shoulders. She held on as sobs jolted the teen's body, trying her best to absorb the shock. For several minutes, they stood that way, Ava's muscles spasming as she struggled for air.

When Ava finally caught her breath, she spent it with a stream of questions. Who had killed her dad? Why had they done it? Did her mom know what had happened? Where would her mother be? Did *they* have her?

Imani rhythmically patted Ava's back in response, whispering the only answer she could give. "I don't know, honey. But I promise you, I will do everything in my power to find out."

CHAPTER SIX

TONYA

Philip didn't fire her. As Tonya stood outside Banque Gauche's front door, scanning for the packs of hungry patrons who'd once put food on her table, Tonya wondered whether the chef's restraint was truly a kindness. At the height of the restaurant's fame, she'd earned $80,000 in a single year thanks to the standard gratuity on hundred-plus-per-person checks, sweetened with extras thrown in by half-drunk executives flaunting their generosity to an affable, attractive twenty-something. But those days were long gone. If Tonya was being honest with herself, they'd faded years before the pandemic.

She scanned the boarded-up storefronts and blacked-out restaurant windows lining the street, reminding herself of how lucky she was to have a job at all. As she took in her bleak surroundings, two prospects rounded the corner. They each wore ankle-length wool coats. One's head was exposed, revealing a sharp haircut. The man had either seen a barber despite circumstances or had a spouse skilled with clippers. Tonya hoped for the former.

She stepped out into the wind. "Ever dine in an igloo?" she shouted.

The haircut turned toward the sound of her voice. His brows scrunched in unmistakable embarrassment. He shook his head and then redirected his attention to his friend, who picked up his pace.

She was too desperate, Tonya realized. If she were auditioning for *Glengarry Glen Ross*, they'd cast her as sad-sack Shelley Levene rather than suave Ricky Roma. Too old to close. Too cold to close. Too female for Mamet, to be honest. It also didn't help that half her face was covered, Tonya thought. Masks, unlike veils, did not create mystique.

A knock caught her attention. Tonya spun around to see Philip on the other side of Banque's glass door. The color had drained from his face. He was now back to looking pale and dour, a washed-out version of the man she'd met ten years earlier with intense blue eyes, reddish brown hair, and skin flushed from heat or, after a particularly good service, a celebratory whiskey.

In the good years, Philip had often ended the nights with a shared toast. He liked Bushmills Black Bush, an Irish malt blend that he boasted spoke to his heritage and therefore calmed his blood. Once, after a particularly busy night, Philip had poured everyone a couple rounds of his favorite spirit, unintentionally encouraging a line cook to over-relax. The guy had teased that "Chef likes straight Black Bush," a vulgar reference to the privates of Philip's Bajan wife. For what had felt like a full minute, everyone in the kitchen had held their breath, bracing for Philip to fly into a rage that would end in the word *fired*.

Fortunately, their head chef had felt jovial that night. Instead of snatching the guy's jacket and slamming him into the walk-in refrigerator—as Tonya had once seen Philip do to a mouthing-off prep cook—he'd raised a glass and said, "The blacker the berry, the sweeter the juice," a literary reference praising dark-skinned women, often slipped into rap lyrics. They'd all laughed like helium had spiked the air flooding back into their lungs, relieved that their good night would end on a high note.

To work in a restaurant was to be at the mercy of one man's mood. Everyone knew that, from the dishwasher to the second-in-command sous-chef. Perhaps that was why Tonya found it so disconcerting to see Philip laid low. It meant that any mercy might be in short supply.

Philip waved her inside. Tonya opened the door, her head at a deferential tilt. "I'm sorry again about the plates. I feel—"

"It happens. Your hands were probably frozen."

Tonya nodded, even though she knew the explanation couldn't have been further from the truth. Much better for Philip to think she'd been reacting to the temperature than to an overheard call with his wife.

"You should take off. Nobody's sitting outside in this weather."

A combination of guilt and hope made Tonya protest. Philip paid ten dollars an hour for showing up. How Tonya earned her real salary was delivering food and drink. "Maybe the after-five crowd—"

"Most folks are working from home, and those in the office are going straight to their families afterward. Go.

Spend time with your kid. You'll get sick hanging out in this cold."

Philip wasn't asking; he was telling. There was no disobeying an order from the restaurant's head. Tonya forced a smile. "Of course. Yes, Chef."

Her down coat was in the front closet usually reserved for guests. She grabbed it off a hanger and then turned to bid Mike good-bye, only to see the bar unstaffed. Apparently, Philip had told him to kick off as well. Tonya looked toward the cooks for a sign-off nod, but they were either too busy with takeout meals or too mortified by her earlier mistake to acknowledge her departure.

Outside the restaurant was even more empty than the inside. Tonya popped the collar of her coat as she stepped onto the sidewalk, an act less about protecting against the cold than attempting to disappear. Tonya didn't want to draw any unwanted attention as she commuted home. It was better for a woman in the city to be invisible, she thought. At least it was these days.

The virus had driven the city's cell-phone-armed social media army behind closed doors. The few folks still out and about often didn't mean anyone well.

As she marched down 47th Street, Tonya felt that she was hurrying through a postapocalyptic landscape. She kept her head down, mask on, and feet moving forward. Once she hit the subway entrance, she hustled down the stairs, avoiding looking at any of the stragglers on the platform. She stared at her shoes until she could board the F train.

There were more people in the subway car, but that didn't make Tonya feel safer. Though many of the passengers wore masks and sat well away from one another, no doubt hoping to make it to work or home without being breathed on, there were plenty of barefaced holdouts with their chins jutted forward, daring anyone to suggest that they cover their mouth and nose. These maskless men and women reminded Tonya of drunks who'd strut around bars with their arms puffed out, commanding more space than they should have felt entitled to, itching for some passerby to unintentionally bump a shoulder. It was best to sit far more than six feet away from them.

Tonya found a corner seat and directed her attention to her phone, trying not to make any confrontational eye contact. She'd taught Layla to ape the same behavior. Her daughter was eleven, old enough to take the subway one stop from St. Catherine's private school to their Carroll Gardens apartment—and smart enough to keep her head down around anyone with an off demeanor. Still, it hurt Tonya to think of her kid sitting in a space that an ill person might have occupied moments before, risking a passerby coughing on her, or worse. Nightly, she prayed that the news reports were right about most kids being relatively immune.

Tonya thought about her daughter the entire thirty-five-minute ride. On some level, she supposed that Layla was always on her mind, her freckled face and strawberry-blond hair waiting behind Tonya's eyelids. Certainly, earning money to support her kid was the only thing that kept her in freezing temperatures outside a makeshift igloo.

In spite of herself, Tonya also thought about Nate Walker. On her cell, she read the *New York Post* article, the one that all but declared that Nate hadn't committed suicide, given that he was found with a gun "arranged" in his hand. Police were still looking for his wife, whom the paper pointedly noted was best known for a twelve-year-old part in which she'd played the unhinged, murderous paramour of a successful lawyer.

The police clearly hadn't done much investigating if they liked the wife for the crime, Tonya thought. Plenty of people had to feel a bit better knowing Nate Walker was no longer in the world. She couldn't be the only one.

In her twenties, Tonya might have been sufficiently naïve to consider herself special like that. But she'd grown up enough to know that she'd been a type: starry-eyed, sexy farm girl with a bit of talent and big-city ambitions. She could not have been the only neophyte whom Nate had cajoled with promises of movie appearances and then pressured into "performing." There had to be others without a child to protect. Women who couldn't be bought off.

Ava Walker entered her thoughts as well, even though Tonya tried her best not to consider her. The girl stormed into her consciousness often, usually due to a casual comment from Layla about who had secured what roles in the school's latest play. Ava was four years her kid's senior, so there wasn't any real danger of them developing a friendship. Even so, Tonya had worried that their mutual interest in theater might shove her into Nate's circle.

She recalled the last time she'd seen him at the school. She'd been sitting stiffly on a bottom bleacher, bracing for Nate's oblivious wife to cease chatting with her hangers-on and meander over with an introduction—or an accusation. Tonya had mentally prepared to either force a smile and point out Layla or claim with all the faux sincerity she could muster that she had absolutely no idea what Melissa was talking about. Pulling off the conversation would have required an Oscar-worthy performance, Tonya knew. Fortunately, Melissa had never stopped socializing with her admirers, leaving Tonya to keep watching her from afar, preparing for the worst.

Nate's death meant never again fretting about such a terrifying screen test. She wouldn't need to steel herself every time she walked into the school for a flash of dark pewter hair and graying five-o'clock shadow. She wouldn't have to worry that Nate's deep-set eyes were fixed on her or that he needed to revisit their agreement. Most of all, Tonya could stop agonizing that he'd one day blab everything to his wife, twisting their history to cast her as the seductress.

———

The train recording robotically announced Tonya's stop. She found herself breathing easier as she exited into the dim late afternoon. Brooklyn was different from Midtown Manhattan. Folks walked to and from grocery stores and corner bodegas. They let their bundled kids scooter down wide-open sidewalks. Some went to friends' apartments for secret, unmasked social hours.

Tonya felt some of her earlier giddiness return as she hurried to her third-floor walk-up. Her apartment wasn't big, but it was pretty with two bedrooms and one bathroom crammed into a well-decorated eight hundred square feet. The largest room was a long, rectangular living area featuring an exposed brick wall and unusable fireplace that she and Layla had filled with electric candles. They'd painted the drywall a grayish beige, selected a few low-profile furniture pieces, and mounted framed art everywhere, all of it created by Layla or Tonya herself. Her favorites were an abstract watercolor that Layla had somehow made at the tender age of four and an image of Layla's and Tonya's profiles as mother and baby, which Tonya had drawn using a mirror and a single, unending line.

Tonya unlocked the main door and then started up the stairs. As she climbed, a voice called out behind her. "Miss Sayre, is that you?"

Her landlord's unmasked face allowed Tonya to appreciate her terse expression. Ms. Bosco was in her sixties and treated the whole building as an extension of her home, probably because it once had been. She did not wear a face covering inside and would not hear otherwise, especially from younger tenants insisting that their only concern was unintentionally passing along the virus to an older woman in a high-risk group.

Ms. Bosco glared. "I need to talk to you."

Tonya descended a step, reducing the number between them from five to four. It was as close as she intended to get without both of them covering their mouths. "Is everything all right?"

"I wanted to ask you that same question."

"I believe so." Tonya knew that this was not the right answer. Her landlord would not be accosting her to simply ask if she was doing well.

"Then why haven't you been paying rent?"

The question felt like a backhanded slap. Tonya's fingers instinctively went to her cheek. "I ... I didn't realize."

"You didn't realize that you'd stopped sending checks two months ago?" Ms. Bosco shook her head in disbelief, freeing her dyed red curls so that they resembled lapping flames. "The first month I ignored because I know times are hard, and the second too. But you've run through your security deposit, and I can't let you live here for free. Things are difficult for everyone. I need the rent for upkeep and to pay my own bills. It's not a boardinghouse. I can't ... "

Tonya tuned out her landlord's tirade as she wracked her brain for some explanation. Every year on August twenty-fourth, Layla's birthday, $60,000 was wired to a private account. The rent was paid automatically from it. "There must be some mistake. I'll look into it."

"There's no *mistake*. I'm not getting the rent. And I really can't keep you here ..."

The sound of her heels clapping up the stairs muffled the rest of her landlord's tirade. Tonya hurried to her apartment door and jammed her key into the lock. Before she could open it, the knob turned from the other side.

Layla stood on the threshold, tears rolling down her freckled cheeks. Babies cried like this, Tonya thought, not preteens. She gripped her daughter's arms, forgetting all the usual protocols about handwashing and disinfecting. "What happened?" She scanned Layla's body for signs of injury. Her daughter's clothing looked clean and intact. Her arms felt solid. There was no awkwardness to her stance. "Are you okay?"

"We need to move."

The panic that had filled Tonya's gut began to drain. "No, honey. I'm so sorry. Did Ms. Bosco say that to you? She doesn't know what she's talking about. The bank must have had a mix-up with the payments. We're not—"

"*He*," Layla said, cutting her off. "He said it."

A chill ran down Tonya's spine. "Who are we talking about?"

"My father."

Though it was Layla who choked on the word, Tonya felt her own throat close. For all intents and purposes, *father* was a term that should never have followed *my* for her daughter. At two, when Layla had first asked about her missing male parent, Tonya had said he'd been a sperm donor. The explanation, and the discussion of genetics that it had necessitated, had been too involved for a toddler. Nonetheless, Tonya had stuck to it all these years. She thought it less of a lie than an analogy. She'd received male genetic material and grown herself a child. Layla was hers alone. No biological father would ever claim her. She knew that for certain now.

"I don't understand," Tonya croaked.

Layla wrenched from her grasp. Her tears, Tonya realized, hadn't been from sadness.

"The lawyer called." She hissed. "My dad can't pay anymore."

CHAPTER SEVEN

RICK

The block was closed. A police car had parked horizontally at the street entrance, preventing traffic from passing through to the avenue. The lights of another cruiser flashed several hundred feet away. No cars were leaving this space, nor entering, Rick realized. There was no escape route.

Rick nudged the man in the driver's seat. Frank clearly wasn't paying attention to the view out the windshield. His head was turned squarely toward the building surrounded by uniformed officers. To Rick, the cops seemed to engulf Nate's townhome, rats crawling up the steps, moving in and out the front door, feasting on whatever remained. They shouldn't be there, he thought. They should be traversing the island, searching for Melissa before it was too late.

Unless they already knew it was too late.

"You don't think slow-rolling the scene of a crime draws suspicion?" Rick asked.

Frank shrugged. "It's like an accident. Everyone takes a gander."

"There's no point in being here," Rick responded.

Frank's knee shifted. He turned the wheel to the right and floored the gas pedal. The Porsche roared as it blindly merged into incoming traffic, a lion leaping into a herd. A horn blared behind them.

"Subtle," Rick quipped.

Frank smirked, acknowledging what they both knew. The man had always been the opposite of subtle. Rick was the nice guy, the one called in to smooth things over after a bad meeting or general bad behavior. He was the talker. The fixer.

Frank was the animal.

"Let's say we head over to the other place." Frank released a hand from the wheel to dig a remnant of lunch from between his teeth.

The sight made some of the vinaigrette dressing from earlier repeat on Rick. He cleared his throat and averted his eyes to the view outside the passenger window. For the first time, headlights seemed to light the sky more than the neon glow of building signs. He'd never seen New York City look so dark.

"That motherfucker will be there, right?"

The curse got Rick's attention. He hated how Frank had taken to talking like a Scorsese character. There were other ways to relay a message than dropping f-bombs—even for guys like his partner.

"I don't know where he'll be," Rick said. "Do you know where he'll be?"

"I thought you two were fucking friends?" Frank said.

Rick rolled his eyes. Neither of them had friends. They

had people. People they lunched with, people they drank with, people who could introduce them to other people or who they could pass around. Friends required feelings that couldn't be changed in an instant by a business decision.

"The whole point of a silent partner is not needing to say a word to anybody," Rick said.

"The whole point of an investment is to get paid, not to pad someone's bank account," Frank countered. "That lying, mother—"

"What are you going to say to him?" Rick said, cutting him off before his ears could be assailed by a barrage of profanity. "'Cause if your opening line is to call him names, I don't think we'll get very far."

The light in front of them turned yellow. Rick slid his hand to the side of the leather bucket seat and curled his fingers around the edge, anticipating that Frank would floor it. Instead, his partner eased off the gas, letting the flat-six engine simmer down to a stop. At the red light, Frank leaned over the center console and popped up a flat panel. He reached inside and pulled out a shiny revolver that looked fresh from a sports' shop display case.

Rick recalled what the newspapers had said about Nate's death. The "arranged" gun. Both their incomes required a certain amount of respect. People had to know that they were not to be lied to, taken advantage of, or otherwise trifled with. But Rick maintained his standing through connections—knowing people who could make life difficult. He'd never given much thought to how he'd react if his connections couldn't come through.

Apparently, Frank had.

The light flipped to green in front of them. Rick gestured to the windshield with his chin, afraid of making any sudden moves with a firearm inches from his thigh. "That loaded?"

Frank shot him a murderous look. "He took our money," he said, dropping the pistol back in the bucket. "If I haven't made it clear before, I'm done fucking talking."

CHAPTER EIGHT

MELISSA

How long had she slept? The same blackness that had enveloped Melissa the prior night still surrounded her. It could have been four or ten or twelve hours later. Without light, there was no time.

But there was sun beyond these walls, she thought. There was Ava.

Her daughter was out there worrying about her, wondering why her mom had vanished after her dad had been shot in the face—maybe even debating whether Melissa had done it. Most people would be questioning her innocence at this point, Melissa figured. Here she was, nowhere to be found, a woman whose last major role had been a femme fatale obsessed with another woman's husband. There would be articles about whether life had imitated art, whether Melissa had captured crazy so well because she, herself, was mentally unwell. If the media found the messages, they would crucify her.

She had to get out of here. Melissa pressed her hand to the

velvety surface that she had stumbled upon after wandering, blind, for what had felt like hours, patting the walls, the floor, the spaces in front of her, struggling to discern differences in texture. The fabric belonged to a couch cushion, she assumed. She'd been able to lie on the elevated cloth in fetal position, placing her head on what felt like a roll pillow.

The cushion was damp, probably from her tears. She needed to stop crying. Conserve water. Dehydration messed with the mind. She would never escape if she got confused.

Melissa placed her feet on the floor. Hardwood, if she had to guess. She rose, feeling the material beneath her butt give way, and slowly advanced, holding her hands in front of her face. Other than the couch, there didn't appear to be any furniture. At least, she hadn't run into anything else.

As she walked, Melissa detected a faint smell. Meaty. Oily. Not rancid, though. Not unpleasant. Her stomach whined, a dog begging for food. She followed the scent like a bloodhound, sniffing the air every few seconds, retracing her steps when it became fainter.

Hunger pushed her to abandon her deliberate pace. After a few seconds, something hard slammed into her rib cage. She jumped back, unsure whether she'd been struck.

"Hello?" she yelled. "Anyone here?"

Nothing answered save the faint hum of something electrical and her own panicked breaths. She didn't sense any change in temperature, no heat emanating from some invisible corner. Watching her was pointless, she supposed. There was nothing to see in the dark.

Melissa returned to what had hit her, patting the air until her hand grazed a slick surface. She ran her fingers over it, searching for bumps or divots in the plane, something to indicate what she was touching. She felt nothing other than smoothness and cold.

The smell from before wafted toward her. She slid her hand toward the scent until it happened upon a round edge.

Melissa knew this material. Hard. Slightly grainy. It pinged when she flicked it with her finger. Ceramic. A plate!

She tested its contents with her fingertips. There were aspects that were soft, a little mushy. Something else was wetter and slick. It failed to snap in her fingers when she bent it, instead peeling away. Tentatively, she brought the freed scrap to her nose and inhaled. It was a vegetable, too bland to have a distinct scent. She stuck out her tongue and tapped the substance on the tip.

Lettuce!

Melissa crunched the leaf between her teeth and then reached both hands out to the plate, patting the top and the edges. It was a sandwich. She was almost sure. The soft part was the bread. She lifted it off and shoved a morsel in her mouth. Yes, definitely bread. Slightly sour. Grainy. There were seeds of some sort in here.

She patted the exposed insides. Something was hard and slightly wet, but she could pierce her finger through it. She brought it to her nose. This was the smell. Chicken. Roast chicken.

She shoved the meat into her mouth and felt around for a glass, tentatively tapping the air. Her nail struck something. She palmed the container, lifted it to her lips, and sipped.

Water. Thank God.

Melissa washed down the half-chewed bite and then

drained the rest of the glass. After, she grabbed the sandwich and ripped off a large chunk. The food tasted like relief. Joy. She couldn't discern individual flavors, but that didn't matter. She was consuming sustenance, something to keep her from starving to death.

Tears wet her cheeks. The plan wasn't for her to waste away in here. So, what was it?

She considered the answer as she chewed. Suddenly, her teeth happened upon something gritty. Quickly, she spat the whole mushy mess into her palm and dumped it onto the smooth surface. It might have been mere gristle, but how to be sure? She couldn't see what she was eating, and she was too desperate to taste if something was off. For all she knew, the whole meal before her had been peppered with rat poison.

Melissa stepped away from the food, ignoring her stomach's pleas to reconsider. Surely killing her wasn't the goal. Nate's murder hadn't been premeditated. It had been a reaction. A mistake. A failed negotiation that all parties had likely thought would have resulted in a different compromise.

But even mistakes had to be paid for. In this case, perhaps the price was too steep to suffer the consequences.

Tears boiled behind Melissa's eyes. She threw her head back and screamed as loud as she could. "Help me. Please. I'm locked in here."

She continued shouting until she was hoarse. No one answered. For all she knew, it was still late. Outside was empty. No one could hear her.

"Help me," she yelled, her voice breaking. "Please. Help. I'm going to die."

CHAPTER NINE

IMANI

Ava was determined to read the articles. As they walked the three blocks to Imani's house, Melissa's daughter kept slowing to type into her phone's web browser. Each time, Imani redirected Ava's attention to a traffic signal or passerby or pavement crack, providing just enough distraction to prevent her from clicking search. By the time they reached her home, Imani had resorted to indicating every sidewalk seam to "watch out for."

She could have confiscated the device for Ava's own good, as St. Catherine's had. But snatching something from someone who'd already lost so much seemed wrong to Imani. Moreover, it wasn't a Melissa thing to do. Her friend had always been a more permissive parent, erring on the side of spoiling her only child rather than enforcing humility and deference to authority figures. It was a parenting style far easier to adopt when there were sufficient family funds to ensure working for the man would never be required. Imani could not afford to similarly indulge her own kids.

"Honey." Imani addressed Ava as if she were a wild horse that might spook. The Walkers lived only a few blocks away. It wouldn't take much for Ava to run there, perhaps breaking through the police tape before some cop stopped her from stepping in blood.

Ava looked up from her cell, moving her head just enough for Imani to make out the shape of headlines on her screen. As soon as Imani opened the door, Melissa's daughter would sprint to some silent corner and start scrutinizing every word written about her dad's death—and every theory in the comments. No doubt some of the speculation would suggest that Melissa had been kidnapped and murdered elsewhere. Other commenters would hint that she'd been involved.

"Remember how your mom would always warn you not to read tabloid stories about your father because journalists like to create drama to sell newspapers? She—"

"The *New York Times* isn't *Star* magazine."

"No. But even reputable papers can make mistakes or have poorly informed sources. This story is developing. You can't assume everything reported is true and that people know what they're talking about. It'd be better to wait until—"

"My dad is dead, my mom is missing, and I'm cold."

Though Ava didn't raise her voice, her flat tone conveyed her fury. Anger was the third stage of grief. Imani figured Ava would circle back through sadness and disbelief once she had a chance to sit. Loss wasn't a one-way subway tunnel. The journey through it lacked the order of emotional platforms that could be stopped at or passed by while advancing to acceptance.

Imani turned the key in the lock and held back the

door, revealing the worn interior of her carriage house. Sometimes she thought her home had solidified the relationship between her family and Melissa's own. Her A-list friend had seen the redbrick exterior of Philip's inherited three-story, five-bedroom in the mews and thought Imani's family much more affluent than they actually were. By the time Imani had revealed the home's origin, she'd already helped Melissa through a miscarriage and named her the godmother of Jay, Imani's healthy baby boy. Their families had been too close then for Melissa and Nate to worry about how the vast difference in purchasing power might complicate their friendship.

Ava passed through the narrow foyer and hung an immediate right, disappearing into the attached garage. Before it had been converted for cars, the area had been a stable. Imani had somewhat restored its original purpose, remodeling it as a hangout for her coltish teens and kicking their infrequently used car onto the street. A large-screen television now dominated one wall of the room. Beanbag couches and bubble chairs were the only seating options. There was a foosball table. Ava had been hanging out there with Vivienne for years.

Imani debated whether to follow her. They both needed solitary time to process their emotions, but Ava wouldn't actually be alone. As long as she had her phone, she'd be connected to a world of strangers chiming in with their uninformed two cents.

Releasing the device had been a bad idea, Imani decided. She removed her mask and shouted Ava's name. "Why don't you come have a glass of water? We can—"

The doorbell interrupted her. Relief flooded Imani's veins. Surely Melissa was on her front step, breathless after having raced from the school but otherwise physically unharmed. Imani hadn't wanted to add to Ava's trauma with any interrogation. In retrospect, she should have at least asked if Ava had seen her parents that morning. The articles hadn't revealed much about Nate's time of death. For all Imani knew, he'd been killed after Melissa had dropped Ava at school, before heading out to have her cell repaired or undergo some procedure in a no-phones-allowed hospital ward.

"Mel," Imani called out as she opened the door.

The woman in front of her was the polar opposite of Melissa. Medium height with dark hair raked into a ponytail, narrowed brown eyes, and a skin tone that read as either Southeast Asian or Hispanic given that the facial features that might have provided additional clues were covered. A police badge adorned the woman's peacoat. Behind her stood a broad-shouldered man several shades darker than Imani. He wore a wool hat and a mask pulled below his chin, enabling her to see the grim line formed by his full, pressed lips.

The woman stepped back onto the sidewalk, leaving six feet between them. She lowered her face covering. "Mrs. Imani Banks?"

Imani knew what the woman wanted before she said it. However, she waited for Detectives Linette Calvente and Roger Powell to introduce themselves and formally request to speak with Ava before saying what she'd planned to the moment they'd arrived. "Can't this wait? Ava learned of her father's death half an hour ago, and her mother should be present when you speak with her."

"Mrs. Banks, this is about finding her mother," Detective Calvente said.

"We can imagine what Ava is going through and understand your concerns," Detective Powell added. "But interviewing her now, when things are fresh, could help us figure out what happened and where her mom is."

Thousands of hours listening to people speak had taught Imani to pay attention to both what people said and the way they said it. The detectives had removed their masks and socially distanced so that they would seem nonthreatening, but their resting hands had remained on their hips near their weapons, on alert for an attacker rather than folded in apology. Their words, too, belied that their main goal was to help Melissa. Police figured out motives and found evidence. They *rescued* victims.

Imani grasped the doorjamb, barring the officers from entering while simultaneously bracing herself. She lowered her voice to a level that she hoped would be inaudible in the neighboring room. "Do you think Melissa's dead?"

Detective Calvente responded with an accusing stare, as if Imani were admitting something simply by posing the question. "Do you believe she's dead?"

Imani tightened her grip on the door's edge. "I think there's a child in there who can't handle hearing about the murder of another parent at the moment. I think, as long as there is hope, she should be allowed to hold on to that."

One of Detective Powell's hands dropped from his hip. "We currently lack evidence to support that. If she's in danger, whatever Ava knows could help us *save* her."

He'd stumbled upon the magic word. Imani's hand dropped

from the door. She stepped back, inviting the officers in. They didn't pull up their masks as they entered, and Imani didn't ask them to. It would be better for both her and Ava to see their full faces.

Imani pointed to the living area beyond the dining room. There was a couch in there across from two swivel chairs with a coffee table between them. "If you take the seats, we can talk in there," Imani said, already negotiating. She needed to establish that this conversation would involve give-and-take. They would not be allowed to use her home as a cozy interrogation room to callously extract information from her best friend's daughter.

"Where is Ava?" Detective Calvente asked.

The question was a bid for control. "If you'd sit in the living room, then I'll get her."

Detective Powell responded with a small smile. Somewhere in the back of her mind, Imani registered the expression as a kind one. The man had a handsome face. Strong jaw. Masculine, broad nose. He was the kind of guy that Melissa would have blatantly checked out before leaning toward Imani and whispering something naughty. Her beautiful friend appreciated attractiveness, particularly in non-actor men and young people because their looks were more likely God's handiwork rather than a plastic surgeon's sculpture. "Good-looking men are like daylilies," Melissa had said once. "No one tends to them, but there they are on the side of the road, just begging to be plucked."

Imani supposed she shouldn't be thinking about the male detective's appearance. But she couldn't help it. The brain was designed to slot people and information into categories, and Imani's mind was working double time. It had already filed Detective Calvente into the hard-ass class, mostly because she'd been first to speak and had answered every question with a question.

Imani watched the detectives' heavy-booted march across her recently mopped hardwood. Another detail that she couldn't help but take note of, despite the circumstances.

"You can open the windows," she called out. "There's a latch at the bottom."

She watched Detective Powell successfully crack open a pane before she walked through to the garage. Ava stood at the door. Her paralyzed body made clear that she knew who Imani had welcomed into her home.

"Honey, the police want to talk to you. Do you feel that you can speak with them?"

Ava's lips pulled beneath her top teeth. She'd removed her mask, enabling Imani to take in the tightness of her jaw and tear-reddened nose.

"I'll stay with you," Imani continued. "If it gets too uncomfortable at any point, you give me a look, and I'll shut it down."

Ava nodded while staring at the floor. For the first time, she seemed young to Imani. She'd always thought of Ava as mature beyond her years, probably because the girl had possessed the confidence of being treated as an equal by her parents. However, the fifteen-year-old before her had been drained of bravado. Tragedy turned even grown-ups into children.

Imani felt less brave herself as she led the way into the living room. However, she tried not to give any indication, keeping her shoulders back and head held high. This was her home, she reminded herself. She was in charge. Not them.

When they entered the room, Imani gestured for Ava to take the couch and then sat beside her, at an angle. She wanted to keep one eye on Ava and one on the detectives.

"Hello, Ava. I'm Detective Calvente, and this is my partner Detective Powell. We are very sorry for your loss. We can imagine the pain you're going through, and we want very much to help find your mother."

Imani stiffened. Where had this empathy been minutes earlier? Had the sight of Ava softened the woman or was this some manipulation tactic?

"Thank you." The phrase barely made it past Ava's lips.

"Can you tell me the last time that you saw your mom?"

Imani rubbed Ava's back, trying to coax out an answer.

"Last night." Ava's voice sounded tinny and rough, metal scraping metal. "My mom came into my room around ten and kissed me good night."

"And when was the last time you, um, saw your dad?" Detective Calvente didn't add the obvious caveat—*alive*.

"Maybe an hour earlier?"

"And did—"

"I was working on math homework, and he came in to help. He's good at geometry." Ava continued, her voice strengthening. "He's a great teacher. Everyone thinks of him as this big, untouchable director, but they don't realize that he's so good at that because he's great at explaining things and getting you to see them. He volunteered to teach an on-line class at the school about visual storytelling. Everyone really loves him. My classmates have been reaching out to say . . ."

Ava's speech dissolved into sobs. Detective Calvente's face softened. Detective Powell, meanwhile, looked down at his meaty hands resting in his lap. He sat with his back hunched and legs pressed close to the base of his chair, as if he were trying to fold his large body into as small a package as possible.

"He wouldn't have killed himself," Ava said. "Online, people are saying he was depressed because he wasn't working. But he'd been busy teaching and spending time with us. He loved us. He wouldn't just leave."

Detective Calvente smiled in a way that she clearly intended to be sympathetic, but Imani suspected was patronizing. "Do you—"

"Do you believe Nate was murdered?" *Quid pro quo,* Imani thought. "Because if you have evidence that Ava's father didn't take his own life, it would be helpful for her to hear that."

Detective Calvente shot her partner a look. He shrugged, almost imperceptibly. "Ava, during an investigation, there are details that we don't want anyone to know so that, if there's a bad guy—or girl—out there, they don't realize that we're looking for them. You understand?"

Though the female detective spoke to Ava, she looked up at Imani, making sure she was on board with whatever agreement the child made. "Yes." Ava nodded.

Detective Powell raised his head, keeping his back bent and his shoulders turned toward his knees. "It might be the kind of thing that you would want to tell people, Ava. You might feel that you need to defend your parents' reputation or correct rumors. But unfortunately, if we talk to you, then you really can't repeat what we say."

If they both hadn't been armed, Imani might have shouted at them to cut the bullshit. It was a simple question. Either the police thought Nate had killed himself or they didn't. "She understands." Imani hissed.

The detectives exchanged another look. "When someone shoots a gun, it usually leaves residue on their hands. There wasn't any on your father's palms. So we don't believe he shot it."

Ava sniffed. "Do you know who did?"

"Do you know what your parents were doing after you last saw them?" Detective Calvente asked, displaying the deflection skills she'd unveiled at the door. "Did they leave the house, or did anyone come over?"

Tears accumulated on Ava's brown lashes. "My dad was . . ." Ava gasped at her use of past tense. She balled her hands into fists and drove them into her jean-clad thighs. "He was in his fifties, and he had hard arteries. He took statins. That put him in a high-risk group, so he never wanted to leave the house, and my mom didn't want to risk getting him sick."

"Well, everyone has to leave their home sometime." The retort came from Detective Powell. He still wasn't sitting fully upright. "Even if for a little walk, change of scenery and some fresh air, right? Or maybe to grab something from the grocery store. Or to let in a delivery guy?"

Ava pressed the heels of her hands into her closed eyes. "I don't think so, but I can't be sure."

"Because your bedroom is on the fourth floor, right,"

Detective Calvente said, her tone telling more than asking. "You wouldn't necessarily hear the front door slam or what happened on the basement level?"

"I have one of those machines," Ava said. "It plays rain sounds and white noise. There's been some construction on the block. Mom bought it so I could sleep past seven a.m."

"And does it work or do you still hear the street sounds?"

Ava's hands dropped from her face, revealing her round, watery eyes, the whites shot through with red. "Do you think I slept through someone attacking my parents?"

The detectives' silence betrayed that they were considering the possibility.

Imani had teenage clients with sleep disorders, kids who couldn't close their eyes longer than a blink because of crippling anxieties, people who needed to be chemically put down every night and caffeine-slapped every morning. She couldn't let guilt turn Ava into one of those patients.

She grasped Ava's shoulder, directing the girl's attention to her face. "Whatever happened is not your fault, honey. Okay? You went to sleep. You're allowed to rest. You must sleep to function and survive."

"But I could have called nine-one-one."

"And you could have been hurt, which would have been the last thing your parents would want."

Tears streamed down Ava's face. She opened her mouth to respond, but no sound emerged.

"You are here, and you're safe," Imani continued. "Believe me, that's what your mom cares about. It's what your dad would care about. And the police don't even know what happened."

Imani glanced at the detectives, silently urging them to repeat what she'd said.

If Calvente or Powell understood what she wanted, they weren't in a mood to listen. Instead, they seemed to take her deliberate stare as permission to continue their interview.

"What time did you leave the house this morning?" Detective Calvente asked.

"I don't know. Around eight, I think."

"You're not sure?"

Imani released Ava's shoulder to return her attention to the cops. Detective Powell was writing in a notepad.

"School starts at eight fifteen, and it takes Ava five minutes to walk there," Imani offered. "Around eight would make sense."

Detective Powell scrawled something in response.

"And did you see either of your parents this morning?" Detective Calvente asked.

Ava shifted to face them head on. "You know I didn't. You know because you've been implying that my dad died last night while I was upstairs. So you know that I walked right out. The den is at the garden level. I never went farther down the stairs than the front door. I walked straight out while my dad was there and—"

"Did you see any sign of your mom?" Detective Powell interrupted, no doubt trying to squeeze in one last question before another crying jag. From the intensity of the cops' attention, Imani suspected that this was what they'd wanted to ask all along. A shudder ran down her spine. They thought Melissa had done it and run off, she thought. Or they were at least considering the possibility.

"I left the house without saying good-bye to anyone, without even looking for them."

"Does your home have security cameras?" Detective Calvente asked.

Ava's eyes remained trained on her hands. "No."

Detective Calvente shot her partner a quick glance, conveying her doubt. Everyone had web-connected security cameras nowadays. Imani remembered a conversation with the Walkers from years earlier in which Nate had adamantly argued that they were all exposing themselves to Russian hackers with their Nest cams.

"Nate was concerned about videos uploading to the cloud, being accessed by strangers and ending up on celebrity websites," Imani offered. "It was a privacy issue."

Detective Powell wrote something in his notebook. "Guess that explains why we didn't find a camera on the door," he mumbled.

"Did you hear anything before you left to indicate that there was anyone in the house?" Detective Calvente asked. "Perhaps footsteps or a television? Maybe water running?"

Anyone washing off blood? Imani stood before their already unsubtle question could become any more graphic. "I think it's best for you two to go now."

Detective Powell rose, revealing the broad shoulders and chest that he'd been trying to conceal. "We don't have too many more questions."

Imani mentally cursed her husband for not coming home like she'd begged. He'd been a marine for four years. An armed police officer wouldn't intimidate him, especially in his own house.

She steeled herself. "Ava has answered enough questions for today."

Detective Calvente gave Ava an encouraging smile. "I think Ava's old enough to decide whether she still wants to talk to us. Right, Ava?"

Imani shot Calvente a look that she hoped was a hundred times more withering than the accusing expression the detective had delivered at the door. This woman knew exactly what she was doing, appealing to a teen's ego, the fervent desire to be seen as the adult that they would become, but were *not*.

"This is my house," Imani said.

"And we're conducting a murder investigation," Detective Calvente countered. "Ava can decide if she wants—"

Imani faced Melissa's daughter. "Would you like to talk to them? Or is it time for them to look for your mom?"

Deciding for oneself was empowering, Imani knew. But telling two armed officers how to do their jobs was far more so.

Ava's back straightened. "I think I'm done for right now. I'll wait until I see my mother."

"Ava, we're trying to find your mother."

Condescension had crept into Detective Calvente's tone. The tightening of Ava's expression indicated that she'd heard it.

"Then find her," Ava said.

The derision that had been present in Detective Calvente's voice wasn't visible in her stance. She rose like someone who'd had a very long day and would endure an even longer night. "I am sorry for your loss," she said.

The finality of the statement seemed to break Ava. Her lip trembled for a moment before dropping open in a silent scream. Imani lowered to the couch cushion. The detectives had done their damage. It was her job now to repair what she could.

She hugged the girl to her side. "Please, Detectives. See yourselves out."

"Just one more question, please?" Detective Powell asked, perhaps sensing that he was the one Imani liked more. He crouched to Ava's level. "To your knowledge, did your dad own a gun?"

Ava turned her head, revealing her tearstained face. She shook her head.

The detectives again communicated silently. A quick side glance and raised eyebrow from Calvente. Pressed lips from Powell. But Imani had caught the micro-expressions, and she knew that they knew.

Nate hadn't owned a gun. But Melissa had.

CHAPTER TEN

TONYA

The lawyer had called. Glen Kelner of Taft, Kelner, and Moore was perhaps the only person certain of Layla's paternity—aside from her biological parents. It was Kelner who'd responded all those years ago after Tonya had formally requested child support. Kelner who'd worked out the DNA test. Kelner who'd determined the annual payment and how that money would be delivered in "the interest of discretion."

Tonya kept the attorney's card clipped to papers within a folder inside a Payless boot box beneath her bed. Unbeknownst to Layla, it had always held their family's most important documents: social security cards, hospital files, and the birth certificate with the blank space after *father's name*. Its bottom was lined with the folder containing Layla's paternity test and Kelner's number.

She withdrew the card and tapped the telephone number into her cell. As it rang, she moved to her bedroom window. Tonya was certain that Layla stood on the opposite side of the master bedroom wall with her ear pressed to the plaster, straining to hear some answer that Tonya had refused to provide.

Her daughter had wanted to know *everything*. Who was he? How many years had he been supporting her? And, above all, why was he paying their rent but refusing to meet her?

Tonya had deflected each question in hopes that her daughter would give up before posing the final one. She'd known every query was a segue to Layla asking why her biological father wanted to remain secret. As Layla had asked her questions, Tonya had felt like she was driving up a stretch of mountain road leading to a summit and inevitable drop-off. On the other side of that last question was nothing but an emotional free fall.

The phone continued to ring. Kelner's secretary picked up, her voice all business and then faux concern. "Yes, I understand. Well, I'll have to see if he's in. You don't have to hold."

"Oh yes, I do."

Every muscle in Tonya's strained neck fought to constrain her vocal cords, to keep them from vibrating at a speed that would produce a harpy's cry. The threat to board the next Midtown-bound train and barge through the law firm's door lodged in the back of her throat.

As hold music played, Tonya paced the sliver of space between her bed and the wall. When she couldn't stand doing that anymore, she opened her window and climbed out onto the fire escape. Her fury kept the cold from registering. This was not how things were supposed to go. The payments were automatically deposited and the bills withdrawn—no matter what. Even in the event of death, the money was supposed to come out of Layla's father's estate.

Kelner came on the line just as Tonya was poised to start down the steps in search of yet more space. She responded to his curt greeting with a seething whisper. "How dare you talk to my daughter."

"Ms. Sayre, I understand you're upset."

"Why would you—"

"Your daughter answered the phone and didn't identify herself. I'd believed that I was speaking with you."

"She's eleven. E-le-ven." Tonya broke the age into three clear syllables. "We sound nothing, absolutely nothing, alike."

"On the phone, that's not clear, and you and I don't speak—"

"What in the hell did you tell my kid?" Tonya shouted.

Dead air answered.

Tonya tilted her head back in a silent scream. She might not sound like Layla, but she was in her daughter's exact position. Just as she knew more than she'd told her kid, Kelner had the information that Tonya needed. It was the attorney's choice—not hers—whether he shared any of it.

The silence on the line made Tonya aware of the sounds below. She glanced through the metal staircase to see a car rumble past and at least one individual lingering on the side-walk, staring up as though she might be a jumper. She raised a hand in apology and slunk inside.

Back in her bedroom, she forced herself onto her mattress and dialed a second time. Ringing resounded until there was a loud click. Tonya clenched the duvet beneath her, deter-mined to keep her tone neutral as she left a message.

"Have you calmed down?" Kelner answered.

The question didn't help Tonya's effort to restrain her anger. She swallowed hard. "I'd like to know what you said to my daughter."

An exhale, loud as rushing water, reverberated in the speaker. "Thinking she was you, I explained that it had come to my attention that the account had been closed and all remaining funds withdrawn, which I understood must be causing some problems."

"How is that possible? I don't even have access to withdraw funds. The rent is direct paid. I—"

"No one is claiming it was you, Ms. Sayre. As I told your daughter, the account is under Layla's father's name, and he controls it."

Tonya sucked in air. "He doesn't control it. He puts money into it and then automatic bill pay does the rest. That was the whole agreement. Neither he nor I touch it. Whatever remains after the rent and the amount that transfers to me quarterly for groceries and incidentals is held in trust for Layla's future college payments. She had nearly eighty thousand dollars in there."

"Ms. Sayre—"

Tonya could tell Kelner was about to give her a lecture about her volume or tone. She knew she wasn't doing a good job of keeping it level. But she also was aware that closing the account breached every agreement they'd ever had. She'd been wronged—multiple times. Her tone should be self-righteous.

"No matter what happens," Tonya said through gritted teeth. "When we worked out this deal, that was the caveat, right? No matter what happens, I don't tell anyone who he is—I don't explain how he manipulated me and lied and cheated—and he pays his child support with a bit extra thrown in for pain and suffering. That's the deal."

"Ms. Sayre, we don't need to relitigate prior matters. Please calm down."

Tonya grabbed her thigh with her free hand and squeezed, containing her anger the same way she might a muscle cramp. "Layla's money needs to be restored immediately."

The attorney cleared his throat. "The problem is that, from an outside perspective, it was never clearly Layla's money in the account."

"Come on, you—"

"Though the account is run for her benefit, it is not a trust fund," Kelner said. "That's an important distinction. If it were a trust account, the funds could not be released until Layla came of age. The account in question was a standard checking account for expenses related to Layla's care. And, as you know, Layla's father had some concerns that the money might be misappropriated—"

Tonya squeezed her thigh harder. "I don't spend my daughter's money on anyone or anything unrelated to Layla's care."

"Again, Ms. Sayre, please calm down and let me finish." Kelner's voice was now the one that was elevated. "There were concerns that the childcare payments could be used for your personal expenses, so we all agreed on an arrangement of setting up an account, controlled by Layla's father, from which your rent would be withdrawn as well as the quarterly stipend you've referenced. Layla's father always had access to the money and could close the account at any time. And he did."

If she hadn't been so close to screaming, Tonya might have laughed at the lawyer's careful use of pronouns and possessives. They'd gone to such lengths to hide Layla's parentage that the attorney didn't even want to utter his name. He was the Candyman or Voldemort, the man so powerful and evil that you didn't dare call him.

"*He*." Tonya stressed the word to show that she was aware of what the attorney was doing, even as she also refused specifics. Layla was right outside and, by and large, eleven-year-olds possessed excellent hearing. "He must pay the agreed upon child support. What did he think? That if he had a rough twelve months he could snatch his daughter's money to make up the difference?"

"As I understand it, the account closure is unrelated to any financial issues stemming from the pandemic."

"The timing—two months ago—suggests otherwise."

Kelner sighed. "His wife became aware of the account and wanted it closed."

"She doesn't get to make that decision. It's Layla's money."

"From his wife's perspective, it was a private checking account that was, perhaps, being used to siphon off marital assets."

This was karma, Tonya thought. She'd been too relieved about Nate being silenced. She hadn't spent enough time thinking of what his death meant for his daughter. The universe was punishing her for being selfish.

"And before he closed the account to make his wife happy, did *he* tell her that he was not siphoning off anything because *he* is legally required to take care of *his* child?"

Kelner cleared his throat. "I am working on reestablishing

a custodial account as per the initial contract. Regrettably, it could take some time."

"My rent is two months past due. I don't have time."

"Well"—Kelner's voice took on a new energy—"I have good news there. There's a moratorium on evictions at the moment. Even if this whole business takes a bit to sort out, you will be able to remain in your apartment. And if I can be of any assistance in that, I'd be happy to help—providing, of course, that discretion continues to be maintained."

Tonya coughed up a *thank you*, aware that her landlord would have a notice on her front door in no time. The phrase left a bad taste in her mouth. She wasn't thankful. She was rageful, furious at Kelner for thinking that a poor little waitress had no choice but to shut up and beg for money that rightfully belonged to her daughter, incensed at Layla's father for canceling the account two months ago under pressure from his clueless wife, and most of all, infuriated with herself for not immediately realizing when the payments had stopped and proceeding as if the money was an automatic bank transfer that would continue without interruption. She should have been more on top of her finances. More careful in dealing with him. More cunning.

Still, Kelner was wrong if he thought that Tonya would simply wait with her lips zipped. Her silence had a price. And, like any past-due bill, there had to be consequences for failure to pay on time. She just needed to determine what those would be, and how she might make them happen.

CHAPTER ELEVEN

RICK

"How did we miss him come out?"

Frank slammed a fist into the steering wheel. His right hand twitched by the gearshift where it had been for several hours, waiting for an opportunity to grab the revolver in the console and wave it around. Rick had convinced him not to enter the building. There were too many burly guys armed with machetes in restaurant kitchens. He was pretty sure that the unarmed half of a two-man team wouldn't make it out alive in that environment.

"He must have left out of a back entrance." Rick pointed to the alley abutting Banque Gauche's brick exterior.

"We would have seen him. It only exits out onto this street. There are dumpsters at the back, pressed against a brick wall."

Rick turned his head toward the passenger window, not wanting Frank to witness his surprise. He hadn't expected that his partner would have done any reconnaissance for this confrontation. Part of him had thought that Frank was simply venting his fury. He'd figured stewing in a car for a couple hours would make his partner simmer down, and he still believed they should try negotiating again without Frank's new toy. Brandishing a gun and demanding to talk about their investment—hours after the man who'd introduced them to the business "opportunity" had been shot to death—would send anybody straight to the cops.

Rick heard the click of locks releasing. Frank pulled the weapon from the console and slipped it into his peacoat pocket before cracking the door. A blast of cold wind barreled through the opening.

"You coming?"

In Rick's opinion, their little stakeout had been ridiculous, and whatever Frank wanted to do next would surely prove more so. He had other things to worry about. His wife, for one. Her divorce attorney, for another. Moreover, the weather outside was bitter. It was bad enough that they'd been idling in the car as the temperature dropped, occasionally running the engine to keep the interior at a manageable level of unpleasant.

"What's the point?" Rick asked, his focus flitting from Frank's furious expression to the pocket concealing his weapon.

"Maybe he didn't get past us," Frank said. "He might have seen the car and decided to hole up in there."

Rick pulled his own wool coat tighter around his neck and began closing the top button. "Let's talk to him tomorrow when our heads are clear and we're not worked up about Nate."

Frank's brow lowered. He had a big square head atop a short body made blocky by too many business lunches.

Usually, Rick found Frank comical-looking, a real-life Lego man. There was nothing funny about the look on Frank's face, though.

For the first time, Rick wondered how new the gun in Frank's pocket really was and whether it had been used before.

"Come on," Frank snorted. "Neither of us could give a shit about Nate, and you know it. He hadn't been bringing in anything but trouble for years." Frank patted his pocket. "And I told you. I'm done talking."

Frank slammed the door and started across the street. Rick watched him step up to one of the restaurant's massive windows and press his face to the plate glass. Were it not for the expensive cut of his coat and the patent leather loafers on his feet, someone might think he was trying to rob the place.

He turned around and waved frantically for Rick to join him. A curse escaped Rick's lips. It hung in the air, a cloud of hot breath carrying his bad language. Frank had seen something in that window—maybe the man himself.

Rick climbed out of the Porsche's low bucket seat and onto the sidewalk. Before he slammed the door, he glanced inside for the key. It would be like his partner to jump out, leave it inside, and then blame him for getting an eighty-thousand-dollar sports car stolen and stripped for parts.

He didn't see a fob in the console. Rick raised his hand and waved until he got Frank's attention. He pressed his fingers together and jiggled his wrist, communicating his question without shouting.

Frank patted his other coat pocket and then tossed his

hand in the air, perhaps telling him to forget it or, maybe, to kiss off. He started toward the alley.

Rick shut the door and hustled to catch up. "You saw him?" The question came out in a theatrical stage whisper. Though Rick didn't want this confrontation to occur, he definitely didn't want to tip anyone off that it might happen.

"I'm telling you, he couldn't have gotten past us." Frank rounded the building's corner, disappearing into the alley.

Rick peered inside before following. The space was lit by the streetlamp and a floodlight over the restaurant's side door. As Frank had said, there were dumpsters, though they were pressed against the other side of the alley, not against the back wall that turned the alley into a dead end.

Frank stood at the restaurant's side door, gloved hand wrapped around the knob. He jostled it aggressively.

The door didn't budge.

Rick felt his shoulders lower. "He locked up and went home."

Frank paced back and forth beneath the light, a lion in a spot-lit pen. "What is he, a damn magician?" Frank pointed at the wall. "You think he scaled that thing?"

The barrier was only about six feet high. Rick imagined that an extremely fit man could reach the top and pull himself over. The easier way would be to push over the dumpster, climb on top, and then amble over the wall, but the dumpster's position indicated that it hadn't been commandeered as a stepstool.

"It's possible." Rick shrugged. "I don't think he's the type, though. He always struck me as the kind of guy who wouldn't run from a fight."

Rick studied Frank's face, hoping that his partner's expression would betray some healthy fear at his warning. Instead, Frank's bottom lip pushed up his top, giving him the look of an angry bulldog. His hands dove into his pockets.

He withdrew the gun in one fluid motion as he whirled toward the door. Before Rick could stop him, Frank pointed it at the floodlight and fired. The shot reverberated against the brick, turning the pistol's pop into a shotgun blast. Glass rained down on the pavement. The alley went pitch dark.

"What did you do that for?" Rick yelled in spite of himself. He needed to be quiet. With luck, there hadn't been a cop within earshot, and they could still make it back to the car without being charged with vandalism or, worse, attempted burglary.

"He needs to know," Frank shouted back. "I'm done fucking playing. I want our money back, and I'm not going to sit tight until he spends it all trying to keep this shithole in the black—'cause there won't be anything to recover then, even if the courts say he owes us. You can't get blood out of a stone. We need to squeeze him now."

Rick realized that both his hands were on his hips, the classic dad-scolding stance. But Frank wasn't some kid he could shame into better behavior. "He'll probably think this was an attempted robbery gone wrong," Rick said.

"Then we'll just have to do something that leaves no doubt," Frank countered.

Rick heard footsteps and felt the thud of Frank's shoulder bumping into his own.

"Like what?"

The fear in his voice was palpable. Rick guessed that

Frank could hear it as well, because he turned around. The streetlamp beyond outlined Frank's square body in light, casting his face in shadow. It was difficult to see, but Rick was almost certain that he could make out Frank's expression. His partner was smiling.

CHAPTER TWELVE

IMANI

A door slam woke Imani. She gasped as though a pair of invisible hands had released her throat. Vaguely, she remembered retreating to her room to read the latest articles and commentary about Nate's death. The coverage hadn't revealed any additional facts about the case, though the army of online armchair detectives had included plenty of speculation about Melissa's culpability and motives. Revenge for infidelity appeared to be the leading theory. No one had posted evidence of Nate having an affair, but his occupation was its own indictment.

Imani supposed she'd dozed off. Guilt at having abandoned Ava overcame the sadness sapping her energy, forcing her from the recliner where she'd fallen asleep. Counseling individuals dealing with trauma was her literal job, yet Imani had left a grieving teen in the care of a fifteen-year-old. "Mother of the year," she admonished herself.

The hallway outside her room was windowless, penned in by bedrooms and the stairs leading both to the first floor and the attic. Her eyes adjusted to the little light emanating from her open door, confirming that both her kids' doors were closed. She cracked the first one, revealing Jay stretched out on his extra-long twin, covered only by a sheet despite the freezing temperatures outside. Imani was tempted to pull up the duvet bunched at the bed's edge, but she restrained herself. Pubescent boys were living, breathing furnaces. He'd only kick it off again.

She headed to Vivienne's room next. Before entering, she listened through the wall, aware that her daughter might be talking to Ava and resent any interruption. When her kids had been younger, she'd retained the moral authority to do nearly anything simply because she was Mom. Now she had to respect Vivienne's and Jay's privacy. Nine months of carrying these beautiful creatures in her belly only for them to constantly demand space a decade later.

Hearing nothing, Imani placed her palm on the door for a full second as if testing for fire. Feeling nothing, she turned the knob like a dial. When the lock clicked, she pulled back the door.

Blond hair shone white on Vivienne's violet pillowcase. Her daughter had apparently given Ava her bed, choosing to sleep on the trundle mattress below in the guard dog position. Imani could make out her kid's ringlets falling from the edge of the mattress onto the shadowed floor.

Imani shut the door. Perhaps it had been best that Vivienne had taken over for her. Fear for Melissa had erased years of Imani's therapeutic training. Instead of actively listening, she'd been spouting unsupported assurances that Melissa would be found safe, exhausting her credibility on lies to make herself feel better. It was little wonder that Vivienne had taken Ava to her room post-dinner.

The lights were off on the first floor. Imani's skin prickled as she stood on the landing, too afraid to descend. Someone operated in the darkness. Someone bigger than her. She could sense the person's size by the sounds creeping up the stairs, the heaviness of the footsteps, and the bang of kitchen cabinets.

"Philip?" Imani whispered his name so as not to wake the children. Though she didn't know the time, it was certainly late. The street noises that were the sonic backdrop to her waking life had completely shut off. There was only the tinkling of liquid hitting glass.

Imani forced herself to step down. Her body buzzed as if she'd fallen into a pool of carbonated water and oxygen bubbles were launching off her every pore. She grabbed the banister to steady herself, held her breath, and strained to hear.

A cabinet shut. "Imani?"

Philip's voice recalled tires on a worn road. It was gravelly and hoarse from the day, yet still familiar. Still her husband's.

She descended the remaining steps and entered the narrow kitchen. Light from a far window illuminated the right side of Philip's face, highlighting a deep-set eye, heavy frown line, and pale skin glistening with sweat. He hovered over the cement countertop, a scotch glass in one hand.

The irony of chefs was that they often ate like food was irrelevant. In spite of possessing a palate that could detect a grain of salt in a spoonful of sugar, Philip would inhale cold leftovers while standing in a corner. At the restaurant, he often wolfed down the trimmings of whatever was on the menu: cod fish tacos filled with the remnants of skinny tail pieces or shredded beef sandwiches made from less-than-prime cuts. Philip didn't take time to dine unless he was sampling the competition.

He also rarely treated his family to homecooked meals. After spending all day in a professional kitchen, her husband couldn't bear to waste time waiting for a stove to reach four hundred or working with a pan that no longer evenly distributed heat. When the family ate at home, it was Imani's efforts that they consumed, most often fashioned from a combination of store-bought shortcuts and online recipes.

"There's takeout pizza in the fridge," Imani said. "It was all I could do to order."

Philip stepped forward as her voice broke on the last word. A long sinewy arm extended, offering to pull her into safety and comfort. She refused to accept it. Philip had left her alone to deal with the disappearance of a woman who might as well be her sister and console their children about the loss of "Uncle Nate," all the while caring for Melissa's grieving daughter. He'd faced a choice between helping her through a harrowing time and attending to his business. He'd chosen the restaurant. Again.

"Babe, come here."

Imani hugged her torso, pulling her sweater tighter around her midsection. "The kids are asleep." Her tone betrayed her disappointment more than her exhaustion. "I passed out sometime after cleaning the kitchen. I don't know when. Since the police came, I've been operating in a daze."

Philip's outstretched arm retreated into his chest. He set down the drink and unbuttoned the collar of his chef's jacket. "The cops were here?"

"They wanted to question Ava about whether she'd seen anything."

Philip unhooked another button. "Did she?"

"I guess she was sleeping with a sound machine on. She has no idea what happened or where Melissa could be."

"So what do the police seem to think?"

The question suggested that Philip had not yet read any of the news coverage. "I think they're leaning toward murder." Imani rested her back against the counter, suddenly too tired to support her own weight. "Apparently, Nate's hands lacked gunshot residue."

Philip wiped his mouth, dragging his former expression into a concerned pout.

"I think they may even suspect Melissa," Imani added, "which is obviously ridiculous."

Her husband's eyes opened wide. "Jesus, really? That's . . ."

As he trailed off, the whites of his eyes took on a wet gleam. In all the years she'd known him, Imani could count on one hand the times she'd seen Philip cry: the birth of their kids, their wedding day, and once back when they'd been dating and had a huge argument that they'd both assumed might end things.

He wasn't crying so much as becoming teary-eyed. Still, Imani was surprised that Nate's death had so moved her husband. Though Philip had hung out with Melissa's spouse a good deal over the past ten years, it was always because of plans involving the families. Nate had been Phil's counterpart in the Imani/Melissa, Vivienne/Ava package. Imani had always thought the husbands' friendship akin to the relationship between her son, Jay, and Melissa's daughter. Her boy was polite, and Ava tolerated him because he was tied to a dear friend.

"That's terrible," Philip whispered.

Imani suspected Philip's tears were truly for Ava. Like Imani, Philip knew what it was like to lose a parent young. Both of his had perished in a car crash before his twenty-third birthday. At the time, he'd been living at home, fresh off a four-year enlistment with the marines, working the bottom rungs in a restaurant kitchen. Philip often brought up his parents after reaching milestones, regretting that they'd never seen him enroll in culinary school, let alone graduate or open his first restaurant.

Philip's vulnerability activated Imani's maternal instincts. Though she was still upset, she embraced him, wrapping her arms around his waist and placing her head between his pectorals. At six-three, Philip was nearly a foot taller than she, so a kiss wasn't possible unless he bent to her level.

"I'm so scared for Melissa." Imani felt her own tears on her husband's shirt. "At first, I kept thinking that she was somewhere and hadn't heard what had happened. But they would have found her by now. She has to be in real danger or..."

Imani couldn't make herself say the obvious. Philip patted her head, unable to run his fingers through the curls that had reasserted themselves in the year since she last visited a hairdresser. "Maybe she's somewhere getting her head straight," Philip said. "She's out there, figuring out what to do next."

Imani looked into Philip's now-dry eyes. "Melissa didn't kill Nate."

"I'm not saying she murdered him, honey. Maybe there was an accident, they were arguing—"

"And what? She pulled out a gun and shot him?" Imani arched her back, signaling to Philip that she wanted out of his vise grip.

He released her. "I don't know. Maybe he had the gun and—"

"Nate wasn't abusive."

Philip reached for his whiskey. "Who knows what really goes on in a marriage?" He punctuated his statement with a sip of his drink, inhaling the alcohol like a smoker taking a pull off a cigarette.

Instinctively, Imani crossed her arms over her chest. "Melissa would have told me if Nate had ever gotten violent with her."

Philip set down his glass. Amber liquid sloshed over the side. Clearly he'd poured himself a double. "There's a first time for everything. I mean, they're stuck in a house together day in and day out, unable to cool off from an argument in their normal ways by having a cocktail with a friend or *whatever*."

The last word was loaded. "I don't know what you're implying."

Philip turned his attention to the fridge. "Okay, then. Never mind."

The fridge's fluorescent bulbs added a yellow glow to the shadowed surroundings, highlighting the tight line of Philip's lips. His face showed a strain that Imani swore hadn't been there before. The therapist inside of her noted it and said to tread lightly. But Imani the wife wanted Philip to explain himself. If even her husband thought her best friend guilty, then what chance did Melissa have of the police taking her safety seriously?

"You clearly have something to say," Imani snapped.

Philip considered the scant selection on the fridge's shelves before withdrawing a jar of kimchi. "I wouldn't be telling you anything you don't know."

"What do I know, Philip?"

He opened the container, wrinkled his nose, and then capped it, shaking his head the whole while.

"What do I know?" she repeated.

"You know that Nate had a wandering eye and Melissa could be . . ."

"What?"

Philip sighed. "Flirtatious."

Imani pulled her chin into her neck, displaying the indignation that she didn't actually feel. The truth was that both Melissa and Nate had loved to work a room. Imani could picture Melissa at a dinner party, moving from guest to guest, asking if anyone needed anything while making elaborate, flattering, and often innuendo-filled introductions to both men and women. *You don't know Philip? Well, let me introduce you to the man of the hour or hors, right? Hors d'oeuvres. I'm being punny because small plates are the specialty of Banque Gauche, Philip's restaurant. You can't judge a man by the size of his plate, though. Just his Michelin stars. High reviews, this one. Isn't that right, Imani? Imani Banks. Philip's better half, but my girl. Keeps me sane, and not only because she's a celebrated psychotherapist. I don't know what I'd do without her living among all these neurotic New Yorkers.*

Imani believed that such coquetry was confined to party conversation—at least on Melissa's part. Though Melissa flirted, she was always checking over her shoulder to see if Nate was noticing. Imani assumed that flirting with others was a game for them. The way they kept their marriage interesting. They'd each endeavored to attract just enough attention to make sure that they held each other's own.

"A penchant for holding court isn't against any marriage laws," Imani said.

Philip put the kimchi back in the fridge and slammed the door. The sound echoed off the high ceilings.

"We can disagree without you waking the kids." Imani hissed.

"It's not that . . ." Philip rubbed his forehead. Whenever her husband had trouble saying something, he massaged the words into his brain.

"I'm going to close the restaurant."

"What?"

Though Imani had heard him, she assumed some mistake. Banque Gauche hadn't been doing well amid all the restaurant shutdowns, of course. But it wasn't an ordinary eatery that would go belly-up after a few bad months. Her husband's place was an institution. Michelin-starred tourist destinations around for a decade-plus didn't simply close down. They perished only after prolonged downturns that left plenty of time for estate planning.

"I'll keep the kitchen open for delivery," Philip continued.

"But the staff isn't earning enough in tips to make a living, and I can't keep paying folks to wait on nonexistent customers."

Imani suddenly understood the source of Philip's tears. He was sad for Ava, surely, but he was devastated for himself. Banque Gauche was her husband's baby, sprung like Athena from his frontal cortex, made entirely in his image. It was the only thing that could compete with Philip's feelings for his family, and win.

"I hope you understand why I couldn't be with you today. Things are bad." Philip threw up a hand. "I mean, everywhere you look. Nate. Melissa's disappearance. People choking to death on their own phlegm. A city that's become a ghost town." The raised hand curled into a fist. It knocked twice on his forehead. "I don't know what to do anymore."

As much as Imani wanted to ask questions, she forced herself to think like a therapist. Her husband's identity was melded with his career. Closing his restaurant had to feel like excising a limb.

She reached for the hand engaged in the mock beating. "No one could have anticipated all that's happened. You've done the best possible."

Philip dropped his fists to his sides. He looked longingly at his scotch.

"Don't worry," she continued. "We'll manage. We have my salary and our savings, and we only have the property taxes on the house. We'll—"

"We owe on the house."

For the second time, Imani had trouble processing the words she'd so clearly heard. They couldn't owe on their home. Philip had inherited the place free and clear from his parents. When she'd met him, he'd been treating his childhood residence as a flophouse, letting rooms to other guys working their way up in kitchens like himself. But that hadn't been about paying any mortgage. He'd wanted to fill the vacancies left by his folks and earn extra spending cash. Debt had never been an issue with the house.

"We can't keep this place, you mean. You want to sell it?"

Philip drained the rest of his whiskey. He poured another as he spoke. "Remember when I revamped the restaurant and added Coffre? I took out a loan—a home equity line of credit. I thought I'd have paid it off by now, but the refresh didn't bring in the level of new business that I'd hoped, and then the pandemic hit and Coffre had to close. Nearly every penny over the past year has gone toward the lease and staff salaries. There's been nothing left over to pay down the debt."

Imani placed a hand on the counter, concerned that her knees might buckle. After eighteen years of living together, surely the carriage house was as much her place as his. How could he have taken out a loan and not told her?

"How much is the mortgage?"

"Six grand a month."

She breathed in through clenched teeth. A back-of-the-envelope calculation wasn't required to show that her salary couldn't cover that kind of a payment, even with the entertainment budget set at zero, their transportation costs cut in half, and no household help. Philip had insisted that they let go of their cleaning lady at the start of the pandemic. Given this new information, Imani couldn't help but wonder if his fear of exposing the children to COVID had simply been a cover for their inability to afford a weekly maid visit.

"Do you think we can renegotiate with the bank?" she asked.

"I'll figure something out. Cut costs. A different menu." Philip was muttering to himself rather than truly explaining anything. "I sold off most of what was in Coffre. But the bar countertop is still there. When restaurants really reopen, somebody will want that."

Coffre's fire sale had already happened. Imani couldn't imagine that whatever was left would be worth more than a few thousand dollars. "Well, school tuition is paid through the year," she said, trying to be grateful for small blessings. "I can cover, maybe, four thousand a month. I'll ask to pick up shifts at the hospital."

Philip set his drink on the counter. "Absolutely not."

"Woodhill is always looking for clinical psychologists."

"Yeah, because the crazy people knife those on staff."

Imani winced at the memory of the case: a Hopkins-trained psychotherapist had been stabbed repeatedly by a patient who'd faked taking his meds after convincing himself that the doctor was trying to poison him. "Patients don't have access to knives," she muttered. The assailant in the case had used a ballpoint pen.

"Over my dead body."

"What else can I do?" Imani snapped. "You took out this loan."

Philip grabbed both of her arms. His fingers tightened around her biceps like police cuffs placed too high. "Listen, babe, I'll fix this, okay? I won't let the bank kick us out of our home. I won't let them shut down my business. And I won't let you risk your safety to help. I'll figure something out."

Imani couldn't imagine what solution Philip would invent. But she couldn't question him anymore. The day's revelations had knocked her down sure as a taxi speeding through a crosswalk. She lacked the energy to speak, let alone argue.

Imani fell into her husband's arms, allowing him to rub her back and whisper lies. *Things will be fine. I can tweak the menu. The customers will soon return.* Tears flowed down her cheeks. The pandemic had been their personal apocalypse. Fighting was futile, Imani thought. Her only option was surrender.

CHAPTER THIRTEEN

TONYA

There was an art to asking a favor. Tonya had learned it through trial and error thanks to farmer parents who'd been overextended in every way that, counted. And the first part of that art was picking the right person to ask.

People you've helped in the past were best. After that, you wanted to hit up folks most likely to sympathize with your situation, the kind of people who would think *but for the grace of God go I*. Individuals with robber baron wealth could perhaps be counted on for lavish charitable gifts, but Tonya knew that such people didn't see folks like her as worthy of their largesse—or even tax dollars. Those who worked for a living were more likely to offer a handout to individuals down on their luck, particularly when the individuals in question were neighbors and colleagues who might one day return the kindness.

Philip was the perfect target. Though he wasn't exactly in Tonya's debt, he knew that she'd been working for him at far below her usual salary and that her skill set would be in demand once the pandemic ended. If anyone would provide a bridge loan or an opportunity to earn more money, it would be him.

Tonya showed up at the restaurant ten minutes before 6:00 a.m., well before the start of her Saturday brunch shift. Typically, the prep cooks arrived at that hour to ready all the ingredients that would ultimately be incorporated into savory crepes and callaloo, poached eggs over cod fritters, and four other Philip Banks breakfast specialties mashing French classics with Caribbean flavors. Since losing his sous-chef, Philip had begun getting in around dawn as well.

Staff did not enter through the front door. Just before reaching Banque Gauche's picture windows, Tonya ducked into a side alley, passing the industrial-sized dumpsters where the restaurant tossed its food waste. In the summer, it was nearly impossible to be in the narrow space without retching from the stink of curdled sauces and accumulated leftovers. But the winter transformed the bins into an outdoor icebox, leaving only a faint metallic scent.

The kitchen entrance was directly across from the garbage. Her shoes crunched on the pavement as she approached the door. She lifted her loafer, revealing what appeared to be glitter covering the rubber soles. Something had broken, Tonya realized. Maybe a glass or a plate.

Tonya winced, recalling her earlier accident with the full tray. She walked through the door with her head down, weighted by the residual shame of the memory and her desire not to call attention to herself. The kitchen's station heads viewed themselves as an offensive line protecting their quarterback from being hit from behind. They would run interference if they thought she was trying to blindside Philip with a request.

As she reached the walk-in fridge, Tonya realized that such caution wasn't necessary. No cooks chopped atop butcher blocks or brought ingredients to and from the pantry. The hustle and bustle that Tonya was accustomed to wasn't simply subdued; it was nonexistent.

The atmosphere recalled a horror movie set. At any point, it seemed a knife-wielding lunatic would leap from behind some stainless-steel cabinet. None of her colleagues would be there to save her.

"Hello?" Tonya called out as she headed toward the main dining room. She pulled the mask covering her face onto her chin, allowing her voice to carry. "Hello?"

A soft thud responded, like the closing of a cabinet. It was followed by a tense silence, the kind in which the body can sense another presence but not see or hear it. Was someone quietly breaking in? Burglaries were more frequent now that many of the city stores and eateries had been boarded up.

Instinct urged Tonya to run back through the kitchen and dive into the alley. But need pushed her forward. There was no bag of money in the dumpster outside. No way to pay her rent or feed her child while Kelner took his time working out a new child support arrangement.

"Hello?" she repeated.

Heavy footsteps answered, the kind made by a man striding toward a target. Tonya clenched her fists and stood her ground near the repurposed security grates. She heard a clatter followed by the sound of things being moved around.

"Who's there?" she yelled.

"Hello?" Her question echoed in a male baritone that Tonya was almost sure she recognized.

She walked forward to find Philip at the dining room bar. A plate sat in front of him, covered by a napkin. He poured a fancy whiskey into a shot glass. Hard alcohol before noon was never a good sign, but it could be excused with the presence of food and a splash of juice. Who didn't enjoy a Bloody Mary with brunch? The mixers were right there on the back bar. Everything Philip needed to turn a shot into a cocktail.

Philip downed the drink without additions. Tonya took a tentative step closer. As she did, she could appreciate the gray undertone of Philip's ivory complexion. He seemed more wan than usual, as if he'd suffered several sleepless nights. Tonya assumed her own face reflected similar exhaustion.

"Tonya. What are you doing here?" Philip asked, as if he'd caught her stealing. He rubbed a hand over his bare face. "Your shift isn't for three hours."

"I was hoping to speak with you, actually."

"Oh." Philip pulled out one of the bar stools. He gestured to it and stepped back, giving her a six-foot berth. He slid his shot glass down several feet to his new post.

Tonya took the seat. For a moment, she gazed longingly at the glasses lined up beneath the liquor bottles on the back bar. A little alcohol would make the coming conversation so much easier. But Philip wasn't offering.

Tonya sighed. "You know it's been difficult lately with the lack of reservations and tip—"

"I do, and I'm sorry for that, Tonya. In fact, I'd intended to call you before you came in today. You might have noticed that the kitchen staff isn't in."

Tonya's nervousness solidified into an icy block.

"I have to close the dining room and furlough the waitstaff until further notice." Philip gestured to the empty expanse surrounding them. "Unfortunately, we don't have enough customers in the igloos to justify the expense of staying open. I know how unfair it's been for you and the others to work a full shift with barely any tips. You all should be able to collect unemployment rather than scraping by on minimum wage." He offered an encouraging smile. "Especially you. You've been with this restaurant since nearly the beginning. I appreciate your loyalty. You deserve much better than what I can provide at the moment."

What she deserved and what she required had nothing to do with one another, Tonya wanted to say. After a decade working as a waitress and then wait captain, she knew that she merited more than a base salary that wouldn't even have covered Manhattan studio rent a decade earlier—without adjusting for inflation. She knew waiting tables at Banque wasn't worth it if she didn't have tips and other perks. But she also knew that she needed money. It wasn't as though she could walk into a vibrant neighboring kitchen with a polished résumé. Everything was closed.

"I'll be keeping on a skeleton crew for takeout dinner service in hopes of maintaining the brand. But I can't..." Philip grabbed for the bottle of Bushmills Black and poured another shot. "I'm so sorry."

Tonya didn't consider herself a crier. However, losing her job the morning after listening to Layla wail about her mother's lies was the proverbial last straw. "I understand," Tonya said, blinking away the tears blurring her vision.

Philip downed the shot. "Over a decade and Banque Gauche never closed. I prided myself on that. So many restaurants come and go, but our doors were always open."

Tonya wasn't sure whether Philip was speaking to her or to himself. His voice was low, barely above a whisper. He tapped his left ring finger against the shot glass, creating a soft pinging sound like raindrops on subway grates. "We tried, eh? Coffre was so beautiful. I really thought it was going to be a new beginning."

He suddenly turned his attention to her, fixing her with that microwave stare—the one that could penetrate a person and grill their insides. "I'm sorry. You'd said you wanted to discuss something."

Tonya looked up at the ceiling, not wanting to see someone like Philip, who'd probably never been behind in a payment, judge her as one of those irresponsible poor people—the kind of person who sent her kid to a ritzy school, the same one her boss's kids attended, no less— even though she couldn't keep a roof over her head.

"My child support hasn't been coming for a few months, and I'm behind in the rent," she said. "I wanted to see if I could pick up some extra work. Maybe cleaning."

Philip's body relaxed into a rounded shape. For a moment, Tonya thought he might cry.

The emotion passed. Her boss's posture straightened, re-assuming the gravitas that a head chef normally commanded. "I don't want to lose a good worker who's been with us for so long. Give me a couple days, okay? I'll see what I can do."

If she wanted to keep her home, she needed more than a casual promise from Philip to perhaps keep her on staff. She'd need to make sure that she had a job—no matter what.

Tonya offered a pained smile and brushed a tear from the corner of her eye, drawing attention to what she knew was her best feature. "Thank you." She moved toward Philip, reducing the social distance between them, drawing close enough for him to appreciate her lineless skin and shiny hair. He was handsome enough, she told herself. Successful. Hardworking. Kinder than Nate, certainly.

Tonya tilted up her chin and looked as expectant as possible. She'd done this move for directors, her Sleeping-Beauty-awaiting-a-kiss impression. "I would really appreciate it," she cooed.

Philip seemed to get the hint. He bit his bottom lip, as if considering how to obtain more clarification, and then glanced at the bar. Maybe she would finally get that shot, she thought. She'd need it.

"What are you drink—"

Before she could finish her question, a harsh ring erupted from her coat pocket. She silenced it almost immediately, but the noise had already done its damage. When she looked up at Philip again, it was clear that any moment between them had passed. Her boss was back to frowning at the reflection in his whiskey.

He palmed the glass and headed toward the kitchen. "I should get home," he said. "I don't want my wife to wake up and wonder where I ran off to. She knows I'm not working."

Tonya tried to parse the statement as she followed him

back toward the exit. Was he rejecting her or simply suggesting that now wasn't a good time? Would he help her stay on regardless?

"Philip, I—"

"I look out for people who do good work," he said, calling over his shoulder rather than stopping to talk. "I really will do my best."

Philip traversed the kitchen, clearing it in seconds with his long-legged stride. Tonya heard the door open. He stood beside it, a doorman booting her from the club.

She thanked him anyway as she headed out into the cold. The door shut behind her, urging her to keep moving forward, to ignore the tears of humiliation building behind her eyes. Again, her shoes crunched on the pavement, as if someone had spread salt by the door.

Instead of examining her feet, Tonya approached the dumpster, curious as to the source of all the glass. One of the cooks might have broken something—perhaps an item more expensive than the glasses she'd destroyed.

The grit beneath her work loafers seemed to disappear as she drew closer. She could feel the regular rough texture of the road. The sound effects stopped.

Suddenly, her foot rolled atop something cylindrical. She hopped back, expecting to see a massive shard, perhaps the stem of a wineglass. Instead, inches from her shoes lay something that didn't belong yet was immediately recognizable— at least to Tonya. A girl didn't grow up on a farm without knowing what a spent shell looked like. And there, at her feet, lay the unmistakable copper casing of a thirty-eight-millimeter bullet.

CHAPTER FOURTEEN

IMANI

Something was burning. As Imani emerged from the shower, she noticed a haze beyond the reach of any evaporating steam. It hovered in the sunlight seeping through her bedroom window, a fog perfumed with the unmistakable notes of smoke, flame, and a pungent mystery odor belonging to the thing being scalded.

Imani squeezed the excess water from her hair and grabbed her robe. She tied it while hurrying downstairs, shame fueling her speed. Vivienne had to be making breakfast. Not only had her daughter taken care of Ava the prior night, but she was also preparing a meal for the entire family, including her scattered, oversleeping mother.

"Vivi, honey?" she called out. "Sweetheart, you got up early, huh?"

"Usual time," Philip called over his shoulder before returning his attention to the task at hand. He stood in front of their range oven, the top of his head nearly level with the hood dangling from the ceiling. Imani realized that he hadn't flipped on the overhead fan, hence why she'd smelled the cooking instead of heard it.

Seeing her husband at home should have brought relief. But it didn't. When she'd woken without him, she'd assumed that all the talk of closing Banque Gauche had been little more than dramatics on Philip's part to excuse his prior absence. But his broad body crammed into her cooking corner meant that he hadn't been manipulating her. He wasn't working. Things were just as dire as he'd claimed. They might really lose their home.

The realization stoked Imani's anger. As she watched Philip monitoring pots on each of the stove's four burners, she had the urge to complain that he was doing something wrong, burning the bottoms of the copper cookware or preparing exotic proteins that the kids wouldn't touch. Unfortunately, her chef husband didn't abuse pans, and plain old bacon graced the griddle.

"You really should use the fan so the whole place doesn't stink of meat." It was the only criticism that Imani could think of other than lambasting him for secretly using their home to prop up his business. She still lacked the energy for that fight.

Philip leaned right to flip a wall switch. The fan whirred loudly. "Didn't want to wake you before," he said.

"Are the kids up?"

Philip stirred a sauce pot, releasing the scent of stewing strawberries. "They will be once I get these crepes going."

France's pancake was Philip's specialty. He made them buttery yet light. Never chewy. Seventeen years of marriage and Imani had yet to properly execute his recipe. Her efforts always resembled stretched-out pancakes with one extra-crisp side and another doughier edge.

Philip knew that everyone loved his crepes. Preparing them was a form of apology, Imani supposed, a consolation prize for failing to provide emotional support or consulting her about the home loan. But she didn't want an edible mea culpa. She wanted Philip to acknowledge what he'd done wrong. More than that, she wanted him to make things right.

"I don't know how much anyone will feel like eating," Imani mumbled, even though the food smells had already drawn out her own appetite.

Philip flipped the bacon pieces with a pair of tongs. "Jay's always hungry." He shrugged. "I got up at five thirty and went to the restaurant only to remember that I'd told everyone to forget about brunch service last night. As long as I was there, figured I'd bring home some ingredients. No sense in letting food spoil."

He was trying to keep his voice light and nonchalant, Imani realized, to avoid adding his sadness to her burden. She reminded herself that, as worried as she was about Melissa and the state of their house, Philip was dealing with his own tragedy, watching twelve years of blood, sweat, and tears evaporate due to circumstances beyond his control.

Imani relented. "Everything smells delicious."

Philip flashed a small smile. "Maybe I should have done an all-day-breakfast diner."

"A Michelin-starred diner," she quipped.

Philip returned his attention to his pots. "A Michelin-starred takeout joint."

Imani couldn't think of a clever comeback that might counter Philip's dejection. "I should get dressed," she said. "We don't know if the police will come back today."

Philip stiffened, a rabbit sensing a coyote. Cops unnerved her husband. He blamed it on all the cases of unnecessary force that made the news. But Imani believed the roots of Philip's discomfort with law enforcement ran deeper. The police who'd informed him of his parents' deaths had made an indelible, negative impression.

"You all right?" Imani asked.

Philip's posture relaxed. "Yeah." He chuckled. "I wonder if they'll want crepes."

———

They were finishing breakfast when the bell rang. Jay sprang from the table, a racehorse reacting to a retracted gate. Imani figured that he would have jumped at the chance to do just about anything. Of the group, her jokester son was the least equipped to deal with the dining room's oppressive silence.

Talking had become taboo. No one dared discuss Nate's death for fear of upsetting Ava. However, compared to murder, no other subject was sufficiently serious to warrant a mention. As a result, they'd eaten without a word, entombed in dead air while trying not to watch Ava's feeble attempts to stomach small bites.

It wasn't until Imani heard the slurp of the door seal breaking that she realized she should have answered the bell herself. Police needed an invitation to enter, and Jay was too young and polite not to provide one. Imani would at least establish some ground rules before allowing detectives Calvente and Powell to question Melissa's daughter again.

"Hello?" Jay's uncertain greeting echoed in the small vestibule.

Imani was up before their visitor—or visitors—could respond. She strode over to her son and tugged his shirtsleeve, signaling him to step back from the threshold.

On the opposite side stood an older man and woman, perhaps in their seventies. Rather than police uniforms, they each wore peacoats that appeared too thin for the season. The man, at least, had a tweed cap covering his head, which rose a full foot above Imani's own. The woman lacked any scalp protection but her short, silvery hair. Neither stranger wore a mask.

The man extended a veined hand. Imani regarded it as though shaking were a foreign custom.

"I'm sorry," she said. "May I help you?"

The hand dropped to his side. "Right. Um. Bill Walker, Nate's father, and this is his mother, Nancy."

The woman struggled to hold a tight smile. "The school said you took in Ava."

"Oh. Right. Yes."

They were the wrong words, but Imani couldn't fathom the right ones. Etiquette demanded that she say how sorry she was for their loss and invite them inside. Fear, however, urged her to walk back her subtle confirmation that Ava was even in her house. For all Imani knew, this nice older pair were opportunists seeking a chance to nab the child of a famous couple who could then be auctioned off in some sick, underground sex market. Her best friend was missing, and that friend's husband had been shot in the face, in a brownstone fortress located in one of New York's wealthiest neighborhoods. Nothing made sense anymore.

"We've come from Tennessee for our granddaughter." Bill stood straighter as he made his announcement, adding another inch to his already-imposing figure.

Nate had indeed hailed from Tennessee. But his birth state was the kind of celebrity trivia that could be verified via Google. Anyone willing to research for a few minutes would know it.

Imani nodded, still wrestling with the idea of welcoming them in. She needed to keep Ava safe. But what harm did she really expect from a seventy-something man and woman when her husband was in the house? Bill was a big guy, but Philip was a fit, decades-younger former marine.

"I-I'm sorry. It's only that we've never met," Imani said, stumbling over her words. "And I'm so sorry for your loss—"

"I understand." Bill stepped forward. "But—"

"And with the case being so publicized and Nate's fame," Imani added, unable to cut off the stream of excuses, "I'm only trying to do what Melissa would want. She's my best friend."

Nancy grasped her husband's arm, either holding him back or holding on for support. "And we're Ava's grandparents. We need to see—"

"Ava!"

Jay's voice echoed behind them. At some point during Imani's babbling, her boy had possessed the good sense to call for the one person able to verify their visitors' identities.

"I think your grandparents might be here," he shouted.

Bill took another step forward. Imani moved left in response, positioning herself in front of him. She grasped the door edge, ready to slam it at the slightest sign of confusion on Ava's face.

Philip approached with Ava a step behind. Seeing her husband relaxed Imani. If these people weren't who they said, Philip would get rid of them without a problem.

"Nana?"

Imani rotated, enabling Ava to better see their would-be guests.

"Pop!"

Ava picked up her pace, spurring Imani to relinquish her hold on the door's edge. "Please come in," she said, stepping back.

Nancy and Bill didn't seem to appreciate her belated hospitality. Ava's grandma extended her arms without entering the house, calling Ava into the cold despite the girl's socked feet and thin school sweatshirt.

"Honey, we're here." Nancy's voice recalled a tuning fork, high and trembling.

Ava fell into the woman's arms, her composure shattering. Bill immediately closed ranks, wrapping his bulky body around both wife and granddaughter, a human shield against the cold and whatever else might come.

They held each other like that for what seemed a full minute, tears streaming down cheeks, shoulders shaking. Imani studied the family portrait with regret. She should have held Ava this morning, she thought. She should have given her a shoulder to cry on rather than a glass of orange juice, a tense family breakfast, and a weak promise to call the cops later and ask if they'd learned anything more.

"Grab your things, sweetheart," Bill commanded. "We're taking you home with us."

Ava withdrew from her grandmother's chest. "But school—"

"We've spoken with St. Catherine's." Nancy grasped Ava's arm as though she feared the child stepping out of reach forever. "They said many students already log on remotely because of the pandemic. We have that fiber internet. You can attend virtually for the remainder of the year until we figure out what to do long-term."

"But I can't just go," Ava countered. "Everything I have is in my house."

Bill rubbed the back of his neck. "The police said we can pick up whatever you need."

Ava seemed to fold into herself, a paper crane crumpling into a ball. The defeatist body language made Imani question whether she should be fighting on behalf of Melissa's daughter. If Ava wanted to finish out the school year, Imani could provide a loving, safe home near St. Catherine's. She could ensure that Nate's parents didn't run off with Melissa's only child. But was that her place? Being a designated emergency contact was not the same as being entrusted with custody. Surely Nate's will had stipulated with whom Ava should stay in the event that his wife wasn't around.

"I can mail anything you need." Vivienne spoke from several feet behind them, where the foyer melded into the living area. "And I'll call you every day."

Ava hurried over to Vivienne and wrapped her arms around her. There was a desperation to their embrace, as though both girls believed that this might be the last time they saw each other. Looking at them, Imani saw herself and Melissa, saying the good-bye that Imani had never had a chance to give or get. That she wouldn't need, Imani mentally assured herself—not since Melissa would be found.

When the girls broke apart, Ava told her grandparents that her things were upstairs. Imani watched all the kids ascend to the second floor before turning her attention to Nate's parents.

"Would you come inside for a minute?"

Nancy pointed to her exposed mouth. "Not sure of the rules. We just got off a plane."

"We can put on masks," Imani offered, hating to add yet another negotiation to the looming one of where Ava should remain. "I have plenty of disposables."

Nancy looked to Bill for permission. He grasped his wife's hand and then entered the house, barely clearing the way enough for Imani to close the door behind him. "Please sit," Imani said, heading to the junk drawer repurposed as PPE compartment.

"That's okay." Bill stood his ground by the exit. "I guess Ava slept here last night as it is, and we really can't stay more than a couple minutes anyway. We have to help her pack and then head out. We don't want to stay at a hotel given everything."

Imani abandoned her errand to join Philip at the edge of the living room. She gave him a pointed look, silently asking permission to suggest that Ava stay with them. Melissa's daughter was Vivienne's best friend, after all, and she clearly didn't want to leave their school.

If Philip understood her stare, he ignored it. "I understand about the hotels," he said, directing his attention to Bill. "Some have rooms that share ventilation, so you can't be—"

"We're always happy to have Ava," Imani interjected. Philip hadn't asked her about taking a loan out on the house, she decided. Perhaps she didn't need his permission for this. "She's been friends with Vivienne since they were little, and she's often here anyway. We could—"

"It's best that Ava come home with us," Nancy said, heading her off before she could get to the point. "It's what Nate would want."

Imani didn't doubt that was true. Able-bodied grandparents, uncles, and aunts were the usual suspects when it came to custody, and in Ava's case, there was only one real blood option. Melissa's mother was in a nursing home with early onset dementia, and her father was long estranged. There was a sister in her thirties. But she'd never been married and didn't want kids, which wasn't a great résumé for the guardian of a teenager.

Still, Nate's wishes were not necessarily Melissa's. Though Imani had never before met Mr. Walker and his wife, their reputation preceded them. Melissa had griped many times about her Kentucky in-laws' refusal to spend a single holiday in Brooklyn, always insisting that Melissa, Ava, and Nate head to their house for a "real" Christmas or Thanksgiving, one that involved cutting down their own tree, shooting their own turkey, or criticizing "Hollywood people's" political opinions.

"Maybe Ava should stay local until we know more about Melissa," Imani suggested. "She might come back soon, and she'd want—"

"I doubt that."

Bill's tone was matter-of-fact and not particularly sad. Imani stared at him, waiting for some sign that he was struggling with the idea of his daughter-in-law's disappearance.

"You mean you think she's..." Imani trailed off, unwilling to utter the word *dead* lest it somehow sink into the universe and change Melissa's fate. "You think whoever hurt Nate—"

"Who hurt him?" Bill made the question sound rhetorical.

"Do you know?" Imani asked.

Nancy glanced at the empty staircase before speaking. "Melissa was seeing someone." She glared at Imani, her blue eyes turning to slate. "Did you know?"

Imani knew that online commentators didn't need facts to weigh in with their opinions. "People are only saying the affair stuff online because of their careers," she countered. "Melissa played some ruthless female characters in the past, so they're confusing her roles with her real life. She—"

"The police asked us if Nate had said anything about problems in the marriage or her being unfaithful," Nancy interrupted. "It's clear they suspect something."

Imani looked away from Nancy's disgusted expression, struggling to bring an imaginary cement wall into focus. "The cops are only speculating, looking for motive anywhere."

"She was privately messaging some guy on Instagram," Bill grumbled.

Imani shook her head, even as she considered the implication of Bill having such a specific piece of information. Germaphobe that she was, Melissa wouldn't have started seeing a stranger during a pandemic. However, if she were completely honest with herself, Imani could imagine Melissa growing bored and possibly flirting online. She and Nate thrived off of attention, and they hadn't been able to get much adoration from strangers lately.

"I'm sure it was nothing," Imani said.

Bill's nostrils flared. "Well, they're trying to track him down. For all we know, she's hiding out with him."

Imani closed her eyes, trying to force the friend that she knew into the character the police had created. On some level, she wanted Bill to be right. If Melissa was hiding out with a lover, then she was definitely alive. But even if Imani threw out everything that she believed to be true about Melissa and Nate's relationship, she still couldn't reconcile Melissa the mother with a woman who would leave her daughter to mourn her disappearance as she galivanted around with a lover.

"Or this guy kidnapped her." Imani said it too loudly. She looked nervously up the stairs and then turned the dial on her voice down to sotto voce level. "I've known Melissa for more than a decade. She would never hurt—"

"Then where is she?" Bill roared.

"Hey." Philip stepped forward, hand raised like a traffic cop. "I imagine this is hard, but—"

"I wish I knew," Imani said, matching Bill's tone if not his volume. "But I can tell you with absolute certainty that she wouldn't run off somewhere without Ava. I'm sure you know how hard she tried to have her and that she couldn't have any more children. She'd never leave her daughter." Imani lowered her voice another notch. "The fact that she's not here means that she's in trouble."

Bill's fair complexion revealed all the blood rushing to his head. "She's in more than—"

"Mom."

The call stopped all conversation. Imani spun toward the staircase, expecting to see a devastated Ava beside Vivienne. Blessedly, only Imani's lanky girl fidgeted atop the fourth step. "Um, Ava says she can't go to the house. She's afraid she might see something."

Nancy's face crumpled. "I understand." The strain from fighting tears showed in the older woman's taut neck. "I'm not sure I want to go myself."

"I'll go." The words were out of Imani's mouth before she considered the implications. Confronting anything that might make her fear more for Melissa's life would be devastating. But she did want to ask the cops about Melissa's supposed internet boyfriend and the rumors that they were spreading. She also wanted to make them see the real Melissa: a woman who'd suffered a miscarriage and then, realizing she couldn't have more children, scaled back her career at the height of her fame to focus on her only child. Secretly, she also wanted to see the crime scene. Perhaps there was something in the house that would strike her as wrong, something that only someone close to Melissa would realize.

"I know the house's layout and what teenage girls need nowadays," Imani said. "And Ava can text me a list of anything special that she wants."

Bill gave Nancy the same pointed look that Imani had tried with Philip moments before, communicating via pupil intensity. Nancy blinked slowly in response, an almost imperceptible movement that Bill, apparently, knew how to interpret. He turned to Imani. "Hopefully the detectives don't turn you away."

Imani went for her coat. Twenty-four hours was all the time she'd had for hope and despair, she decided. The period of mourning was over. It was time to help the police find her friend.

CHAPTER FIFTEEN

TONYA

A missed call from a child left home alone was disturbing. Five was downright terrifying. Tonya froze atop the subway stairs as her cell flooded with notifications bearing Layla's name. She clicked on the first voice mail, her heart beating in her throat.

"Mom. You have to come home!"

The panic in her daughter's voice shook Tonya from her paralyzed position. She jogged up the remaining stairs, clearing two at a time until she could take off into a run.

"They're moving everything to the street!"

Tonya whizzed past an older woman and then wove around another with a stroller, eliciting a sharp "watch it" as she brushed the bassinet. She was too focused to apologize. All she could hear was Layla's frantic explanation. *"Ms. Bosco says they're allowed to be here. Where are you? Mom! Pick up your phone! Please!"*

Tonya picked up speed, drawing upon some adrenaline source reserved for evading predators. She clicked on the subsequent message, holding the phone to her ear as she ran. *"Mom."* Layla's voice was suddenly, unnaturally flat. *"Ms. Bosco says to tell you that I'm in her apartment and am welcome to stay here until you get back."*

In the background, Tonya could hear the landlady dictating her daughter's speech. *"Tell her you're safe. Tell her to hire a moving truck."*

By the time Tonya rounded the corner of her street, she was panting hard, sucking her cloth mask into her mouth with every breath. She didn't see the sidewalk crack. It snagged the toe of her right work loafer, stopping the nonslip shoe like a brick wall. Her body pitched forward. Though she wrenched her back to compensate, the effort only changed her fall's direction. She hit the ground like a fouled basketball player, dramatically sliding back and skinning her thigh through her work pants.

Grit dug into her exposed palms. Tonya pressed them to the pavement regardless, forcing herself into a standing position. She could not confront the men before her while weeping on the ground.

"Hey!" Tonya limped toward the moving guys. "What are you doing?"

The question was solely to get their attention since its answer was pretty obvious. Two men dragged her queen mattress down the building's front steps. They hadn't bothered to remove the linens, which seemed to be complicating the job. Her fitted sheet caught on a cement stair, pulling the duvet into a heap in front of them.

A wall of a white guy grunted. He made brief eye contact with her as he kicked the comforter out of the way.

"Should have paid your rent," he grumbled through a neck gaiter.

"There was a mistake at the bank," Tonya shouted, drawing closer. "I told Ms. Bosco."

"And she told us to take your shit to the street." The guy descended onto the sidewalk and then gestured with his chin to the curb, a signal for his moving partner to dump her bed on the side of the road beside the pile of wooden boards that Tonya recognized as her bed frame supports.

She tried stepping in front of the other guy. He was younger and thinner than the one who'd spoken, and he was avoiding looking at her, indicating he felt some remorse for helping remove her from her home in the middle of winter during a pandemic.

"Please, you can't do this."

The younger guy sidestepped her without lifting his gaze. Her mattress hit the pavement with a dull thud. A flop followed as the bed flipped onto the angled side of the street where the gray snowmelt ran into the gutter.

Tonya couldn't let her blanket end up in the same position. She hurried to the stairs, scooped up the comforter, and headed to the entrance.

"Uh-uh," the larger man shouted. "You're not putting anything back."

Tonya turned around, the duvet spilling from her arms. "This isn't even legal. There's a moratorium on evictions."

The man's gloved hand grabbed a dangling end of the comforter and yanked it forward, threatening to take Tonya down the stairs with it. She released the blanket and grasped the banister, saving herself from another fall.

"There's a moratorium on taking advantage of old ladies too," the guy quipped.

"Please. This is a misunderstanding, really."

The guy dumped the blanket atop her mattress. Tonya noticed that her coffee table had also been brought outside. It teetered on the curb's edge, piled high with the framed artwork apparently removed from her walls.

Tonya pulled out her phone and stared at the screen, too overwhelmed to make a call. The pieces of her life were simultaneously falling around her, and she didn't know which ones to try and save. Should she grab the picture frames on the precariously balanced table, run in and calm her daughter, beg Ms. Bosco to give her more time to resolve the rent issue, or hire a moving truck with the little money left in her checking account?

"You can't do this," she shouted. "It's not right."

"Get a lawyer," the man yelled back.

She had a lawyer! Tonya scrolled through her recent calls and dialed Glen Kelner's office. The secretary put her through as soon as she uttered the word *eviction*.

"They can't do this, right?" The desperation in her voice made her sound like Layla, Tonya realized. Kelner's mistake wasn't so outlandish after all.

"What are you talking about, Ms. Sayre?" Kelner said, evidently annoyed that she'd taken him up on the offer of representation so soon.

"You said New York City isn't allowing landlords to throw out renters."

Kelner grunted. "Well, the problem is that you have to file paperwork showing financial hardship, and I only started it for you yesterday. Sounds like your landlady is throwing you out at the moment."

"Isn't there a rule about eviction proceedings? Don't I get time?"

"You do." His voice had become soft and calm, which Tonya found infuriating. She wanted the guy to care about saving her apartment. She wanted him yelling. Fighting. "The landlord is supposed to provide a written fourteen-day notice and then file an eviction lawsuit," Kelner continued. "And, even then, technically, only the county sheriff can actually evict a tenant."

"She hasn't done any of that!" Tonya shouted. "There's no sheriff here."

"Calm down, Ms. Sayre."

Recalling how Kelner had hung up on her the prior day, Tonya held the phone to her chest and forced out a long exhale.

"You can call the police," Kelner continued, his voice emanating from the cell's speaker. "They can stop them and give me time to file the paperwork."

"I'll do that." Tonya panted. The effort of keeping her emotions in check was greater than the exertion of her earlier sprint.

She hung up and started dialing 911, mentally rehearsing what she would say to the operator. She was being illegally evicted from her apartment. She needed the police to force the movers to cease and desist. They should slap Ms. Bosco with a summons.

The sight of Layla stopped her from completing the three-digit call. Her kid stood on the landing several steps above, her masked face red from crying. Tonya leaped up the two steps and pulled her daughter into a hug. "It's okay." She petted Layla's reddish blond hair as she reassured them both. "I'm going to fix everything. They're not allowed to throw us out."

Ms. Bosco emerged from the building, boldly barefaced as usual. She shook her head at Tonya, a principal scolding a student. "I didn't want to do this."

"You're not allowed to do this," Tonya shot back. "I'm calling the cops. You can't evict me. You have to give notice and file a grievance with the courts. There are rules."

"Rules." Ms. Bosco spat on her own stoop. "I know all about Cuomo's unfunded mandates. Telling people like me and my husband who worked our way up to buy a building decades ago when this area was filled with crime and drugs, when it wasn't safe to raise a family here, that we have to starve on our social security while supporting other people who get their real money from God-knows-where doing God-only-knows-what. You don't want to call the police. I'll tell them about you and your kid's private school and paying for this apartment all on a waitress's salary."

The threat stifled the arguments on the tip of Tonya's tongue, forcing them back into her throat where she could choke on them. The police would want names of the men responsible for each of those checks—names that she couldn't provide lest she risk losing both sources of income.

"You can't do this," Tonya said for the umpteenth time, knowing that her tone no longer sounded convinced. "It's against the—"

The sound of glass shattering overpowered her last word. Layla's head turned toward the source of the sound, giving Tonya a preview of what was happening from her expression. The wall of a man had picked up one of the framed art pieces and smashed it on the pavement. He held another in his hand.

"Stop!" Layla shouted.

"You gonna leave my ma alone," the man roared, "or do I have to make sure there's nothing to move back in?"

"You can't—"

Before Tonya could finish, another picture hit the pavement.

"Stop!" Layla screamed. "Stop it!"

Another crash.

"Stop!"

The man picked up the broken frame with his glove-protected hands and pulled out the art inside. It was Layla's watercolor. "You gonna go?" He started to tear the paper.

"Why are you doing this?" Layla screamed.

The man ripped the painting in two and grabbed for another of the artworks. Layla turned into Tonya's chest, her tears adding a slick to the waterproof coating of Tonya's coat. The phone was in her hand, Tonya thought—91 was on the screen. One more digit and she'd be on with the police. The cops would arrive within five minutes, maybe less. Maybe she could give them a fake name to explain the child support payments?

The younger man appeared. He stood by the coffee table, his foot near one of the four legs. He wore workman's boots, Tonya noticed, the industrial kind with reinforced heels and toes.

The police would stop them, she assured herself. But by the time they did, what would she and Layla have left to save?

Glass shattered. The young man's foot recoiled.

"Okay," Tonya shouted, directing every ounce of energy into her voice. "Okay. We'll go."

She raised her phone like a weapon. "I'll call a moving truck."

Behind her, Ms. Bosco cleared her throat. "Call one with a storage company. It's cheaper."

CHAPTER SIXTEEN

IMANI

A supermarket tabloid that Imani often flipped through had a feature called "Stars—Just Like Us." It showed various celebrities engaged in the mundane necessities of modern life: paying parking meters, hailing cabs, picking up takeout, or pushing a grocery cart. The point of the feature was to convince readers that folks who earned millions of dollars for three-month shoots still donned their pants one leg at a time like the rest of the hoi polloi, that these folks were relatable, despite the very fact that they'd been photographed doing regular old activities and then had those pictures mailed out by a publicist or sold to a magazine.

As Imani approached the Walkers' front door, she considered that her friends had lived like "the rest of us," only everything they'd owned was bigger, brighter, and worthy of a close-up. Their brownstone had the same taupe exterior and black-trimmed windows as so many of its neighbors, but it was bathed in sunlight, mere feet from the tree-lined promenade. It was also surrounded by paparazzi.

Imani and Bill kept their heads down as they dodged camera lenses and the paparazzi's questions. The photographers
backed off once they hit the first stair, restrained by New
York City's private property laws and the dour expression of
the uniformed, armed officer guarding the door.

Bill nodded at the cop as though they'd been previously
introduced. "Ava couldn't come. I brought her friend's mom
to help."

Imani wondered if Bill knew her name. She tried recalling
whether she'd introduced herself and then decided it didn't
matter. Nate's dad had enough to process. As long as the
officer let her in, Imani was fine with the "friend's mom"
attribution.

The cop cracked one of the brownstone's arched double
doors. He gruffly gestured for them to enter, more annoyed
bouncer than gracious doorman. As soon as Imani's feet hit
the tiled vestibule, the door shut, locking them in the small
vestibule between the front door and true apartment entrance. Usually, Melissa left the second door open, enabling
visitors to shed their coats and shoes before heading right
in. Imani tried the knob only to find it locked.

She knocked on the interior door's walnut-stained wood.
A shadow advanced through the frosted window, ultimately
filling it with darkness. Imani had a flash of Melissa on the
other side of the glass, broad smile that she so often covered
with her fingers when laughing, as if afraid to give hidden
photographers a shot of her molars.

The door retracted, revealing Detective Calvente beyond the
threshold. She gave Imani a what-the-hell-are-you-doing-here
glare before realizing that Nate's father stood beside her.

"Mr. Walker."

If pity had a sound, Imani thought, it would be the trailing rumble to that final *r*. Again, Imani wondered why the detective struck such a different tone with her.

"Come on in, please."

Nate's dad led the way into the Walkers' rotunda. Imani found it odd that the hallway looked as it always had. She'd expected yellow police tape and evidence markers, props from crime scene investigation shows. Instead, there were the familiar wide-planked herringbone floors, untouched by chalk, covered by the same Persian rug that Imani had always believed belonged on a museum wall.

"Mrs. Banks."

Detective Calvente pronounced her name like a question.

"I'm here to help Ava collect what she'll need," Imani explained.

"My granddaughter wasn't up to coming," Bill added.

If the detective was disappointed by Ava's absence, she didn't show it. Instead, Calvente told Bill that she was required to accompany them, as the house was a crime scene and nothing could be removed from the premises without inspection. "If you'll follow me," she said, finishing her spiel.

The detective marched toward the narrow staircase with Nate's dad in tow. Imani followed at a snail's pace, spying into each room off the hallway, scanning for something out of place that might scream where Melissa had been taken or, at least, profess her innocence. Everything appeared more or less as Imani remembered, save for the black-jacketed police officers.

She headed up the curved staircase to the third story. The fact that the level above the entrance wasn't the second floor was one of the oddities of brownstone living. Often, the entrance was located up a flight leading to an elevated "parlor floor." The story right below was typically the true first floor or "garden level," as Realtors liked to say, despite only the priciest homes possessing backyards. The Walkers' residence had a yard, however, right above the basement level, which housed the media room, gym, a closet-turned-wine-cellar, and Nate's den.

As Imani rounded the staircase landing, she couldn't help but wonder about the room somewhere below her in which Nate had been killed. Was it covered in blood? Were there footprints? Had the police found evidence in there of a woman running from the scene? Was that why they'd honed in on Melissa's Instagram?

They passed through a narrow hallway lined with closets and headed to Ava's room. Melissa had given her daughter the second-biggest bedroom on the floor, as it faced the water and overlooked the promenade. Across from it were two guest bedrooms, the larger of which had been converted into a teenage hangout space.

Detective Calvente held the door back. To Imani, the teen's room had always seemed as if its designer had smoked a doobie in Restoration Hardware. It was a wealthy person's idea of bohemian chic, too many blankets artfully draped over too-expensive surfaces. Imani had a room that was truly boho-chic, filled with Craigslist finds and hand-me-down pieces that her father had found too painful to keep after her mother's death. The combination was an eclectic mix of things that didn't match but were united by loved-in wear and tear. This was not that.

Even so, Imani could guess where things were kept here. She opened the top drawer of Ava's dresser, wanting to prove that she meant to help before confronting Detective Calvente about Melissa's supposed boy toy. If she asked about him too early, she feared the cop might escort her back to the exit.

Imani selected warm, casual clothing, the kind of wear-all-day gear that one could sleep or cry or work out in. Sweatshirts and yoga pants. Sweaters and jeans. She also grabbed handfuls of panties, bras, and socks, as well as a box of maxi pads tucked in the underwear drawer.

"Any word on that list from Ava yet?" Imani asked as she put the pile in the center of Ava's unmade bed.

Bill hovered by the exit, avoiding eye contact with his granddaughter's undergarments. "I'll call Nancy," he said, stepping into the hallway.

Detective Calvente moved closer to the door, perhaps to keep an eye on both of them. Imani decided it was now or never. With all the detectives' innuendos in his head, Bill might try to shut down any defense of Melissa.

"You're wrong, you know," Imani said, folding one of the shirts. "You don't understand Melissa at all."

The detective widened her stance, a defensive maneuver that wasn't quite as obvious as crossing arms over one's chest. "What do you mean?"

"You told Nate's parents that she was having an affair."

The detective looked over her shoulder to where Bill was pacing. "I asked about the state of their son's marriage."

Imani stopped folding to fix the detective in her sights.

"You suggested that she was carrying on with some guy from Instagram, which Nate's parents will probably repeat to their granddaughter even though it's not true."

Detective Calvente held her gaze. They were two dogs, Imani thought, testing who would snap first.

After a moment, the detective stood down. "I was planning to ask you about it," she said, pulling something from her pants pocket. "Since you're here, might as well check out the photo."

Imani expected to see the pebbled green of Melissa's phone case. Instead, the detective typed a code into a plain black phone. She tapped the screen, typed again, and then turned it to face Imani. "Recognize this guy?"

On the screen was an actor's headshot if Imani had ever seen one. The photo was taken straight on, flaunting the near-perfect symmetry of its subject's face. He had black hair and a matching five-o'clock shadow that looked dusted onto his boyish jawline. His eyes were deep-set and dark brown, but so luminous that they almost appeared another color, something belonging in the hazel category.

There was something vaguely familiar about him, though Imani doubted she'd ever seen him before. He had a leading-man face, Imani figured, the kind with features that Hollywood found again and again as the original model grew too old to play the same characters. The man's handle meant nothing to her: MickyKline_Drinks. Was he an alcoholic? What kind of person bragged about drinking post-college?

"I don't know him," Imani said.

Detective Calvente tilted her head, like she suspected Imani of lying.

"He seems like the kind of person who might have been

working on a production with her," Imani said. "What kind of messages did they exchange that make you think there was something going on between them?"

"They were very complimentary."

"He's a good-looking guy," Imani said. "There's no crime in telling someone that."

"They'd exchanged phone numbers."

"Maybe she thought he'd be good for a future project that she was attached to." Imani said it, though she didn't believe it. Melissa hadn't worked on anything where she would have clout with the casting director in a long time.

Detective Calvente gave her a dubious look.

"I know you have this idea of Melissa because she played cheating characters," Imani said, resuming folding. "But she loved her family. She wouldn't have blown up her life for a pretty face."

Detective Calvente rotated the phone so that the image faced her. "A young guy like this. Maybe she figured it was worth the risk."

"No." Imani shook her head. "She loved Nate."

"How do you know?"

How did anyone know? Imani thought. It was an impression, she supposed, formed from little acts of kindness and longing. The admiring way that Melissa looked at her husband when he wasn't watching. The frequency with which she laughed at jokes of his that were only marginally funny. The way that Nate had been able to upset her with words said or withheld, betraying that his opinion mattered. And a million other things. Imani simply knew what long-term love looked like. She'd been married for a long time.

"I'm a therapist," she said. "I see dozens of couples a month."

"Well, then you know that love is a leading cause of murder."

The statement seemed flippant given the circumstances. "Well, what are the other ones?"

"Money," Calvente said. "People kill to inherit everything or to take something they wouldn't get otherwise. Safety. That's a popular one with women in the cases of abuse. And, of course, mental breakdowns." She glanced over her shoulder in the direction of Nate's father. "People kill when they don't understand a situation or assume something untrue because their mind is playing tricks."

"Melissa didn't snap. She'd called me the prior night looking to hang out. She sounded fine. Rational." Imani pointed at the detective. "But Melissa could have had some crazy stalkers. Nate too. Are you looking into that?"

"It's been a while since Melissa or Nate were on anyone's radar like that," Calvente said. "But we're exploring the possibility."

Imani doubted that the detectives were spending much time "exploring" given their focus on Melissa's love life. If they were truly searching for her, they were looking in all the wrong places.

She placed the last piece of clothing on Ava's mattress and then snapped her fingers, emphasizing that she'd just gotten an idea without divulging just what it was to the detective. "I need a suitcase for all of this. If you'll excuse me."

Before Calvente could object, Imani was out the door and heading down the stairs. "Mel keeps them in her room," she shouted.

She exited off the landing and hurried through to Melissa's bedroom. The space was expansive, large enough for a king bed, two walk-in closets, and, above all, a nook that was Melissa's workstation. In Imani's home, Philip handled the finances. But Melissa had been responsible for paying the bills in her family. Nate had considered himself the consummate artist. Bothering with anything as mundane as making sure people got paid had been beneath him, Imani supposed. Moreover, Melissa had said multiple times that he was a poor investor. "Easily swayed by a sales pitch, that one," she'd quipped once. "He'd buy Florida swampland if someone suggested it was prime for development."

That Melissa would not fall for such scams had gone without saying. She possessed the financial savvy of someone who'd made a fortune in her twenties and knew well that she had to make it last through her eighties. In all the years that Imani had known her, she'd always been careful with money. Generous, certainly. Yet also frugal.

Thinking about her friend's talents felt like gathering anecdotes for a eulogy. Imani pushed the thoughts from her mind and hurried to Melissa's paper-strewn desk, withdrawing her cell from her pocket. She wouldn't be able to abscond with anything, Imani knew. But maybe she'd be able to snap a photo of something that struck her as worth further investigation.

A metal rack held recent mail. Imani noticed the name at the top of an opened letter: TKM Advisors. She pulled out the document and scanned the front. It appeared to be a law firm. The sight chipped away at her convictions about Melissa's marriage. She hadn't seen her friend face-to-face in months. Maybe Philip was right. Perhaps the forced time together had eroded Melissa's relationship with Nate. It could have even been why Melissa had wanted to see Imani in person, despite her fears of catching the coronavirus.

Somewhere behind her, Imani heard footsteps. She snapped a photo and continued rifling through the documents. There were the standard heating, water, and tax bills. A letter from St. Catherine's regarding a scholarship—no doubt one that the Walkers had endowed. They'd been very involved in the school, giving money as well as time, especially Nate. In addition to volunteer teaching, Nate had been on the scholarship committee and the admissions board.

"Mrs. Banks?" Detective Calvente called from the hallway.

Imani rushed to the closet and flung back the door. At the top, above a rack of Melissa's dresses, was a shelf holding a set of soft Louis Vuitton suitcases. Imani grabbed a vacant hanger, stood on her tiptoes, and then swatted the metal hook in the air until it snagged one of the bag handles. She heard the detective enter the room as the bag hit the ground.

"I got it," Imani called out.

The detective hovered by the closet door, right behind her. She frowned at the suitcase. "I need to watch everything you take out," she said.

"I know," Imani quipped. "I'm taking this bag. You can check it."

Calvente eyed her as if she knew that Imani had taken longer than necessary to pull down a suitcase. However, she didn't accuse her of anything. Instead, she turned on her heel. "Bring it upstairs."

Imani grabbed the bag and followed the detective back

to Ava's room. As she ascended the stairs, she kept thinking about other alternative suspects to suggest to the police. She'd already offered up an obsessive stalker. Who else might want to hurt Nate and Melissa? Someone jealous of them, perhaps? Someone upset that Melissa had taken a role seemingly meant for them, or angry that Nate hadn't jumped on a movie idea? Maybe someone who believed that Melissa and Nate were preventing them from doing something or blocking them in some way?

The answer came to Imani with such force that it stopped her on the stairs. "Detective," she called out, "have you checked with the school?"

Detective Calvente continued up the stairs. "About Ava? We informed them what's been going on and—"

"About Nate." Imani felt something akin to excitement bubbling in her stomach. "He's been on the admissions' committee for at least a decade. Maybe someone was upset that their kid didn't get into St. Catherine's."

Detective Calvente stopped walking. She faced her, eyebrows pinched in a disapproving V. "Most of the admissions happen in kindergarten, right?"

Imani nodded. "That's right."

"You think Mr. Walker was murdered because someone was mad that he didn't think their five-year-old was preschool material?"

Imani ignored the sarcasm. She had kids in the school system and had seen the level of vitriol thrown at the admissions staff up close. "This is New York City," she countered. "Folks would kill to get into St. Catherine's."

CHAPTER SEVENTEEN

TONYA

The moving truck came with a driver but not a "mover." Legally, Will, the wiry guy behind the wheel, wasn't allowed to lift anything onto the truck or into the storage unit because then he could be responsible for breaking it or throwing out his back. Drivers were insured for car accidents, he'd explained, but not compensated for injuries sustained helping out single moms. He hoped she understood.

As Tonya rode in the front passenger seat with Layla squeezed beside her, she realized that every part of her understood. Her neck. Her back. Her thighs. She'd dragged both her and Layla's mattresses into the truck, as well as suitcases and paper grocery bags overflowing with all the clothing and linens that they owned. One of her neighbors had offered to help with the couch, but she'd decided that the five-year-old piece of furniture wasn't worth saving. The large storage facility was double the price of the medium. She couldn't afford to house her sofa if she wasn't sitting on it.

Layla's head rested on her shoulder. She'd gone from

screaming about the forced move to silent acceptance. Tonya brushed her daughter's copper bangs from her fair forehead and kissed the center. Layla's mask was covering her cheek.

"Where are we going to go?" Layla whispered.

Tonya turned her face to the open window, pretending not to have heard over the blasts of cold air. She'd been struggling with that question since they'd started driving. Her parents would take them in, Tonya knew. But fleeing to rural Pennsylvania meant disrupting Layla's schooling. Her folks were probably some of the last people in America not to have high-speed internet. They owned cell phones with patchy signals and tended to call her when they were "in town" on an errand.

City hotel rooms were relatively cheap at the moment, Tonya knew. But that was for good reason. Sharing common areas and ventilation systems was dangerous nowadays, and the places that Tonya could possibly swing had given half their rooms to the homeless. She didn't want to expose Layla to folks who'd been on the streets and may be suffering drug problems or mental health issues.

Moreover, she couldn't afford a hotel room for very long. Even if Kelner expedited setting up another account on Layla's behalf, Tonya doubted the money would materialize before the end of the month. In the meantime, she had a little less than a thousand dollars in her checking account, two hundred of which would be going to the storage facility for a one-month rental and administrative fee. She would run through her cash far before the school year's end.

Tonya rotated her phone in her palm. Who did she know

who might help? She had no one to crash with. Despite all her years in New York City, Tonya had never found a tribe that could relate to her working all day as a waitress and then happily rushing home to be with a kid. Women her age were all chasing their dreams, free of such "bummer" responsibilities. Her fellow school moms had always been significantly older, richer, and not exactly enamored with the idea of commiserating with a single young woman. At some point, Tonya had stopped trying to find female friends. Layla had been friend enough.

And Mike. Tonya called up his number on the screen, debating whether or not to have a conversation with him in front of her daughter. Layla knew her mom had a special friend who she saw sometimes. Not a boyfriend, exactly. Tonya didn't have time for dinner dates, movie nights, or dreaded conversations about where things were going. But she had needs, and every now and again Mike fulfilled them, taking her back to the small apartment that he shared with two other NYU grads juggling day jobs and auditions.

Mike's place was too small and crowded to put up a woman and a child, Tonya decided. More than that, the favor was far beyond the bounds of their friends-with-benefits relationship. Even if he was valiantly willing to surrender his room and bunk with one of his buddies, the ask would change their relationship forever. She wasn't ready for that, and she doubted that he was either.

"Mom, where are we going to go?" Layla asked again.

Tonya kissed the top of her head. "I'm figuring it out."

———

By the time Tonya fit the last of their furniture into the walk-in-closet-sized storage unit, she still had not determined where she'd take her daughter. She sorted through her clothing for the warm items she'd need during the next few weeks, avoiding looking at her kid lest she again hear the question burning in her blue eyes. It wasn't easy. Each task she gave Layla to do was done staring at her, silently demanding an answer.

"Mom," Layla said.

"I'll check the truck for any loose items," Tonya said, putting a pile of clothes in an emptied duffel bag. "Put what you'll need for the next few weeks in here, okay?"

Tonya hurried out of the storage room before Layla could respond. She raced to the back of the truck, heart pounding and her breath short. When she finally got inside the metal walls, she let it out, all the fear and shame and fury that had been building up inside her, not just since Ms. Bosco had kicked her out, but since this whole pandemic had started, maybe from long before. Homelessness was not supposed to happen to hardworking people. Her acting career might not have taken off, but she'd held on to a job with the same company for more than a decade. She'd worked her way up to head waitress, in charge of the whole dining room of a celebrated French fusion restaurant in Manhattan. How could she not have anywhere to go?

Tonya kicked the truck's metal interior and screamed. The cry belonged to a harpy, high and visceral. She slammed her hands over her mouth, realizing that Layla might hear, and continued yelling into her palms. Afterward, she dropped to her knees and took out her phone. She'd given her life to

Layla, the restaurant, and her secrets. The truth was, they were all she really had left.

Philip answered on the second ring, uttering "Hello?" with the wary tone of someone concerned that they might have inadvertently answered a telemarketer.

"Hi, Chef." Tonya cleared her throat. "I mean Philip. Mr. Banks."

She pulled the phone away from her mouth, giving herself a moment to exhale and correct her stumbling introduction. "It's Tonya Sayre."

"Hello, Tonya..." Movement added clattering sounds to the end of her name. Philip was taking the phone somewhere. "How are you?"

He already knew the answer, Tonya thought. How often did an employee call their boss hours after being furloughed with news of getting another gig or winning the lottery? "Um, I'm calling because you said this morning that you would see what you could do about keeping me on in some capacity, and I really need the work. I could clean the kitchen, perhaps, or deliver food. I was thinking I could use Citi Bikes or, maybe, get a bicycle off of Craigslist with those baskets."

Philip sighed. "I'd really like to keep you on but—"

"I'm good at cleaning," she interrupted. "You should see my house. It's always neat and..." Her voice started to break. "The truth is, Philip, Layla's child support usually covered my rent. But since it hasn't been paid in a few months, the landlord kicked me out. All my stuff was out on the street when I returned today. I need to have a job to rent anywhere else. Landlords will want to see employment. Not to mention first and last month's rent. And..."

The reality of her words overwhelmed her. Who was she kidding? Tonya thought. She wouldn't be able to scrape together first and last month's rent anywhere, even with Philip keeping her employed. Her call was pointless. She'd have to return to Stoney Hill, Pennsylvania, the failed actress limping back to the farm with her tail tucked between her legs. Layla would have to say good-bye to school and her friends, squeezing her gifted little mind into whatever box the public school could provide. She'd have to get used to standardized tests and learning things not because they interested her, but because that's just what people learned at that point in public school.

Layla wouldn't have it easy in Stoney Hill Middle School, Tonya thought. She'd tried to show her daughter how the other half lived and learned so that Layla would have something to aspire to, so that she'd feel comfortable dreaming big and working to achieve whatever her mind could imagine. But all she'd really done was show Layla what she couldn't have.

Philip waited for a break in her sobs before saying anything. "Tonya, we have a guest suite on our top floor that isn't in use. Why don't you come see it?"

Tonya stopped crying, not out of gratitude but out of fear. Was Philip taking her up on her earlier, desperate flirtation? She'd meant to suggest that they could work something out, but she hadn't really intended to follow through with it, she told herself. In her experience, the suggestion that sex might be in the offering was often enough to make men do what she wanted.

"Is your wife home?" she asked.

Silence answered her question. Tonya felt her eyes refill with tears. How desperate was she? Would she really? Was that all she had to offer?

A grumble sounded on the other end of the line. "You should meet her," Philip said. "Maybe we can work something out."

CHAPTER EIGHTEEN

RICK

Seeing the house made Rick angry. Most Brooklynites crammed their entire lives into apartments scarcely bigger than a McMansion kitchen. Even the relatively affluent like himself—or, perhaps, his former, non-divorcing self—worked, raised children, and cared for pets inside spaces far less than two thousand square feet. But here was Philip Banks, failed restauranteur, with three entire floors and his own garage.

"See what I mean?" Frank snarled beside him. "This is the guy you want to talk to, this guy using our fucking money to pay the mortgage on his fucking New York palace."

Technically, Philip had been using their investment in Coffre to cover the monthly lease on the entire restaurant space. According to Nate, that was why his friend was claiming that all their cash had been spent, despite Coffre being open less than four months and earlier assurances that their capital contributions would enable the new restaurant to operate for nearly a year at a loss.

But Frank's point was still valid. Cash was fungible. Philip had been misappropriating their funds, stealing money earmarked for the new, cool spot that they'd partially owned to pay for the no-longer-popular albatross that was his baby. It was thanks to Philip's theft that Rick's wife had become concerned about his investments and begun combing through the bank accounts, inevitably stumbling upon hotel room receipts and flower orders.

Rick exited the car into the dark, cold afternoon. The sun set around five in the winter, taking the day's little warmth with it. He stood just beyond the reach of a streetlight, staring into Philip's illuminated windows.

Philip was home. Rick could make out his hulking silhouette shuffling around in a back room. A Black woman sat at the dining table in the foreground, her eyes glued to a computer screen. She was attractive—the kind of girl that guys like Philip got when they had recognizable names and houses like the one he was looking into.

Behind him, Rick heard a door open. "Can't have the wife calling the cops," Frank said.

For once, the menace in his partner's tone didn't bother Rick. "Open the trunk," he said.

"What's in the trunk?" Frank asked.

"Open it."

Maybe it was the fact that Rick's tone finally matched his partner's, but Frank didn't object. Rick heard the pop of the trunk unlocking, followed by the mechanical creak of it rising. He stormed over to the open compartment and dipped his head inside.

"What are you looking for?"

Rick didn't answer, partly because he wasn't sure. Something physically substantial. Heavy. He'd know it when he saw it.

A tire iron glinted atop the trunk's gray fabric interior. Rick grabbed it and headed toward the house. He kept his head lowered, eyes to the ground, as if he weren't too angry to feel the presumably cold air swatting his exposed skin.

The street was dark, a consequence of the hour, the season, and the lack of tall buildings in the area with omnipresent lit windows. The bottom half of his face was already covered by a black face mask. They wouldn't see him, he thought. More importantly, he no longer cared.

Blood rushed to his head, drowning out the street sounds. Still, on some level, he heard the car door slam and the rumble of the Porsche's engine. For all his bravado, Frank apparently wasn't sticking around to see what happened next.

Rick gripped the tire iron like a baseball bat. He extended his arms behind him, martialing all the rage and adrenaline coursing through his veins. *Let's see how you like your home disrupted,* he thought. *Let's see how you deal with destruction.*

The tire iron flew through the air and smashed into the picture window with a tremendous crash, a thousand times more satisfying than the noise made by the weak little alley light shattering into a million pieces. A long crack immediately formed on the pane, an artery branching off into thousands of spidery veins, ruining the reflection.

Inside the house, the woman bolted upright and screamed. Her audible terror snapped Rick out of his rage-induced trance. He began running, his black peacoat whipping behind him. He needed to flee the neighborhood. He needed a damn taxi. Fucking Frank.

As he cleared the corner, he heard the roar of a sports car engine. Over his shoulder, he glimpsed the Porsche's matte-black exterior. It screeched to a stop beside him. "Get in, you fucking nutcase," Frank shouted.

Rick rounded the vehicle and dove into the passenger seat. Frank floored the gas pedal as Rick frantically buckled his seat belt. "Do you think he'll know that was from us?" Rick shouted.

Frank chuckled, a nasal sound that was less laugh and more snort. "If he calls for a meet, then we'll know."

"And if he doesn't?"

Frank ceased laughing. "Then we'll have to refine our message."

PART TWO

CHAPTER NINETEEN

MELISSA

This was how people broke down prisoners of war, Melissa thought. They stripped their hostage of every human necessity and then, ever so gradually, doled out morsels of kindness in the form of basic luxuries. A little food. A little water. A light over a toilet.

There was a cost to these gifts, Melissa knew. She had to be good. She couldn't scream herself hoarse as she had been doing. She couldn't make a mess of her meals or piss on the floor, as had happened a bit earlier.

There'd been no helping that. Like most people, she relieved herself after waking. Her bladder was trained to expel its contents minutes after she got up in the morning. She couldn't have held it, even if she, supposedly, hadn't been trapped *that* long.

Time was relative. In the dark, it became elastic, stretching the hours, vibrating with tension. Her argument had resonated with her captor, which she would call *It* from now on. Names belonged to human beings. Killing something with a name was hard. Melissa was determined not to hesitate if she got the chance.

It had opened an unseen door and turned on the bathroom light, revealing a sink, the unpainted space where a mirror had once hung, and a solitary stall. She sat in there now, clothed bottom atop the toilet seat, her need to urinate previously satiated on the hardwood floor. A toilet paper holder had gleamed from the wall, beckoning like a knife. She'd managed to pry it loose and had been using it to bang on the faucet. Her goal was to break the pipe and perhaps cause a flood, something that would need to be addressed, hopefully by someone other than It.

She'd been hitting the thing for what seemed like hours. Breaking the pipe no longer seemed possible. The noise, however, might attract attention.

Of course, any sound could also draw It back to revoke her bathroom privileges. It liked to punish, Melissa thought. It had already said that she wouldn't be getting dinner, given that she'd refused to eat the prior offering, "irrationally" claiming fear of poison. Such thoughts were ridiculous, It had insisted. The goal wasn't to kill her. She was here simply to "settle down" so that they could have a discussion about how things needed to be going forward. What they should do.

Melissa had overplayed her hand. She'd demanded to be let out, insisting that she couldn't believe anything while locked up in whatever godforsaken space It had trapped her inside. As a result, It had left, promising to return when she'd calmed down and was more ready for rational conversation. It would clean up the urine then, too, so the smell wouldn't attract rats.

The threat could not have been more clear.

Her arm was tired from the repetitive motion of drumming on the faucet. She stopped and sat back on the toilet seat, thinking of her next move, tearing up as one failed to materialize. In her head, she heard a voice telling her that she had a purpose, that life wasn't over. She just needed to give herself time.

The advice came from a memory. She and Imani had been at the local swim club, watching their first graders dolphin kick while a swim coach explained in a thick Russian accent the necessity of a good butterfly. Years later, Ava had told her that she hadn't understood all the animal analogies and had partially believed that she might metamorphosize if she only kicked hard enough. Melissa had found the revelation both hilarious and heartwarming. There was something wonderful about being so new to the world that magic seemed not only possible, but also everywhere.

That day, though, she hadn't had much faith in anything, let alone transformation. Imani had been nursing Jay in public, unaware of how painful it was for Melissa to glimpse his little mouth latched on to her dark nipple, of the hot rush of liquid that filled Melissa's own breasts at the sight. Her baby had been too small to suckle. Too tiny to do anything but die. Melissa had still been tearing up unexpectedly, even though seven months had passed since she'd lost her child—even though she'd been mourning for longer than she'd been pregnant.

Imani had seen something on her face and asked what was wrong. "I don't know what I'm supposed to do," Melissa had explained. "I mean, I know I'm supposed to take care of

Ava, but other than that, what? Work? Nobody wants a post-partum actress twenty pounds overweight. I'd had all these plans for the next few years of my life, and they'd all involved being a mom to a baby. But that's not going to happen."

Melissa had said similar things to other people in her life. Her sister. Friends from past theater productions. Her gynecologist. All had suggested ways to solve her problem: adoption, fostering, surrogacy, medical advances that might repair her broken uterus. She didn't need to keep mourning, they'd subtly suggested. Replacing a baby was eminently possible.

Imani hadn't given her such solutions. Instead, she'd silently waited for Jay to de-latch and then passed over her contented, sleepy six-month-old. "You have so much to give," she'd said. "You'll find new ways. I believe in you."

Melissa was surprised to find the memory brought fresh tears. She'd cried so much, off and on, that she'd believed all her emotion spent. But the wetness on her face was real, as was the melancholy that came with it.

Hollywood liked to show how fraught friendships between women could be. It dwelled on the competition, the sexual jealousy. It depicted female companionship as existing to attract male attention or being in a state of uneasy truce brought about by solid male relationships.

But Tinseltown was wrong. Women were designed to bond with one another, to build one another up so that they could all share in collective power. Imani had known that. Her friend had never acted intimidated by her fame or tried to one-up her by bragging at times when Melissa had been feeling low. Imani had been a listening ear and a sounding board, and all she'd asked in return was the same respect, secrecy, and attempt at wise counsel.

Her friendship had been real and deep, Melissa told herself. Imani loved her. Surely, she wouldn't simply let her disappear.

CHAPTER TWENTY

OKSANA

Oksana marched through the massive gray skyscraper's revolving doors into the frigid air. She leaned against a limestone pillar, pulled a cigarette from the pack in her right coat pocket, and lit up beneath the giant news ticker affixed to the building's facade. The spot was shielded from the wind and as good a place as any to figure out her next move.

Fascists, the lot of them! The editors had refused to buy the photos. Worse, the blond, bifocaled brat behind the counter—the same woman who had eagerly written a check for Melissa's skin care regimen—had the audacity to suggest that her taking the pictures warranted calling the cops.

American laws were so hypocritical, Oksana fumed. The country couldn't care less about privacy when it concerned the living. It let companies tailor advertisements based on personal emails and permitted devices that listened in and recorded people without their consent. People could walk around videotaping an entire street via internet-connected glasses, for God's sake. But try to sell a picture of a dead body—show a person who couldn't possibly care anymore what anyone thought of them—and that was a violation. That was the sacrilege!

Fortunately, Oksana knew that America's true religion was capitalism. Its golden rule was that demand must be supplied. Give the people what they want, with legal caveats indemnifying the deliverer, of course.

Folks would want to glimpse the end that had befallen a famed director, to see secondhand that even the so-called beautiful people died ugly. Internet sleuths would want to examine all the little details she'd been sure to include in the shots, each a potential clue as to whether Nate had killed himself or was murdered. The picture was the human version of a five-car highway pileup. Who would be able to resist following a link with the headline *Nate Walker's Blood-Soaked Last Scene!* It was clickbait on crack.

Oksana took a long drag, pulling the cigarette smoke deep into her lungs. Every puff of nerve-calming nicotine came laced with cancer-causing chemicals, but she didn't care. Fate had to have other plans for her than an oxygen tank. She'd probably die far earlier from something unexpected, a hit-and-run accident or a fall down the stairs, ignored back pain that proved the early warning sign of something more sinister. What killed you was rarely what you saw coming. It was something you'd missed.

What was she missing? Oksana wondered. Other than the money that should have been fattening her pocket.

The money! That was it! The perennial motive behind so many actions. The newspaper probably hadn't bought the photos for fear that its advertisers wouldn't want their products associated with a near-severed head. But there would be other companies that didn't care about selling ad space alongside articles, firms that charged people to see exactly what they were looking for.

Oksana exhaled the smoke in a long, swirling line and then stubbed the cigarette on the limestone column. She slipped it back into the box in her coat pocket. There was no sense in wasting good tobacco, she thought. But she needed to make the call before her cousin went to sleep.

She connected her cell to the building's guest Wi-Fi, clicked the WhatsApp icon on her screen, and called up Grygoriy. Three rings later, he answered, his voice thick with fatigue and vodka. He thanked her for calling and asked how she was, both formalities. Their relationship was transactional. They each called the other when something was needed.

"You remember that site you told me about?" Oksana asked, her native language buzzing on the tip of her tongue. "You said they paid in crypto. Explain for me."

CHAPTER TWENTY-ONE

IMANI

Imani ducked when the glass shattered. Later, she would wish that her first reaction had been to run for her kids, that she'd performed some heroic act of maternal self-sacrifice as she'd always imagined she would if her family were threatened. But her instinct had, regrettably, been to hide beneath the table at which she'd previously been sitting.

Her second impulse was to scream for Philip.

He shouted for the kids to get away from their windows while sprinting toward the door. Imani watched through chair legs as he stood guard, his hands in fists and his right foot extended forward.

Outside, a car engine roared. The squeal of tires followed it along with footsteps. The latter noise was the most frightening to Imani. Their assailant was coming, she thought. He would be armed while her husband had only his bare knuckles.

She crawled toward the pushed-out chair that she'd previously occupied. Her phone was atop the table. If she could get to it, Imani thought, then the police would come. Their assailant would be arrested.

"Stay where you are!"

Philip's instruction rang out as loud as the earlier bang. Imani reacted to his volume in the same way she'd responded to the seeming gunshot, dropping her stomach back down to the floor. "My phone is up there," she explained. "I—"

"Don't call the police."

Imani didn't understand the negative. Their circumstances were the exact ones for which law enforcement existed. "Cops are armed," she shouted.

"Exactly." Philip hissed. "We're not inviting in a bunch of scared patrolmen with automatic weapons and minimal training who just want to get home to their families after their shift ends. That's how we get our kids killed."

The footsteps grew fainter. In the distance, Imani heard a car door slam. Still, she waited for Philip to back into the dining room before emerging from her makeshift bomb shelter.

Imani grabbed her phone as she headed over to the window. She scanned the glass for a circular hole. A large crack ran from the window's center to its right corner. Hair-line fractures extended off a broken line. But there didn't seem to be a bullet entrance.

"Was it a drive-by shooting?" The question felt foreign to Imani, as if she were speaking in another language. When she told people that she'd grown up in the Bronx, they often pictured her living in an area where drivers rolled their windows up, the kind of place with corner drug dealers and omnipresent housing projects. But Riverdale was not an area that '90s rappers wrote rhymes about. It had been—and still was—a wealthy suburb on the outskirts of Westchester County populated by affluent professionals and two-parent, office-working households.

Philip ran his thumb over the window crack. "A gun didn't do this." He tilted his head to see through an undamaged section of glass. "An idiot threw something at the window."

The dismissive "idiot" was supposed to make her feel better, Imani figured. But idiots often caused the most damage. "Do you think this has something to do with the Walkers?"

Philip turned from the darkened street. "Why would it have anything to do with the Walkers?"

"I don't know. Nate is murdered, and Melissa is missing. Ava came home with us. Maybe someone wants to hurt them and thought she was still here. We should call the police. Her grandparents. Maybe—"

Philip shook his head, as if disappointed. "The pandemic has nearly sixteen percent of the city out of work, babe. People are angry. They want someone to blame. They see the lights glowing in one of these houses and think to hell with those rich bastards. You know how it is."

Imani shook her head. "It has never been like that."

Philip shrugged. "First time for everything, then." He started toward the kitchen. "I'll duct-tape it for the interim. Tomorrow, we can get quotes to replace it and call our homeowner's insurance."

Imani felt her adrenaline reduce into annoyance. They'd been attacked. Yet her husband thought the problem could be fixed with duct tape. She followed him toward the kitchen, waving her cell. "We should call the police."

Philip whirled around, a fighter shaking free of someone on his back. "I said no." His sudden volume and the redness of his face forced Imani to retreat a step. "Please go check on the kids. They're still in their rooms wondering what the heck is going on. I'll be up after I tape this."

Though Imani wasn't done with the discussion, guilt over her earlier failure to protect their children made her turn toward the stairs. She climbed to the bedroom floors, calling her kids' names. "Vivienne? Jay?" She shouted in the direction of their closed bedroom doors. "Everything's all right. Where are you? It's okay."

Vivienne emerged first. "Mom?" Though her brow was knitted, there was a surprising lack of tension in her face. Imani heard the massive bass line of a Travis Scott song. "What's up?"

"You didn't hear?"

Vivienne gestured behind her to a speaker. "I was listening to music as I finished my homework."

Imani opened her mouth to explain and then abruptly closed it. Nate's death had surely caused her children enough concern for their safety. They didn't need to know that angry miscreants were running around destroying property. "Nothing," she said. "The window broke downstairs."

A creak sounded behind her. Jay's curly head popped out the door. "That's what all the shouting was about? I thought you and Dad were just arguing."

Blood rushed to Imani's cheeks, heating her face like a blast of hot air from a subway grate. "When do we yell at one another?"

Jay shot his sister a look, as if to ask whether or not he

should answer. Imani recalled the prior day's conversation about Philip's restaurant. Clearly, they had not been as quiet as she'd believed. "I shouted because I didn't know what was happening," Imani said. "Glad to know you're both okay."

Her kids exchanged another glance. Imani interpreted this look as pitying. It was the kind of side-eye that she imagined adult children gave one another when they realized a parent was suffering the beginning stages of dementia.

Protesting her sanity would only solidify their opinion, Imani decided. She headed to her room, slumped onto the bed, and opened her phone. The Instagram profile that she'd been perusing before the window broke was still on-screen. In the center was the name MickyKline_Drinks. Below it was the message that she'd started to write.

"Hello Mr. Kline."

Imani deleted the greeting. Use of honorifics and last names on Instagram would read as a call for charity. *You don't know me, but my daughter is sick...* Better to get straight to the point, she thought.

"I'm a friend of Melissa's and understand that you were also," she typed. "I'd like to speak with you."

It read like a Twitter dating request, Imani thought. She needed something more enticing than a simple call for conversation. If the police were correct and this Micky had been sleeping with Melissa, then he wouldn't want to advertise his cuckolding a dead man. It made him a murder suspect. In fact, for all Imani knew, he was Nate's killer. He could have become obsessed with Melissa, shot her husband, and kidnapped her.

"The police are already trying to find you," Imani wrote. "Maybe I can help."

Or maybe I can rescue my friend and send you to jail, she thought.

She appended her telephone number and email. As her phone sounded with the whoosh of a sent message, her bedroom door opened. Quickly, she exited the application. Philip would not appreciate her messaging handsome, young strangers, let alone people of interest in a murder investigation.

His coloring had returned to normal, though his body language seemed more beaten down. Philip entered with his hands in front of his stomach, knotted into a ball like he'd been praying. The pious posture unnerved her. Philip was not a man to come pleading about anything.

"What's wrong?"

He rubbed his forehead, working out the words. "I think I have a possible solution to our financial problems. But it will require some flexibility."

Flexibility was earned through pushing muscles to the point of pain. The last thing Imani wanted was more of that. She put her phone down to give Philip her full attention. "What do you mean?"

"I think—"

The doorbell's ring cut him off. Imani stared at Philip, wordlessly urging him to resume guard at the entrance. He winced. "I'm sorry, babe. I guess she's early."

CHAPTER TWENTY-TWO

TONYA

He hadn't told her. Tonya could tell by the smile plastered onto Philip's wife's face, a cemented expression, ready to crack. The woman's pupils darted from Tonya's large suitcase to their masked faces and back again as Philip welcomed her and Layla inside.

"So, Imani, as you might remember, this is Tonya, the head of my waitstaff, and her daughter, Layla."

Tonya placed the hand not holding her massive bag on Layla's back and pushed her forward. Her daughter offered a small wave along with brief eye contact. Unlike Tonya, Layla had never been an actress. She didn't know how to cover the utter humiliation that Tonya was certain they both felt standing out in the cold on a strange front stoop, a pair of starving alley cats begging for a warm box and milk dish.

Philip reached for the suitcase handle. "Let me help you with that."

Imani's brown eyes widened as she watched him wheel in the massive bag. Had Tonya known that Philip hadn't discussed things with his spouse, she would have shown up with little more than the clothes on her back. As it was, she'd packed for the foreseeable future, bringing most of Layla's wardrobe and much of her own, as well as notebooks, folders, and other items that Layla would need for school. The Bushwick storage facility was easily an hour away by public transport. Tonya hadn't wanted to make too many trips.

"I really can't thank you both enough," Tonya said, directing her gratitude to Imani. "This whole thing happened so suddenly. Layla and I weren't sure where we were going to go."

Imani's smile seemed to soften. "Well, we do have the rooms upstairs, and I understand your concern about hotels given the virus. Speaking of"—she pointed to her uncovered face—"I suppose I should grab a mask. Just a minute."

Imani stepped into what appeared to be a dining room. Tonya could see a long table with six chairs and a sitting room beyond. Presumably, the kitchen was on the other side of the wall.

Philip, still maskless, waved them inside.

Tonya urged Layla forward and then stepped inside just enough to clear the door. It shut behind her, locking them in. There was no going back now.

Philip took several steps into the dining room. "I don't think masks are really necessary, honey," he said, addressing the bent back of his wife, who was already opening drawers in the hutch. "They won't be sleeping with them on, so they're ultimately sharing the same air. The Band-Aid's got to come off sometime."

Imani made a noise, part hiccup, part stuttering start to some objection. She turned toward Philip and delivered a hard stare. A million words were passing between them at the speed of light, Tonya knew. She couldn't read all of them. But she got the gist.

"We can wear one in the common areas, if you'd prefer," she said.

The tense smile on Imani's face turned sheepish. "I'm sure you're healthy. It's only that we wouldn't want to unintentionally be carrying something around and make you sick."

Philip pulled the embarrassingly huge suitcase farther into the house. "The kids are all tested every week at St. Catherine's. I'm sure we're fine." He gestured toward Layla. "You were just tested, right?"

Beside her, Layla nodded. Tonya noticed Imani's expression change from concerned to surprised. "You're a St. Catherine's mom?"

Avoiding such amazed reactions was why Tonya rarely told anyone where her kid attended middle school. St. Catherine's had a well-deserved reputation among New Yorkers as being an Ivy League farm team with a cost exceeding many colleges. Everyone knew that a single mom wouldn't be able to afford it on a waitress's salary. In most people's minds, that left only three options: Her child was a genius on an academic scholarship, her rich parents were willing to support their granddaughter but had cut off their own kid for some horrible transgression, or Layla's absentee dad was loaded. Two of the assumptions may have been correct, but Tonya wasn't allowed to confirm or deny any of them.

"Layla has gone since kindergarten." Tonya shot her daughter an encouraging look. "You love it, right?"

Layla stepped a little farther into the room. "I like the writing programs a lot," she said.

"So does Vivienne." Imani gave Layla a more natural smile. She pointed to her own bare face. "I suppose since you guys are all regularly tested anyway."

Layla turned to her, wide eyes begging permission. Tonya reached behind her kid's strawberry-blond locks and unhooked the ear loop. The mask fell away, revealing Layla's freckled nose and fair skin. Seeing her child's bare face while indoors in someone else's house nearly made Tonya gasp. It was like running into a forgotten and once-loved friend.

"Vivienne, Jay," Philip yelled up the stairs. "Come and meet our guests."

Tonya bristled at the term. A guest was the recipient of hospitality, someone who might be expected to repay the favor at a later date, in a way yet to be determined. She was a renter. Philip had told her that he'd charge eight hundred a month for the two-bedroom guest suite on his third floor. She intended to start paying once her unemployment checks arrived, four to six weeks hence. Philip had said she could work off the first month in the restaurant washing dishes and cleaning the floors during the takeout dinner shift.

She addressed Imani. "I am really glad to be renting from someone I know," she said. "Philip mentioned eight hundred per month."

Imani glanced at her husband. Again, they exchanged inaudible information. Tonya felt a needle of regret. She'd never been close enough to anyone to speak wordlessly, save for with Layla. And things were lost in translation when the conversation was between a parent and child. Adults could convey so much more via gesture and glance.

Imani clapped sharply as she shot Philip another look. Tonya couldn't tell whether the sound was to emphasize Imani's excitement or displeasure. "That sounds fine. Let's show you the rooms."

Philip heaved the bag over his shoulder. "Welcome to our bubble," he said.

It was Tonya's turn to force a smile. Though she understood what Philip meant, she didn't like the comparison. Everyone knew that bubbles had to pop.

CHAPTER TWENTY-THREE

IMANI

As a therapist, Imani would claim the key to a good marriage was mutual respect. As a friend, she'd append a caveat, *and avoiding temptation.* As she shut her bedroom door behind Philip, Imani couldn't help but think that he'd staked their relationship in a greedy gamble to keep their home. Tonya was fit and blond—a youthful, Bette Davis–eyed idealization of Philip's own mother. Freud had studied Oedipus for a reason.

Imani walked through the room to the sliding glass door leading to the slip of balcony overlooking the postage-stamp patio behind their house. Jay and Vivienne had heard them fighting the other day. This conversation needed to take place as far away from the hallway as possible.

She gestured to their bed, inviting Philip to sit and start explaining. She intended to stand.

"We need help with the mortgage." Philip walked past the mattress, positioning himself in front of her. "And I know eight hundred might not seem like a lot given the size of our loan, but it could really help once her unemployment checks start coming in a month and—"

"Wait." Imani shook her head, shaking off the verbiage buzzing around it. "What do you mean once they start coming? Are you saying she can't pay now?"

"She'll clean in the restaurant for free this first month until her unemployment kicks in."

Arguments flooded Imani's throat, threatening to choke her if she didn't immediately spew them out. "I understand the desire to be charitable, Philip, but we're financially drowning. This isn't the time for us to be throwing anyone a life preserver."

"It's not charity, honey. She's a hard worker, and she'll eventually pay eight hundred a month."

"A drop in the bucket. We—"

"Nearly all commercial loans have a force majeure clause for unforeseeable acts of God," Philip interrupted. "The pandemic has to count. I'll renegotiate the loan, get it down to something that can be paid with her rent and whatever the restaurant is bringing in."

"And if you can't, then what?" In spite of her promise to keep the kids from hearing, Imani found her voice rising. "The bank takes the house, kicks us all out, and all we'll have gained from bringing in another family is additional exposure to a deadly virus. It's not like we can tell a grown woman who she can and cannot see and how cautious she should be outside our home. What do you really know about her and who's in her bubble, huh? Does she have a boyfriend? What job does he have? Does Layla see her father multiple times a week? Are we actually exposing ourselves to two families? To three?"

Philip pointed to the ceiling, indicating their new tenants' quarters and, perhaps, reminding her to keep her voice down. "Tonya's not going to take any risks with her health or her kid's well-being. I'm sure she's more afraid of contracting the virus than we are. She's the one who won't have health insurance soon. One of the reasons she took us up on this deal is because she's grateful not to be living in a hotel with a bunch of COVID patients."

Imani turned her attention to the window. She needed to both calm down and come up with another way of framing her objections that wouldn't seem cruel. Of course, she didn't want a single mother and her young kid renting a room in some hotel booked with infected folks who were recuperating away from healthy loved ones. But Philip's employees shouldn't be her problem. She had enough on her plate working to keep food on the table and make a dent in Philip's massive loan while trying to find her missing best friend. She couldn't add Airbnb host to all her other responsibilities.

A snowy film coated the windowpane and potted trees in their strip of backyard. Imani had once found such frost beautiful, a glitter coating on the gray city. The sight now made her feel withered. It resembled dust, she thought. They were all rotting away inside while the world went unused.

Warm hands landed on her shoulders. Before she could turn around, Philip enveloped her in his arms. His chin lowered to the top of her head. "Please give it a chance. She'll pay rent, and I'll renegotiate."

A sob stopped his words. Imani separated from him to see his face. The fire was out of Philip's typically intense blue eyes, finally doused by real tears.

"Babe." His voice was pained. "I want to do something good.

I've been firing and furloughing people who have dedicated so much to my restaurant, taking away live—" He coughed, fighting the emotion that had reddened his fair skin. "Livelihoods. Upending lives. I *need* to do something good."

Imani wanted to argue that all Philip *needed* was to be there for his family. But she knew it wasn't true. Her husband valued the people who worked for him in the same way that she considered her own dear friends, she supposed. He could no less ignore a loyal employee's predicament than she could forget about Melissa's disappearance.

The last of Imani's objections evaporated in a long exhale. "Only a month of this labor-for-rent arrangement, though, okay? You don't need an indentured servant. If she can't start paying a reasonable rent in a month, she has to go elsewhere."

Philip pulled her in for a tight hug. "I love your heart."

Imani collapsed into him. She'd given in not because of her heart but because of insufficient energy. After everything that had happened, she lacked the stamina for a long, emotional argument. It was easier to let Philip do what he wanted and hope to God he was right.

CHAPTER TWENTY-FOUR

TONYA

Ask ten diners what the worst job in a restaurant is, nine of them will say washing the dishes. Before Tonya had landed the gig with Banque Gauche, she might have made the same mistake, imagining a group of low-paid workers in rubber gloves, elbow-deep in soapy, food-particle-filled water, wiping grimy sponges over dinner plates. She'd since learned better.

Doing the dishes wasn't nearly as messy as people imagined. More than anything, it was a sorting and loading exercise. Plates were blasted by a power hose capable of sending all food scraps into a sink strainer. After, they were racked and pushed into a massive stainless-steel contraption that sanitized them with chemicals and boiling hot water.

The grossest and perhaps most dangerous kitchen roles were cleaning the equipment. Grills. Meat grinders. Ovens. Everything had to be washed, sprayed with chemicals, and descaled by hand. In some cases, as with the grinders, the machines needed to be partially disassembled for proper sanitization and then reassembled before the next service.

The scraps inside many of the cutting machines weren't even cooked. Whoever got the job needed to wipe raw, extruded proteins out of holes and gears, then dry each piece, and then rewipe them down with food oil to guard against rust. It was a dirty, greasy, labor-intensive job.

Fortunately, Tonya didn't have to do that one. At least, not yet. Philip was taking it easy on her. In addition to the dishes, he'd asked only that she mop the floors and squeegee the outside of the walk-in fridge.

The first task had been pretty much done by the end of dinner service. As the meals were all takeout, the plates and cutlery were recyclable one-use items thrown into bags. Only the pots, pans, and cooking utensils had required washing.

Tonya had moved on to the rest of her responsibilities. She dipped the mop into the soapy water in the yellow bucket at her side and then slapped it onto the floor. Sliding the cloth ribbons back and forth across the gray tile felt good, satisfying in a way that standing outside, desperately trying to attract patrons, hadn't been. The latter role had made her permanently anxious. She remembered hours of shivering, trying not to look as uncomfortable as she'd felt and hoping that her hourly wage would reflect a generous tip or two, deep down knowing that it wouldn't.

There weren't any unknowns in her new role. No need to fake a smile behind a mask and attempt to exude sex appeal through a boxy uniform shirt. She would clean for several hours a day, six days a week, during and after the dinner shift. In exchange, she'd receive two furnished, sunlit bedrooms and a private bathroom in a beautiful home located mere blocks from her daughter's school.

It was a fair deal, Tonya thought. She continued to glide the mop over the floor, feeling pride in the wet gleam on the tiles, the emerging whiteness of the grout, and the disappearance of the black rubber marks left by skidding work shoes. In some ways, the job reminded her of farm work. Repetitive and tiring, but also visible. She'd have something to show at the end of the day. Or night, as it were.

Because her new gig required cleaning after dinner service ended, Tonya's shift had swung to an after-hours schedule. She would work until ten thirty most nights, returning to Brooklyn long after Layla had gone to bed. Tonya told herself it was temporary and didn't matter at the moment. Her daughter was in a locked house with an adult in a safe neighborhood. Or, at least, what had passed for one until Nate's murder.

Tonya shuddered, perhaps at the thought of Nate, dead on the floor of his multi-million-dollar mansion or, more likely, the unshakable eeriness of her own surroundings. As soon as the clock had struck ten, Banque Gauche's kitchen staff had all rushed off to spouses and children or late-night drinks, leaving Tonya to listen to the fridge's hum and the slap of sopping cloth against stone.

Tonya finished up around the baseboards and then twisted the mop into the wringer at the top of the bucket, squeezing out the dirty water into a separate compartment. She then pushed the contraption into an out-of-the-way corner and grabbed the chemical spray, squeegee, paper towels, and a shammy. Wiping down the kitchen counters and fridge were the sole tasks left on her to-do list.

As she started, a door slammed. Tonya froze, her arms filled with weapons against grime, but nothing that could fend off an attacker. The last line cook had locked the staff entrance behind him, hadn't he? Or had he expected her to do that? Had the door been cracked all this time, beckoning some drug addict or thief hiding out in the alley to come in from the cold?

Tonya backed toward the sink and lowered the contents of her arms into the basin. She scanned the counter for knives. Banque Gauche's cooks typically brought their own custom tools. But there had to be house knives for when they forgot or when a blade grew dull.

The counter was empty save for the butcher's station. A variety of stainless-steel appliances sat on the space, each outfitted with sharp blades—on their insides. Seeing nothing else, Tonya crouched below the fry station and grabbed one of the large, cast-iron skillets. Abused women killed husbands with these things. She could knock a man senseless.

Philip entered the kitchen, carrying a plate and some wadded napkins. His head was down, as usual. His shoulders were rounded. Her boss had the physique of an attacker but the posture of a victim.

Tonya set down the frying pan. Though she tried to accomplish it softly, the weight of the thing made an attention-grabbing thud as it landed on the counter. "Sorry," she murmured.

Philip whirled around, his body language shifting from downtrodden to defensive in a blink. The plate turned sideways as he raised his hands in a fighting stance. Tonya felt that same shiver from earlier, only stronger.

"Oh. I thought someone had broken into the restaurant for a second." Philip's body seemed to shrink back to its former state as he bent to pick up the food that had fallen to the floor. "I didn't realize you were still here."

Tonya took a deep breath. Philip's presence was something to take comfort in, not fear. Her boss was tall, broad, and, as she'd just witnessed, ready to protect them if needed. Tonya recalled a joke between Philip and one of the guys in the kitchen about combat training. She wondered if he'd had any.

"I'm finishing up." Tonya walked back to her cleaning supplies in the sink. "But if I was a robber, I don't think I'd want to tangle with you."

Philip came closer, stopping to throw the food and napkin in the trash. "Sorry about that. I'm jumpy lately."

"You looked ready to throw down for a minute," Tonya said, bundling her items back into her arms.

Philip shrugged. "Once a marine..."

"You were in the marines?"

"Only four years active." Philip walked his plate over to the same sink and pulled down the power hose. "I enlisted straight out of high school many, many moons ago." He raised his voice to be heard over the spray. "It wasn't really for me. Too much yelling. My body seems to remember more of it than I do."

Philip shut off the water and put his plate in the dishwashing rack. "Don't worry about that tonight. It costs too much to run the machine for one plate." He pointed to the bundle in her arms. "Sorry you're still working. The job will go quicker once you find your rhythm."

Tonya looked up at Philip's lined face. His bottom lip folded under the top in a faint, forced smile. He wasn't exactly handsome—certainly nothing like Mike—but his face had a certain masculine, older man appeal.

"It's fine," Tonya said, spritzing the counter with chemicals. "Your wife's home."

Philip's translucent smile faded completely. Tonya wondered if he'd taken her mentioning his wife as an aggressive attempt to dissuade flirtation. Nothing he'd said had warranted her telling him to back off. In fact, she'd been the only one to hint at something happening between them.

"It's great for Layla to have an adult in the house," Tonya added, trying to soften the comment. "Whenever I worked the dinner shift, I would often ask one of the neighbors to check in periodically. Lately, I'd been leaving her at home alone without anyone popping in, though, which wasn't really good. I forget sometimes that she's only eleven. It's great to know she's safe in your house. And the guest rooms are so nice. It's really incredible to have a house like that in Brooklyn."

Tonya realized that she was talking too much, making up for an unintentional and likely unperceived slight. She stopped herself on the last compliment, even though it failed to bring back Philip's slight smile.

"It belonged to my parents." Philip grabbed a paper towel from a nearby rack and picked up the spray bottle that she'd set on the counter. He drenched the cloth and began doing the job that she, clearly, wasn't accomplishing fast enough. "I grew up there. They left it to me when they died."

Tonya resumed cleaning her section, unsure what to say in response. *I'm sorry they're dead, but nice they left you a mansion?* It was difficult, given her own financial problems, to feel too devastated about how Philip had received his inheritance.

Philip rubbed down the fridge's exterior. "It happened a long time ago. I was a kid, just back from the aforementioned marines."

Tonya peeled off another paper towel sheet. "They were young, then?"

"Yeah. Though I suppose I didn't think that at the time. But they were barely older than I am now."

"How did it happen?"

"Car accident."

The flat way Philip said it made Tonya stop working. Philip, however, continued cleaning as he spoke. "I'm pretty sure my father had been drinking, though the cops never said. He was a prominent guy, and back then, the media covered up that sort of stuff for wealthy people."

"Drinking and driving, you mean?"

Philip snorted. "Drinking and driving. Smacking your wife around. Child abuse. Wealthy people have always had a kind of carte blanche." He tossed the cloth into a laundry bin. "Anyway, they reported that he might have had an allergic reaction or something."

"Was he allergic to anything?"

Philip took another paper towel from the rack and began to dry the areas that he'd previously wiped down. "Peanuts. I am, too, actually." He ran the towel over the walk-in's handles. "My father was always pretty careful about asking what was in his food, though. I can't see him actually ordering anything with peanuts."

Philip balled up the towel in his hand, looking away as he

squeezed it in his fist. "Anyway, he crashed the car with my mom in it."

"Geez."

Tonya realized she was simply standing there, listening rather than working. Yet she couldn't do anything else. It was one thing for Philip to clean a counter while sharing the news of his parents' deaths, distracting himself from the emotional weight of his story. It was another for her to do so. She didn't want to appear dismissive.

"Is it possible to crash a car because of a food allergy?"

"If you go into anaphylaxis, then sure. The body can become starved of oxygen. You can have a heart attack. Food allergies can be pretty serious." Philip threw the second used towel in the laundry bin. "I wouldn't want to stand beside the fryer when it's bubbling with peanut oil."

Tonya glanced at the dormant contraption. It sat in a corner, its metal baskets suspended over empty wells. "You use peanut oil even though you're allergic?" Tonya asked.

Philip shrugged. "It has the highest smoke point, which means it's the best for frying chicken. And it's not like I can get really sick from breathing it alone." He placed his hands on his hips and surveyed the room. "I think we can call it for tonight. Why don't you get the rest of your stuff? I'll drive us home."

Tonya thanked him distractedly. She grabbed her coat, still thinking of his sad story with his father. "Are you as allergic as your dad?"

Philip slipped an arm into a wool jacket. "I can't know for certain. But if I swallowed a bunch of it, I suspect it would definitely kill me."

CHAPTER TWENTY-FIVE

IMANI

He'd driven her home.

The thought streamed in the back of Imani's brain, an unwanted radio signal periodically interrupting her connection to the screen in front of her and the woman at its center. Her patient was a thirty-eight-year-old marketing consultant and mother who, up until the pandemic, had deftly managed a demanding career and caring for two elementary schoolers. She'd done so with the assistance of a nanny, a weekly cleaning service, and in-person school—none of which were currently in her life.

"I can barely think between all the food preparation. I mean, they eat constantly. Constantly. Mommy, can I have a snack? Mommy, it's our lunch hour. Mom." The woman wiped her dark bangs off her forehead. Her hair had a stringy quality, like it hadn't been brushed or washed in a couple days. "And then there are the interruptions with help for school and the laundry and the packages. Every damn day something else needs to be opened and unpacked and recycled. And I'm on deadline for a major project—not that anyone cares in my house."

The complaints became a background beat to the refrain that Imani couldn't ignore. *Philip had driven Tonya home.* Her husband would be spending hours at work with this woman and then ferrying her back to the house where they all lived. The two of them would be alone in the car for thirty minutes at least, sharing their day and dreams, their frustrations and failures. They'd have more quality time together than she had with her own spouse—than she'd had with him for years thanks to the constant demands of his restaurant.

"Do you know what he said to me when I asked him to please come down and fix the internet connection so that the kids could log on?" Her patient continued. "'Derivative traders don't multitask.' He suggested that simply asking him was putting millions of investor money at risk."

"You both are under a ton of pressure. Are there any things you can scrape off your plate?" Imani asked, aware that her thoughts of Philip and his work were bleeding into her language. "The house, for example, doesn't need to be as neat as it once was."

"I can barely walk in it as it is," the woman said. "Seriously, I look like a hoarder. You can't see it because I'm having this conversation with you from my bed and only showing you the headboard. If I rotated the camera, you'd think I needed medication."

"Being stressed is understandable," Imani said, offering a platitude because she was plainly distracted. "You're doing more than any one person should have to do."

"I'm going to have to leave my job." Her patient looked away from the camera, possibly at the unseen mess. "It's impossible otherwise."

The feminist in Imani woke up at the statement. She wanted to demand that her patient keep her career and force her husband to take on more. But she stopped herself. Her role wasn't to tell a fellow female how unfair it was that she felt the need to choose between work and family. "Well, what would that look like?" she asked. "Would you be happier?"

Would she be happier? Imani wondered. If she and Philip stopped struggling so hard to hold on to their home and their careers, if they both settled for smaller lives in less expensive hamlets somewhere that didn't require taking on renters, would that make them happy? Would it solidify their relationship or add more strain?

"So, no, I wouldn't be happier."

Imani realized she hadn't heard her patient's prior answer. "Well, something has to give," she said. "So, let's consider what that could be."

———

By the time Imani had finished her counseling session, neither she nor her client were any closer to determining what they should relinquish. But Imani knew the next task on her agenda. Call Melissa's lawyer.

She scrolled through her photos to the picture of the TKM Advisors letterhead that she'd taken in Melissa's apartment. Carefully, she input the number into her phone and placed the call. The woman who answered offered a dry, "Taft,

Kelner, and Moore" without inquiring how the firm might be of service, implying that they might not want to be. TKM, apparently, did not beg business from cold calls.

Imani recited the introduction that she'd invented the prior night while staring at the ceiling, mind racing with concerns about her new rental arrangement. "Yes. I'm a friend of Melissa Walker. I'm caring for her daughter, Ava, and am hoping to get in touch with the person who might have been representing her and her husband's affairs."

The secretary told her to hold. As she listened to a tinny classical song on the line, Imani remembered a conversation she'd had with Melissa at a restaurant playing similar Muzak. They'd been sharing oysters on a sunny summer day. Imani had ducked out between clients to see Melissa on the way back from an audition. As usual, Philip had been at the restaurant, and Nate was off somewhere, no doubt hustling to get some project made. Imani had been complaining about a client leaving her husband.

"She says the spark is gone," Imani had said.

"She means the lust is gone," Melissa quipped. "And that's not love."

"Well, it's part of it," Imani countered. "Love is initial attraction plus shared experiences multiplied by time."

"You've broken it down to a mathematical equation, huh?"

"In a way." Imani chuckled to show she was being somewhat facetious. "And whether a couple should stay together is that love calculation minus the anticipated pain and loneliness of leaving plus the possibility of finding love in the future, which is its own equation based on temperament and age."

"And Tinder," Melissa added.

Imani giggled while listing more things that might aid in finding a new lover. Botulism. Green juice. Money. Older children. "Therapy!" she shouted. "Lots and lots of therapy."

Melissa had guffawed, immediately covering her mouth with her long, slender fingers. She'd palmed her wineglass and begun tapping a nail against the goblet, creating soft pings like windchimes. "Love is something best left unexamined, I think. I mean, I'm not exactly sure why I love Nate. Sometimes I believe it's because I thought he was sexy and more established in Hollywood than me, and everyone else seemed to want him. Sometimes I suppose it's because he gave me Ava. Sometimes I figure it's because we've simply gotten used to each other. I mean, he makes me laugh, occasionally. I admire his creativity. I still find him handsome. But I'm impressed with a lot of people's creativity and looks." She sighed. "I guess Nate's just been in the background for so long that I can't imagine him not there."

Imani had watched Melissa sip from her glass, feeling suddenly sad. Thanks to the restaurant, Philip was also in the background of her life. The people involved in her day-to-day activities were her children and her clients. Melissa. Perhaps the school. When was the last time she and Philip had enjoyed a deep conversation? Imani had asked herself. Or engaged in more than perfunctory sex?

She'd taken a gulp from her own glass. "So, love is a lack of imagination. I should tell my patients."

Melissa had reached out, placing her hand over Imani's knuckles. "Not love," she'd said. "Staying."

"Hello, this is Glen Kelner. With whom am I speaking?"

The abrupt question snapped Imani from her reverie. "This is Imani Banks. I'm a dear friend of Melissa Walker."

"And why are you calling me?"

"I understand that you were handling some of the Walkers' affairs, and I wanted to better understand what they were so that I can help take care of Ava."

"Mr. Walker's will and testament was provided to his parents, who I understand are caring for Ava. Ms. Walker's affairs, like the affairs of all clients, are privileged. Good—"

"Wait!" Imani shouted. Her lie had backfired. "Please. I'm Melissa's friend, and I'm very worried about her. I'm sure you know that she is missing, and the police seem more concerned with pinning Nate's death on her than her safety. If she was divorcing her husband, their suspicions will only get worse, and—"

"I am not a divorce attorney, Ms. Banks."

Imani exhaled. "Well, why was she working with you, then?"

Kelner cleared his throat. "Clearly, I can't get into specifics."

"It's only that, if there is anything you know, anything at all that can help police focus on finding Melissa rather than blaming her, anything that she was working on with you that would indicate she and Nate were not at each other's throats or that there were other issues that might have made someone angry or—"

A surge of emotion cut her off. Imani held the phone away from her mouth, taking a moment to compose herself. "Please. She's my best friend, more like a sister. I'm scared for her, and I just want to help in any way that I can."

Kelner breathed on the other end, a soft whistle, the kind

made by a slightly stuffy nose. "I can tell you that my typical role is to discreetly handle delicate financial matters."

Imani was silent, struggling to process the job description in relation to Melissa.

"I help separate marital assets to limit spousal liabilities or ensure that certain debts can be paid without involving both parties," Kelner continued.

Though the lawyer wasn't a divorce attorney, it sure sounded as though he shuffled money around in preparation for a separation. "And you were doing this because Melissa wanted to leave Nate."

The exhale that followed this time sounded more annoyed than resigned. "None of this can come back to me, understand? I'm only saying anything since you seem to think Ms. Walker is in trouble."

For a moment, Kelner went silent. Imani could only hear her own anxious breaths on her end of the line. "Nate had made some questionable decisions," Kelner said. "Melissa wanted to make sure that her earnings were siloed and untouchable in case he found himself owing people."

Imani again recalled Melissa's quip about Nate's lack of business acumen. *He'd buy swampland in Florida...*

"Did he invest with bad people?" she asked. "People who might kill him and kidnap Melissa?"

"He wasn't in bed with the Mafia, if that's what you're thinking," Kelner said. "If I'd thought Nate had gotten himself mixed up with people committing fraud or any other kinds of crimes, I'd have come to the police before anything had happened. Not doing so would have risked my license."

The last part made Imani doubt Kelner's honesty. If the guy

had failed to come forward with information that might have stopped Nate's murder, he might lie in hopes of indemnifying his practice or, at the very least, avoiding bad publicity. However, if that were the case, Kelner would have been smarter not to have divulged anything in the first place.

"But Melissa was afraid these people would come after them?"

"Nothing like that." Kelner loudly exhaled for the umpteenth time. Apparently, Imani was tiring to him. "As I said, I can't go into details. My point in telling you any of this is to urge you to let the police do their jobs. They know what to focus on."

Silence rang in Imani's ear. She ran Kelner's words back to herself, looking for some clue that would suggest a different meaning than the obvious: Melissa's own lawyer thought her guilty.

So why didn't she? Imani wondered.

Maybe because fame was blinding, Imani thought. Perhaps because, despite a decade of friendship, she'd still seen Melissa in a halo of stage lights, her flaws blurred by good makeup and an ability to project emotions barely felt. It was possible that she'd wanted so badly to be associated with Melissa that she'd placed more importance on their interactions than she should have, elevating her friend to a status that she should never have occupied. That Melissa herself had never really wanted.

Imani tasted something salty and bitter. She was crying, she realized, bawling for a friendship that might never have been as deep as she'd felt, yet that she missed so badly that her bones ached. Maybe love in any form was never meant to be deeply examined, Imani thought, because it hurt too much to learn that people weren't who you'd built them up to be. Each revelation about Melissa caused her physical pain, cutting like knives into her vital organs.

Or bullets, Imani imagined. A bullet—just like the one Melissa had put in Nate's skull.

CHAPTER TWENTY-SIX

TONYA

She smelled like a storm drain. It was the clothes, Tonya realized. Garments, hastily piled into paper bags, had spilled onto the grimy floor of the moving truck. Every scrap of clothing she owned stunk of the runoff water that had coated her mattress. Even the off-shoulder T-shirt and pajama bottoms she'd slept in the prior night, which had always been in the suitcase, balled and stuffed between breakable frames, had the odor of stale, dirty water and sweat.

During the prior night's drive home, Philip had offered use of his house's washing machine. Still, as she carried an armful of clothing to the closet at the end of the second-floor hallway, Tonya couldn't shake the sensation that she was stealing something. If she'd been renting a real apartment, she'd be expected to visit a laundromat or put quarters into a basement machine.

The front loader made a cringe-inducing popping noise as she opened the door. It also released the musty smell of wet newspaper. Someone had apparently run the wash and then forgotten about it. A white-and-black lump lay inside the barrel, drying in a damp ball.

She shook out the dark garment, revealing a pair of men's trousers. Tonya opened the dryer door below and tossed the pants inside. She then pulled out the bunched white fabric. The texture of the collar's terry-cloth lining told her it wasn't a normal garment before it unraveled to reveal the embroidered Banque Gauche logo and cursive *Philip Banks* beneath.

Philip's chef jacket needed another go-round. Rust-colored flecks, no doubt from some splattered sauce, dotted the jacket's right sleeve and chest. Tonya spread it on top of the washer and then gathered the clothes that she'd dropped by her feet. She tossed them inside, grabbed the detergent off the narrow shelves crammed beside the machines, and squirted some into the bottle's cap.

She was figuring out where to pour it into the machine when she heard another door crack, followed by a slam. Tonya listened for some sign of who had entered the house. It was too early for the kids to return from school, which meant either Philip had come back from wherever he'd gone earlier or Imani was home from work.

Keys hit a counter below. Footsteps approached the stairs. Their lightness indicated that they belonged to a woman.

Tonya figured out the location of the soap tray and, with the speed of shame, filled it and started the cycle. She started toward the stairs before realizing that footsteps were already on the lower staircase. They would reach the landing before Tonya could escape to her floor. Imani would find her just outside the master bedroom, a pedestrian caught in the crosswalk as the light changed.

She retreated to the laundry area. As Imani appeared, Tonya grabbed Philip's jacket and a spray bottle of stain remover. Helping remove the spots on Philip's laundry would justify her throwing in her clothes instead of rerunning the load that had already claimed the machine.

Imani noticed her immediately. Her chin retreated into her neck before she adjusted her posture to something more welcoming. "Hello, Tonya."

"Philip said it would be fine if I put in a load. I hope that's okay."

Imani's stance stiffened, but she didn't object. Instead, she pointed to the jacket in her hand. "Is that Philip's?"

"It had a few stains on it," Tonya said. "Figured I'd spray them and let it soak."

The invisible screws at the edges of Imani's tight mouth rotated another turn right. "You shouldn't be doing that."

Tonya lay the garment atop the washer. "I was trying to be helpful."

The vein throbbing in Imani's thin neck belied her cheery tone. "I mean, you don't have to do our laundry. I hope Philip didn't make you feel like you should."

"Not at all."

"Don't worry about it." Imani marched over, as if to inspect the jacket. "I'll deal with my husband's clothes."

Duly chastened, Tonya sidestepped out of her way before turning toward the stairs. Imani did not want anyone messing with her family's stuff, especially the new boarder. The next time she had to do laundry, Tonya resigned herself to scrounging together enough quarters for the laundromat.

"So, Tonya."

The call stopped her retreat. Imani held the stain spray bottle, perhaps ready to repeat the work that Tonya had already done. The prior plastic smile stretched her mouth. "It was nice to hear that you are at St. Catherine's. I really love the school."

"Us too."

"What teacher does Layla have?"

Was she testing her or simply making polite conversation? Imani's expression was a cinched veil, obscuring whatever she was really thinking.

"Ms. Brown," Tonya said.

"She's good. I know her." The smile pressed Imani's large brown eyes into almond slivers. She was a pretty woman, Tonya found herself thinking. Pretty with a PhD, if Tonya remembered correctly. And a handsome celebrity chef husband. And a giant carriage house in Brooklyn.

"I actually have to go to the school later today," Imani continued. "I'm on a bunch of committees. When I was trying to get my kids in, I thought volunteering was the best way to get an edge, you know? But once you're in, you can't get out. It's like the Mafia."

Imani winced as she said the last word, like she'd made an off-color comment.

"I should do more of that," Tonya said. "It's just that—"

"You're a single working mom. I have some flexibility. Some days, like today, I only have a handful of patients. Got to do something with my time. I don't have many hobbies."

Tonya wasn't sure if the comment was an invitation to ask Imani about her extracurriculars or share her own outside interests. She couldn't get a read on the woman. Imani was like a gas fire. Her presence gave off a heat but didn't exactly crackle with warmth.

"So, um, does Layla see her dad much?"

The question felt like Imani had grabbed a fistful of her hair and pulled. "Not at all, actually." Tonya heard the edge in her tone, though she couldn't control it. She hated Layla's father too much. "He was never really in Layla's life. She doesn't know him. We don't discuss him."

Tonya caught the warning in her tone as she said the last part. She'd intended it, though perhaps not as blatantly as it had come out.

Imani's eyes went wide. "Oh. I was only wondering if he might be coming here to pick her up or, I don't know, it's none of my business. I shouldn't have asked."

Her guard was too high, Tonya decided. She was reading too much into Imani's forced politeness. The woman was simply trying to establish a rapport with the strange adult female in the house. "So, you saw patients this morning?"

Imani's face relaxed. "Yes. A woman overwhelmed with homeschooling and having some issues with her husband because of it all. Not that unusual really..."

Suddenly, Imani's full lips pressed together. She blinked up at the ceiling.

"Are you okay?"

"I'm sorry." Imani covered her mouth. "I've been emotional lately. My best friend was Melissa Walker. I'm sure you heard about what happened."

Tonya tried to look saddened even though she didn't actually feel much of anything—save for that awful twinge of relief that so frequently accompanied thoughts of Nate

Walker's absence from the earth. She mustered what she hoped resembled compassion. "It's awful."

Imani wiped a knuckle at the corner of each eye. "They were St. Catherine's parents too. Did you ever meet them?"

For the millionth time, Tonya tried to deduce the reason behind Imani's question. Were they still having a polite conversation? Was this a test? Had Imani heard anything?

Again, the woman's expression revealed nothing except a forced earnestness. The quicker she could exit this conversation the better, Tonya decided. She might have been an actress, but faking sympathy for Nate Walker would be too difficult.

"Nope. I never met them." Tonya covered her lie with the same pained expression painted on Imani's face. "I do hope they find your friend."

CHAPTER TWENTY-SEVEN

IMANI

Melissa would say she was crazy. As Imani passed through St. Catherine's surprisingly quiet halls, she could almost hear her friend admonishing her for bringing that woman into her house. It was one thing for Philip to see flashes of Tonya at work, her slender body covered by a boxy button-down, work slacks, and an apron. It was quite another for him to stumble upon a beautiful young woman in his home, bra peeking from the wide neck of a thin T-shirt, casually doing his laundry. "She's not paying rent?" Melissa would shout, incredulous. "You've taken on a sister-wife, and you're not even Mormon."

Imani chuckled at the thought and then hiccupped as she thought about Melissa's secrets and her giggle threatened to morph into something else. Whatever Melissa had done, she'd been a real friend to her, Imani decided. Melissa had been her confidante, the person who would break from her busy day to grab a glass of wine and listen to Imani rant about her insecurities or frustrations with a challenging patient. With all the demands of the restaurant, Philip had never had the patience to hear her go on about her *issues* or *feelings*.

Imani leaned on the hallway wall, taking a minute to compose herself before entering room 203. Typically, the space was used by the drama teacher. According to the front office, he'd temporarily moved his classroom into the auditorium to allow students to space out, leaving this tighter space for her and Barbara, a sixty-year-old theater critic, St. Catherine alumna, and head of the Parent-Teacher Organization.

The PTO lead was essentially a full-time, unpaid position. Though all committees had a chief, those positions were largely ceremonial. Nate, as head of the admissions committee, had ultimately rubber-stamped most student résumés that had come blessed by the faculty and Barbara. It was Barb who really did the work: organizing meetings, gathering applications and teacher addendums, liaising with the staff, and digitizing damn near every document.

Imani opened the door to see Barbara already seated at a desk. Unlike in many schools, St. Catherine's workstations weren't in a spaced line but arranged side by side, forming a horseshoe with the teacher at the center. The setup reminded Imani less of a school than a conference room.

Barbara acknowledged her with a warm, albeit mask-muffled, "hello" before lamenting the stack of financial-aid-contingent applications. "It's bigger than I've ever seen it," she said. "And it includes a bunch of students who've paid full freight for years."

"The pandemic has been devastating for many families," Imani muttered through her own face covering, thinking of her personal predicament. Had her husband not hidden the home equity loan, she would have filled out two aid applications herself. But it was too late now. The deadline had passed months ago. St. Catherine's senior teachers had already weeded out those they'd felt undeserving. She and Barbara were providing parental input on the finalists.

Imani approached a seat that Barbara had already furnished with a stack of petitions. She unzipped her coat. As she began to remove it from her shoulders, a blast of frigid air from the room's cracked windows changed her mind. The best part of the pandemic ending wouldn't be removing her mask, she thought. It would be feeling warm inside public places.

Imani pulled the first packet from the stack and began reading. According to the parents of five-year-old Angelique, their daughter had "it," an amorphous star quality that people immediately recognized. The essay went on with examples of little Angelique's giftedness, some of which had to be exaggerations. "Making her own short films?" Kids that age couldn't hold a camera steady.

The parents included a TikTok link to their daughter's "comedic monologues." Imani brought up her phone and painstakingly copied the address from the printed form.

A big-cheeked, dark-haired girl with cartoonish eyes stared at the camera as if she wanted to devour it. "What super-hero do I want to be?" Angie's face screwed in disgust. "Why would anyone want to be a superhero? Flying around with their unnecessary masks. You can't catch a cold in the sky. Who can sneeze that high?"

Imani laughed. "This would have been one for Nate."

The name hung in the air. Imani stiffened, hoping it might dissipate without additional commentary. It was one thing to speculate about what had happened in her own mind. Another to open the topic with Barbara. Melissa's disappearance wasn't simple school gossip to be whispered about with other St. Catherine's moms.

Barbara peered at her from over a pair of red bifocals. "Oh. It's awful." She removed her glasses and set them down on the table. "You were good friends with his wife, right?"

"I am friends with her," Imani said, correcting the past tense even though she had her doubts. Even if Melissa was alive, Imani wasn't sure what she should call herself. She'd loved Melissa like family. Perhaps the feeling had never been mutual.

"They gave so much to this school." Barbara rapped her knuckles against her six-inch application stack. "Nate in particular—volunteering for committees, teaching a virtual class during the shutdown. He even endowed a scholarship. It pays for a kid's entire tuition from kindergarten to graduation—half a million dollars, all in."

Imani had figured Nate and Melissa as the kind of people to give back, but the extent of their generosity was impressive. It was the kind of thing that should be mentioned in a *New York Times* obituary or an In Memoriam on behalf of the school. "Do we know which child? Maybe we could reach out to the press or Nate's family with the information. The child might even want to record something nice that the family could play at the funeral."

Though she hadn't heard anything about a service, Imani assumed Nate's parents were having one. Likely they were keeping it small and local because of the pandemic. Immediate family. Real friends.

"That's a great idea." Barbara rose from her seat and moved toward the blackboard at the head of the room. A laptop sat on the teacher's desk. She lifted the screen and then leaned over the keyboard, standing to put in her administrator password to access the school records. "I remember him mentioning a candidate when he'd endowed the scholarship—years ago. He wrote this long letter about the need to consider not only ethnic diversity but also economic diversity and experience."

The clatter of computer keys echoed in the room, overpowering the street sounds slipping through the cracked window. Imani turned her attention back to Angelique's application. If she hoped to make a dent in the pile before her kids came home, she'd have to read an application every fifteen minutes.

"I found his letter!"

Barbara's victory took ten years off her face. She looked like the girl she'd once been, brandishing an A-paper.

"Who is it?"

"Looks like"—Barbara scrolled down a page—"Layla Sayre."

She'd said something else, Imani thought. The brain often substituted familiar names for others. "Layla Sayre?"

"This is what I was talking about," Barbara said, reading: "'While ethnic and religious diversity is key to developing the world that we want to live in and create via St. Catherine's, so too is economic and occupational diversity. Layla is a smart, hardworking, dedicated little lady with considerable academic promise being raised by a single mother with Appalachian roots. Layla's grandparents are farmers, and her mother has mentioned to me that she grew up working the land. Our city-dwelling students could learn a thing or two about America from Layla's upbringing and her mother's experience. Imagine reading Steinbeck's *Grapes of Wrath* and gaining the perspective of a kid who visits grandparents and works on a farm? Full disclosure, mom is an aspiring actress who has auditioned for me multiple times and spoken at length about how her background developed her work ethic. I have witnessed how Tonya's experience rounds out the characters that she portrays. Surely, her daughter will enrich her classmates' experience as well.'"

Barbara kept reading, but Imani had heard all she'd needed. Nate had clearly met Tonya multiple times. Yet the woman sleeping upstairs in her house had claimed not to know him. In Imani's experience, such lies meant only one thing: an affair.

"Nate's scholarship pays for Layla to go to school," Imani said, confirming the news to herself.

"Yes." Barbara sat back, impressed. "She'll be in the middle school now. We can reach out to her mother and—" Barbara looked up at her, brow furrowed. "Is something wrong?"

Imani could only imagine the expression visible on the top half of her face. She tried to picture a blank wall, but the only image her brain would serve up was Tonya from earlier, her head cocked toward an exposed shoulder, denying that she ever knew Nate.

"I . . . I just remembered that I have a patient." Imani gathered her purse from the table. "I'm so sorry. I'll read these later. Okay? I'll find time to come in—"

"Don't worry," Barbara said. "I don't know how you juggle everything. I'll send you the files via email."

Imani thanked her as she rushed out the door, her feet fueled by a bad feeling. Tonya was a liar and a cheat. And she'd left her alone, in her house, with *her* husband.

CHAPTER TWENTY-EIGHT

TONYA

"You don't smell like a puddle."

Mike sniffed Tonya's neck while pulling her into his apartment. "Gardenia, baby powder." He kissed her and then smacked his lips together, a sommelier searching for the right notes to describe a fine wine. "Maybe coffee. A touch of strawberry."

Tonya rolled her eyes. "I haven't eaten any fruits in twenty-four hours."

"It must be all the sweetness mixing with..." He inhaled behind her ear where skin had sweated beneath a wool beanie. "Just a touch of sour."

Tonya laughed. "So a little dirty, then?"

"Aren't we all?" She felt a wet tickle as Mike's tongue flicked her ear.

"See why I had to do that laundry?" she asked, referencing her earlier phone rant about Imani's offended reaction to her attempt at fixing Philip's soiled jacket. Tonya laughed to show she was over the incident—even though she wasn't—and stepped farther into a living room that could have been the stock photo for "bachelor pad." Black leather couch. IKEA coffee table. A notable lack of other furnishings.

"You can come over smelly," Mike said. "Most of the time I stink of spilled liquor. Well, I did."

Tonya extended a hand, inviting him to join her as she flopped onto the couch. "Maybe the layoffs are a blessing in disguise. You can focus more on auditions."

Mike sat beside her but didn't make eye contact. Instead, his gaze drifted to a shelf of liquor bottles. Light shone through empties, testifying to a recent binge. "Yeah. Maybe," he said.

Tonya understood his lack of enthusiasm. The entertainment industry was perhaps the only arena hit harder by the pandemic than the service industry. Broadway was shut down. Moviemaking had been put on an indefinite hold. "I also didn't want Imani coming home to a full dryer," Tonya said, changing the subject back to their flirty banter about her laundry. "It's bad enough that she caught me swapping out Philip's clothes for my own."

Mike's gaze retreated to the hands in his lap. He'd folded them, Tonya realized. Around her, they were never stationary. His hands were always busy. Pouring drinks. Snapping for orders or attention. Caressing her body.

"That's one of the things I wanted to talk to you about," he said.

Conversation was actually on the agenda? When Mike had asked her to come over and "talk," she'd assumed the chatting part was a euphemism for another four-letter word. She and Mike didn't do deep conversations, though Tonya was guilty of several drunken, postcoital confessions.

She scooted over another inch, wanting the extra distance in case Mike intended some grand romantic gesture like asking her to move in with him and his roommates. If she was going to break something, she wanted to be on the edge of the impact zone, not in it. "You wanted to talk about my living arrangements?"

Mike ran a thumb over his knuckles. "Not exactly," he said. "More about Imani."

Hearing Philip's wife's name on Mike's lips made Tonya shift onto another cushion. She'd been wrong about him, she quickly concluded. Mike was a womanizer who'd gotten entangled with his boss's hot wife. Tonya could imagine how it had happened. Imani had come to the restaurant, seeking her husband. Philip had been too busy to pay her any attention, so she'd sat at the bar chatting up the handsome man behind it, ordering drink after drink after...

"She messaged me on Instagram."

Tonya felt as if she were taking her own pulse. That's how conscious she was of the beating in her chest. "Why?"

"She says the police are looking at me in relation to what happened with the Walkers."

Of all the responses Tonya had suspected, that had not been one of them. As far as Tonya knew, Mike had never met the Walkers. "Why?" she asked again.

"Don't be mad," Mike replied.

The phrase worked like an electrical pulse, lighting up Tonya's nerves. As a parent, Tonya knew that such a request always preceded a terrible admission. *I colored all over the*

walls. I lost what you said to make sure stayed in my pocket.
I had an accident. I told them . . .

"Say it." Tonya's voice came out a whisper, smoke in
the air. She'd entered Mike's apartment full of fire and
sexual energy. It was gone, turned to ash by his ominous
statement.

"I messaged his wife."

"Imani? I thought you said she—"

"No. Melissa."

Tonya felt a hollowing in her stomach, as if someone
were chiseling out her insides with an ice pick. "Why would
you—"

"Because of what you said that night." Mike finally made
eye contact. He had a puppy-dog stare, providing the puppy
was a Doberman. "You were so nervous that she'd find
out what her husband did and blame you for it. After
everything you went through with him, that wasn't fair. I
wanted—"

"You told her what happened to me?"

"I didn't use your name." Mike's gaze retreated to his
hands. "But I messaged her and said I wanted to talk,
claimed we had common friends. To be honest, I didn't think
she'd respond. I was so angry, and I wanted to do something
to hold him responsible. She must have been bored, I guess,
because Melissa replied."

The hollowing expanded through Tonya's body. She was
being scooped out from the inside, reduced to a shell to be
filled up with whatever others gave her. Whatever Nate had
given her.

"We met in a park," Mike continued. "I got right to it, told her that her director husband was cheating on her and abusing his power, pressuring young actresses that I knew into sex acts and stuff under the guise of auditioning, implying that their compliance would show how far they were willing to go and help them land parts in his films."

The bachelor pad blurred before Tonya's eyes, becoming a different room. Its lights lowered to a candle's glow. Chocolate-leather chairs appeared in front of overbearing bookcases decorated with tomes chosen for their colors rather than content. She saw Nate leaning back in a barrel chair, face lit by a reading lamp and the glowing end of a cigar. She heard the doors close as the waiter exited, emphasizing that the hotel bar's back room was truly private. They could do whatever they wanted. Whatever Nate and his friend wanted.

"Your audition starts now." His voice was deep and rumbling, distant thunder in the dark. There was power in it. Threats. "You're playing the part of a waitress attracted to the brooding, wealthy man in the corner."

"What's my line?" she asked.

"Improvise."

She strutted to the couch, palm in the air to balance an invisible tray. She lowered it and then plucked the pretend stem of a martini glass from space, placing it on the table beside him. "Your gimlet." She offered a wide smile. "Is there anything else you'd like, or will that be all for the moment?"

She punctuated the question with a flick of tongue against bottom lip. Her character was supposed to be flirting.

"What else is on the menu?"

"The kitchen's open," she cooed. "Are you in the mood for salty or sweet?"

Behind her, the friend laughed at the line. Nate didn't seem to find it as funny. He sat back in the chair and examined her as if looking at a handsome sweater that he'd just noticed had pulls in the fabric. His smile twisted into a frown. "I don't believe you."

An actress couldn't receive a worse note. The job was to embody a part, to lose oneself within a character's skin. How was she failing? The part wasn't a stretch. She was a waitress in real life, after all.

"What am I doing wrong?"

"I don't believe you want me." Nate's eyes narrowed. "Make me believe it."

Tonya considered Nate anew as her character, donning imaginary glasses that filtered out the fact that he was far too old and too married for a single twenty-something. She focused on the boyish cut of his auburn hair and intense blue eyes, ignoring the scruffy salt-and-pepper beard drawing down his cheeks. She reminded herself of his successful films and the mind that worked behind that forehead, what it was capable of—a godlike power. Nate could create a character perfect for her. He could make her a star.

"Do you want a part in one of my movies?" Nate asked.

"Yes." The word came out breathless, reflecting the twin desires held by her and the character she was pretending to be.

"Then think about what you're willing to do."

"I'll do anything." Tonya didn't know who was speaking anymore. Her? The lustful waitress? They were the same person. No, she told herself. They weren't. She wasn't even in the room anymore. There was only the character.

"Whatever you need. Anything. Absolutely anything."

"I have a room," Nate said.

Tonya shuddered, the memory of her voice bringing her back to reality. She channeled all her residual shame and anger into the look she shot the man in front of her. "It happened to me. It wasn't your story to tell."

Mike reached for her hand. She pulled it into her chest. He couldn't touch her. She was certain she'd never let him touch her again.

"I felt like it was my burden, though." Mike scratched at the stubble on his cheek. "I mean, I understand why you didn't want to come forward. I get not wanting your name dragged through the mud and needing to protect Layla. I know the fact that he helped with Layla's school complicated things. But once you told me, I knew. And I kept thinking that, unless somebody said something, this predator was going to keep getting away with it. I thought, maybe if I told his wife, she'd hold him accountable in a way that didn't involve you."

Tonya wanted to run from the room. She forced herself to stay still, though. Mike was confessing his betrayal for a reason: Her landlord wanted to talk to him. "We both work at Imani's husband's restaurant. It doesn't take much to draw a line from you to me."

Mike nodded, conceding the point. "That's why I wanted to discuss it with you before speaking with her."

Instinctively, her arms crossed over her chest. "Now you want to talk it over."

"Listen, the cops must have found the messages between Melissa and me. They were kind of cryptic. I wanted her to come out and meet me so I could tell her. I may have been a little effusive in my compliments. As a result, I think the police think we were romantically involved. At least, that's kind of what Imani implied."

It didn't take a genius to see where Mike was going. To clear his name with regard to Nate's murder, he'd have to explain that he wasn't a jealous lover but a concerned citizen in the acting community. He'd have to tell Imani and everyone else all about what had happened.

"You can't use my name."

Mike picked at a hangnail on his thumb. "I'll say that I'd heard about Nate through the grapevine, and I thought that his wife should know. Hopefully she'll tell the police and that will be the end of it."

Tonya threw up a hand in frustration. Mike couldn't really be this dense. "You don't think the cops will want to talk to you after? You don't think they'll demand names?"

Mike bit off the jagged piece of skin. "Worst-case scenario, they'll talk to us, and that will be the end of it. It's not like you or I could have done anything. The newspapers said Nate was killed Thursday night. We were together at your apartment."

"How convenient." Tonya again rolled her eyes. "You think they'll believe that?"

"I took the subway to your place. I'm sure I'm on a camera somewhere. They'll have to look. I have my MetroCard too. That probably scans somehow. And Layla knows I was over, or that someone was."

Tonya closed her eyes, imagining how Mike's conversation would inevitably play out. He'd talk to Imani, revealing Nate's bad acts. Imani would tell the police.

Or not, Tonya realized. Knowledge of Nate's actions gave Melissa motive for murder. If Imani was truly Melissa Walker's best friend, then perhaps she wouldn't want to give the cops any more ammunition against her. Perhaps she'd stay quiet, let law enforcement figure out Mike's identity on their own.

"The police didn't message you?"

"Not that I know of." Mike examined his irritated finger, perhaps avoiding eye contact. "I did get a random message from some stranger claiming to be a producer seeking talent for an East Village production. I checked all the usual posting sites, though, and there wasn't anything about it. Nothing on Backstage or even Craigslist."

If the police were being cagey about interviewing Mike, then they wanted to do more than simply talk to him, Tonya thought. They wanted to trap him in case he'd somehow kidnapped Melissa so that he couldn't get rid of the evidence. Finding the real identity of an Instagram user couldn't take that long. For all Tonya knew, the cops already knew who Mike was. They could be spying on his apartment—or on their way over.

Tonya jumped up from the couch. "I have to go."

"Please, don't leave. I'm sorry." Mike finally looked directly at her. "I never wanted to cause trouble for you."

"Well, you did." Tonya started toward the door.

"I'll do whatever you want," Mike shouted.

Absolutely anything.

Tonya shook the memory of her earlier statement from her head. "Do what you need to, Mike. Just leave my name out of it. If she pressures you, make something up."

"Like what?"

"You're an actor." Tonya pulled open the door, calling over her shoulder as it swung back, "Figure it out."

CHAPTER TWENTY-NINE

IMANI

Imani returned to the smell of curry. It struck her as she entered the house, a cloud of cumin, ginger, and other pungent aromatics combining to form a scent so strong that it had physical presence. She pushed through it to enter the kitchen where she could crack the window that Philip should have opened when cooking. He'd made lunch, she thought. Perhaps for both of them.

Neither Philip nor Tonya appeared to be downstairs. She could see nearly every room from the kitchen entrance, and they were all empty. Even the bathroom door was cracked, revealing a darkness beyond that suggested no one was inside.

Imani headed to the second floor, half searching for the house's occupants, half fleeing the overwhelming odors. By the time she hit the landing, the scent had sufficiently dissipated for her to shift focus from smell to sight. The bedroom doors were all closed, she realized. That wasn't unusual for Vivienne's and Jay's rooms, as they routinely shut their doors to deter her commentary on the pigsties they'd left behind. But her door should have been cracked. Imani closed it only to sleep. Air smelled odd when trapped in tight spaces. She approached her room, Philip's name on the tip of her tongue. A sound stopped her. She could just make it out through the door: a guttural moan followed by a high-pitched wail that could have been a ululation—or orgasm.

Imani pulled back her door. Some women that she counseled swore they wouldn't want to know if their husband was having an affair. They professed that they'd prefer to live in willful ignorance rather than shake up their comfortable existences and upend their children's lives. Imani always doubted that they meant it, though. Their very presence in a therapist's office meant that such ignorance wasn't bliss. Not knowing was killing them as much as knowing. Deep down, nobody could stand being kept in the dark.

Philip's head was tilted back against the bedframe. His eyes were wide. His mouth open. His chest exposed in all its blinding whiteness. A duvet, one or two shades lighter than Philip's skin, moved up and down above his waist, a back arching and flattening, or a head lowering and raising.

The moan sounded again. Philip ignored it, turning his head toward the door. "Imani?" The covers abruptly stopped moving. "You're home early."

His tone wasn't alarmed enough for a man caught in bed with another woman. Imani tentatively approached, unsure of what might pop from beneath the covers. As she did, the moans continued. They emanated not from beneath the duvet, she realized, but from the television atop the credenza.

Before she could see what was on the screen, Philip rolled

toward the nightstand. She got a flash of bare bottom. At the same time, the television went dark.

"I didn't mean to interrupt anything," she said.

Philip's face reddened. His blush was one of the features she'd always found attractive on her husband. There was something innocent about the ability to be so blatantly embarrassed. "Sorry," he said. "I was home and had nothing to do."

Blood rose to Imani's cheeks. "It's fine. I get it."

"Didn't expect you to walk in."

Her husband's persistent shame made her wonder if he'd been watching something particularly offensive. Bondage, perhaps. Or, worse, a Tonya look-alike going at it with an older Irishman. "Maybe I'm glad I did," she said, trying to keep her tone flirty. "What were you watching?"

Philip eyed her as if she was hiding something behind her back.

"What?" She kept her pitch high and playful, knowing that her face was likely advertising her concern. "I'm not allowed to see?"

"Sure. I'll show you."

Philip clicked the television back on. The video continued from where it had left off with a dark-haired, bronze woman, perhaps Afro-Latina, obviously faking enthusiasm for a man with tanned arms and a belly even paler than her husband's own. The woman didn't exactly look like her. However, she definitely didn't resemble Tonya.

Imani felt her shoulders drop from the tense position level with her clavicle. She smiled at him, remembering her earlier musing about perfunctory sex. Surely she was to blame for that as much as Philip. "Well, now that I'm here, I suppose I can put on a little show."

A grin erased her husband's prior expression. He patted the bed beside her. "The real thing is always better."

Imani pulled off her top, momentarily forgetting what had urgently driven her home. Tonya was not seducing her husband at the moment. She was.

The shock of her arrival hadn't completely calmed Philip. A few kisses to her breasts, a grab of her buttocks, and he was ready to perform. She concentrated on his face as they began, forcing herself to think only about the relationship between her movements and his expressions, what he liked, what made him lose control. Several times, she suffered a pang of guilt. Her friend was missing, and she was making love. Surely there was something callous about that. Something cruel. Each time she thought about it, she instructed Philip to go harder, bringing her back into the room. Real physical pain was always easier to bear than its emotional counterpart.

The session lasted longer than usual, perhaps because of everything else weighing on their minds. When it was done, they both went to the bathroom to wash off the sex and the lingering scent of spices. Philip got into the shower first. Imani talked to him while pinning up her hair.

"I learned something disturbing today," she said, loud enough for Philip to hear beneath the spray. "Tonya knew Nate. Apparently, she auditioned for him several times. He wrote this glowing letter to get Layla into the school, and he was even paying for it. Layla attends St. Catherine's because of a scholarship that he funded."

A squirt from the shampoo bottle was the only response.

"It was disconcerting because I was talking to her about Melissa earlier today and specifically asked if she knew the Walkers. And she'd said no."

Philip rubbed the soap over his hair. "Maybe she thought saying yes would indicate that they were friends, and she didn't know them well."

Imani stepped into the shower, appreciating the warm mist from the water on her goose-pimpled skin. "But you wouldn't say you don't know them, then; you'd say that you didn't know them well." She turned on the handheld shower hose and held it to her body. "And, judging from Nate's letter, he knew her pretty well. He talked about her background."

Philip dipped his head under the water.

"Why would she lie?"

"I don't know if it's a lie, exactly." Philip's words came out garbled from the spray in his mouth. "She probably wanted to avoid talking about him since it would lead to conversations about his death."

"So she completely omits the fact that Nate advocated for her kid to go to St. Catherine's and pays her tuition. I mean, he really pushed for Layla to get this scholarship that he sure seemed to have specifically endowed for her."

Water tumbled off the bumps in Philip's forehead generated by his raised eyebrows. "I wonder if he met Tonya at the restaurant..."

"It's possible." Imani grabbed the soap from Philip and lathered it over her chest. "From the way he wrote about her, their relationship had to go further than chitchat post-audition. I think they were having an affair."

Philip dipped his head back under the water. "I suppose it's none of our business."

The soap slipped from Imani's grip. "Are you kidding me? Melissa is missing. Nate's dead. If he was sleeping with Tonya—"

"Then Melissa would have more cause to shoot him in the face," Philip said.

Imani watched Philip pick up the soap, feeling like her jaw was somewhere beside the dropped bar. "You can't really think that."

Imani heard the doubt in her own voice. Of course he could think that. She was wondering the same thing, after all.

"Well, what are you suggesting, then?" Philip asked. "That Tonya's been having an on-again-off-again affair with Nate for years and that she finally got fed up and shot him? And then did what with Melissa? Kidnapped her only to move into the house of her best friend?"

As he spoke, Philip concentrated on soaping his body, dismissing her theory in both words and withheld eye contact. Imani had to admit that it sounded ridiculous the way he put it. But she knew from experience that people often acted irrationally under extreme stress. Irrational acts were, by nature, kind of insane.

"I don't know," she said, taking back the soap. "All I know is that she lied."

"Maybe she simply didn't want everyone knowing that Layla is a scholarship kid," Philip said. "It must be strange going to a school where everyone has so much money."

Imani winced. How would it be for their own kids next year? she wondered. Would they even be able to afford two tuitions?

"The police are looking into all of the Walkers' relationships," Imani said, bringing her focus back to something she could do about getting the woman who'd been sleeping with her friend's husband out of her house. "They found out Melissa was talking to some guy on Instagram. If there was something between Tonya and Nate, the cops are going to ask about it."

"So, let *them* ask about it." Philip quickly rinsed off, emphasizing that he was done with the conversation by exiting the shower. Imani watched him approach the towel rack, water droplets dripping onto the marble tile, creating dark, circular impressions. "It's their job, Imani. Not yours."

"Melissa's my friend," Imani said. "And if Tonya was sleeping with Nate, she shouldn't be here."

Philip wrapped a towel around himself and then grabbed one for her. He tossed hers over the glass shower wall. "We don't know anything, and we need the money. So there's no need for you to be running around playing amateur detective. Let the police do their jobs. We have enough problems."

Philip dropped his voice as he said it, the head of the household delivering the final word.

Imani appreciated it about as much as Vivienne when she heard it. But she was too old to say something only to have the last word. Moreover, her husband was right. They did have enough problems.

And she'd be damned if Tonya became one of them.

CHAPTER THIRTY

MELISSA

The sound of a dozen metal pins snapping into place stopped her banging. For a moment, Melissa gripped the metal paper towel dispenser, wielding the rod like a too-short, too-thin billy club that, at best, would add a few ounces of force to a feeble punch before being knocked out of her hand. She was too out of shape to counter It effectively. Juice cleansing off the quarantine pounds had cut her bodyweight while failing to build any muscle. Outrunning anyone would be impossible, let alone fighting.

But she needed to do something. The noises meant there were now two of them in the darkness. Her and It. And It was stronger.

Melissa placed the rod beside the toilet bowl. The metal pinged as the rod made contact with the ground. Quickly, she flushed to make the sound appear related to the mechanics of using the facilities.

"You need to tell them what really happened." Its voice echoed in the other room, commanding but also pleading, struggling to strike a balance between an order and a request.

Melissa emerged from the stall into the main room. The little light emanating from behind her revealed Its outline as well as a long stick in Its hand. She heard the wet slap of soaked fabric hitting the floor.

Her urine, Melissa thought. It was mopping up her mess.

For a moment, she felt a rush of gratitude. It was not going to leave the smell to attract vermin. Maybe, deep down, part of It was still human. Perhaps It cared about her. She could appeal to that.

"I'm not sure I know what happened," Melissa said.

In the darkness, her trembling voice became tangible, standing in for her physical presence. Part of Melissa wanted to pull it back. If she stood out of the bathroom light and didn't speak, she was as good as invisible.

"An accident." It worked the mop back and forth. She could tell, not because she saw the mop moving, but because she sensed a repetitive change in the air molecules. "Nate and I were supposed to have a civil conversation, but I suppose I got a bit worked up, and he became drunk and aggressive. He pulled the gun on me."

Melissa hadn't witnessed how the weapon had entered the picture. When she'd joined the scene, It had been standing over what had been left of Nate. The gory image had seemed like horror movie special effects, so much so that she hadn't even screamed. She'd simply watched It clean off the gun with an antibacterial wipe and place it in her husband's hand.

She hadn't even thought to run until it was too late. By then, It had been gripping her arm and pulling her from the house, warning her that she didn't want Ava to come down-stairs, promising that everything could be explained and a rational solution developed. Next thing, she'd been in Its car, a gun at her side telling her to drive, not to make any sudden movements, and then ordering her out of the vehicle.

She'd started screaming then. *You killed him. You murdered him.* In response, It had pointed the gun and ordered her into this hole. Instructing her to take time to calm down.

She was no more relaxed than she'd been when It had first shut the door. If anything, she was wilder, a dog made mean by abuse. Without light, she'd grown comfortable with her own darkness.

"I was defending myself," It continued.

Melissa had imagined every director's cut of the missing footage, picturing how Nate would have found himself on the other end of the barrel of his gun—really her gun, as it had been used as a prop in her big film and then gifted to her as a memento. She guessed that It could have asked Nate to put the weapon down and then, after he had, grabbed the thing. Or maybe It could have stolen the weapon in a scuffle. Nate, having never intended to really shoot, wouldn't have known what to do. Her husband had always been full of bravado and bluster. He'd liked to imagine his life a movie in which he nabbed all the main parts. Loving husband and father. Hefner-esque playboy. Mobster Capo. But Nate wasn't a real actor. He could never become the character.

The moment the gun had come out, Nate's time was over. It had responded with genuine fear and desire for self-preservation. Nate, faking his way through, had never stood a chance.

"He wouldn't have shot you," she said.

"You don't know that. When a man points a gun at your chest, you should expect him to mean business," It countered. "I reacted."

"And what about bringing me here? Was that a simple reaction too?"

The mop stopped moving back and forth. It leaned on it. "You were going to call the police, and I needed time to think. Obviously, things looked bad."

Melissa moved closer. It had gotten in through the main door, but how did It intend to get out? The exit didn't seem to have a key or a handle or even a knob. She'd felt around for one in the dark and only made contact with cold metal. It would leave at some point. She needed to follow It.

"You've had time to think," she said, taking another step toward It.

"And I think you should tell the police what happened, but as a first-person witness. You should say that you saw Nate become aggressive with me and pull the gun, and I reacted in self-defense."

"How do I explain why I am only coming forward now?"

It threw up a hand. Or, at least, Melissa guessed that's what had happened. She'd felt air whip toward her. "Say you were afraid and hid out for a couple days."

"Leaving my kid to wonder if I'd died. Leaving Ava."

Melissa's voice broke on her daughter's name. Aside from escape, Ava dominated her thoughts. She pictured her child in that house, mourning her father, fearing for her mom. It had to know that there was no way she could believably confess to letting her daughter go through that. "How is she?"

"Safe." For the first time since the shooting, she heard an emotion other than panic or resolve in Its voice.

"Did she . . ." Melissa trailed off, her voice crumbling. "Did she see her father?"

"No. The news said the maid found Nate while Ava was at school."

Relief dribbled through her, damaging Melissa's resolve. She would need every ounce of aggression to follow It out of this place. Every bit of strength to do what was necessary. Yet she was crying. She couldn't stop crying.

"So, what do you say?" It asked.

Melissa couldn't answer through her tears. She couldn't even process the question.

The bucket started to roll across the floor. Melissa could hear the sound of wheels on wood. It was backing into the shadows. Departing. "You can have time to think," It said.

She ran toward where It had vanished. The little light from the bathroom didn't reach more than a foot outside the small closet. Again, she was plunged into blackness, into a space so dark that she couldn't see her own hands at the tip of her nose. Then, suddenly, a sliver of light became visible, the last stage before a new moon.

Melissa dived toward it. A force shot out of the void. Without sight, it felt like some strange reverse gravity had slammed into her chest, propelling her backward. Her foot slipped against a slick spot on the floor. Her butt slammed to the ground. Her head followed.

Its voice emerged from the blackness. "I didn't want to hurt you. But I can't have you running to the cops. I have a family to protect."

Dazed, Melissa rose to one knee, cradling the back of her head.

"Don't force me to choose," It said.

Before she could ask what the choice was between, a bang silenced her. She stepped toward the source of the reverberations, knowing that it was too late. A dial turned. Pins snapped into place. All those bars, she thought, sealing her away in the darkness.

CHAPTER THIRTY-ONE

OKSANA

"Half Truths" Director's Last Scene.

Oksana clicked the website link. Her picture loaded into view line by line, a product not of a slow internet connection but of the malicious code that was probably downloading onto the library computer with every painstakingly revealed pixel. She saw the blood-splattered suede wallpaper. The bookcase backdrop. The desk in the foreground. Nate's body took at least a minute to fully appear. His head, or what was left of it, was last of all, an unintended consequence of the angle of the shot, which the photo's buyers had to be happy about.

Oksana admired her work for a minute. In another life, maybe she'd have been a good crime scene photographer. She hadn't simply captured the gore, which was what most people would want to see, but also the little things that suggested what had happened. The gun was visible in Nate's hand, its lazy positioning indicating that it had been placed in an open palm by the real killer. The uncapped whiskey bottle and glass with a sliver of amber liquid, both visible on the desk, suggested that he'd been drinking, perhaps with someone. In her opinion, definitely with someone.

She double-clicked the image, zooming in. Again, the pixels took their time appearing, no doubt pulling additional packets of malware into the machine. New details emerged. The faint ring of a glass on the desk. The black label on the whiskey bottle. The glint of a wedding ring on Nate's finger. There was something almost beautiful about the whole image. All the rust colors and ambers against neutral furniture. If not for the gruesome subject matter, it might be modern art.

She'd been paid for it as if it were a painting. A flat fee for the original. It could be copied, of course, but that had nothing to do with her. She had her digital currency. The internet's armchair detectives could pass it around all they wanted now. Maybe they'd also notice what she had. Maybe they'd put it together.

Either way, that problem was above her pay grade. She couldn't risk her neighborhood clients hearing that she'd gone to the cops with information gleaned while cleaning in the background. Nosy was a bad brand for a maid, and people talked. Most of her patrons were client referrals.

The trip to the library was really about cashing in. Oksana closed the webpage with Nate's body and opened the address to the currency exchange that her cousin had provided. It reminded her of the places in airports that displayed exchange rates to the local tender on a ticker, except here everyone was selling money denoted by ones and zeroes, saved on ledgers posted to computer servers across the world.

Oksana opened her account. She clicked a few buttons, advertising her "coins" available for purchase. Fifteen minutes later, she had an offer for far more than her photo purchasers had negotiated. She clicked accept.

Oksana smiled to herself as the US dollar equivalent of her cryptocurrency entered her account. The Walkers had been good clients, she mused. But they'd never paid her as much alive as Nate had dead.

CHAPTER THIRTY-TWO

RICK

Rats crawled behind the dumpster. Rick heard them scratching and squeaking as he stood in the restaurant alley, waiting for Banque's side door to open. The noises set his skin ablaze. In the dim light, it seemed that the vermin were climbing up his pant legs or scampering down the neck of his shirt. They'd become more aggressive since the shutdowns. Starved by a dearth of overflowing restaurant dumpsters, they'd begun venturing out in daylight and invading apartments. Eating each other. He would swear that he felt their claws.

"Will you stop that?"

Frank hissed at him from the opposite side of the alley. They'd chosen their posts with care. Rick was directly in front of the exit, as his job was to call for Philip's attention as soon as he appeared, distracting him from Frank at the door's side. Before Philip could run, Frank would have the pistol pressed into the chef's left flank along with wire instructions for the $350,000 that Philip owed them.

"What am I doing?" Rick spat.

"Scratching."

Rick wanted to ask how Frank could see him that well. The only light in the alley was a diffuse glow from a side-walk streetlamp and a window several stories up in the neighboring building. Frank was shrouded in darkness. Rick had thought that he'd been as well.

"Every second you're pawing at something," Frank contin-ued, silencing Rick's question. "The back of your neck. Your sides. Your hair. Stop being so freaked out. You're giving me the jitters."

Rick took offense at the characterization of him as the nervous Nellie. Frank liked to pretend that he was the big man, the guy with the gun ready to play real-life cops and robbers. But Rick was the brave one. What had Frank done when Rick had thrown a tire iron at Philip's window? Peel off in the Porsche. That was what.

"You try standing next to Ratatouille's extended family and see if you don't itch," Rick said.

Frank chuckled. "That was a decent payday."

"Yeah. Brad turned out to be quite the voice actor, huh?"

"Well, he was always better suited for cartoons than ro-mance flicks. I told him when we signed him that he could clean up as the heavy. But it's too out of character for him. Audiences can't buy it after seeing his comedy."

"He's too nice a guy," Rick agreed. "No one believes he's going to blow anyone's head off."

As soon as he said it, Rick regretted it. He worried that Frank would take the statement as a challenge, a sly sugges-tion that Mr. Brand-New Revolver didn't have the guts to fire at anyone. Shooting someone didn't take courage, in Rick's opinion. It took fear and anger. A lack of control.

He still didn't know whether Frank's emotions had gotten the better of him when talking to Nate about their failed restaurant. Rick hadn't asked his partner point-blank because he didn't really want to know. Better for him to continue operating under a cloud of plausible deniability, to be able to say that he hadn't turned Frank in because he'd been certain that Nate had died after a marital dispute with his wife. She was probably the more likely suspect anyway. If Melissa had learned half the crap that Nate had pulled over the years— half the things that Rick had smoothed over and kept out of the headlines—then she would have had more than enough cause to shoot him in the face.

A rustling noise sounded from the opposite side of the alley, followed by a crack and a whoosh. Rick was still struggling to make sense of the noises when he saw Philip in the doorjamb, illuminated by the kitchen light behind him. He held a large, black plastic bag, near bursting at the seams.

"Philip," Rick shouted, stepping into the center of the alley where the light reached. "We need to talk."

Philip continued toward the dumpster as if Rick hadn't just surprised him in a dark alley. As if he found his presence nothing more than slightly tiresome. "Money's spent, man." He flung back the dumpster's metal lid with one hand and tossed the bag inside. "There's nothing more to talk about."

"Like hell." The gun caught the light as Frank emerged from the shadowed area at Philip's right, extending from the hand at Frank's hip like a hook affixed to an amputated arm.

"Your staff is working," Frank shouted. "We watched them all come out. You're paying them with our money."

Philip spun to face Frank. As he saw the weapon, his hands rose in the air. "What's with the gun?"

"You need one when dealing with a fucking thief."

"I don't know what you're talking about." Philip stepped toward the weapon, hands still in the air. "Coffre's money went down with the restaurant. My staff is being paid off Banque's receipts."

"What receipts? You can't have receipts when the restaurant's closed."

"We're doing a decent takeout business."

"Thanks to us covering the rent, even though you know that was never the deal."

Philip took another step toward Frank, his hands still in the surrender position. "Coffre was located inside Banque. It used Banque's kitchen. Its staff. There was no Coffre if Banque went under."

"Bullshit," Frank said. "You should have prorated the cost of the space, and you know it. The deal was never for our money to bail out the bigger restaurant. Our investment was to make sure Coffre could run for twelve months at a loss. The bar was open for fucking four. You owe us two-thirds of the money that we laid out. At least."

Rick agreed with everything that Frank was saying, but he didn't like the way he was saying it. With every sentence, Frank seemed to raise the gun a bit higher until it was pointed, not at Philip's legs, but at the man's center mass. Because of the darkness still obscuring Frank, the weapon seemed to hang in the air, its metal slide catching the light from the above window. It vibrated as if on a string and not in his partner's gloved hand.

"I should never have let you all into the business." Philip took another step toward the hovering handgun. "You guys never got how restaurants work."

The gun was nearly touching Philip's chest. "You going to shoot me, Frank? That the plan? How are you going to make your money back without any food coming out of the kitchen?"

"You're coming with us," Frank said. His voice didn't sound as confident as before. "You're going to go to the bank, take out the money you're running this shithole on, and wire it to our accounts where it rightfully belongs."

"That a double-action pistol?"

Before Frank could answer, Philip's right hand was gripping the gun's slide and pushing it toward the floor. His body was wrenched back at a sideways angle, away from the weapon. Rick heard the pop of the gun firing and the sound of a bullet slamming into something hard, pavement or brick. Philip's other hand covered the gun. Frank yelped as his body tilted in the direction of his sharply turned wrist.

Rick stepped forward, a calculated delayed reaction to Frank's obvious need for assistance. His partner was not a marksman. He'd feared Frank accidentally shooting him while aiming for Philip. But he was more afraid of what Philip might do now that he had the gun.

He heard the click of the slide retreating and snapping back into place. One of Frank's hands shot up in the air. The other remained wrenched at an unnatural angle by his chest. "Philip. Let's talk," he said. "That's all we really wanted. We just need to understand—"

The gun rose. In the dim light, Rick could see not only the weapon but also the torso of the man behind it. His chest inflated and sank. Philip's adrenaline was up. His blood was pounding.

Rick dropped to the ground. He tucked his chin to his chest and put his hands over his head, an instinctual hedgehog defense. Philip might still shoot him, but he wouldn't be facing the bullet. He didn't want to see his life end.

He fell over from a sharp pain in his side. The blow had come with a dull thud but not the click or pop of a firearm's discharge. Rick remained curled up as another kick landed to his rib cage. "You come to my house, break my window, scare my wife, stalk me at my work." Kicks punctuated each whispered phrase. Philip wasn't raising his voice because he didn't want the cops to come, Rick thought. He wanted to beat him to death in this alley.

"No. I—" Rick couldn't complete the phrase. He was choking on fluids, blood or spit or tears, he couldn't tell.

"Philip, stop. You'll kill him. Stop."

The kicks ceased. Rick moved the arm over his head to see Philip standing over a kneeling Frank, the gun pointed at his head, execution style.

"Get him and get out of here." Philip sneered. "And don't let me ever see either of you again."

Rick watched Frank crawl over to his space. He felt his partner's left arm slide under his armpit. The pain in his side became excruciating as he was half lifted to a standing position. Philip had broken one of his ribs. Maybe several, Rick thought. But he could breathe. He was alive.

He leaned heavily on Frank's stocky body as they limped

toward the light outside the alley. The gun was on them. Rick could sense its barrel aimed at his back, hear Philip's huffed breaths over his own shallow ones. He refused to look back to verify, however. There was no need for any more confirmation or conversation. The money was gone because the man with the gun said so. It was a sunk cost. A loss. And he and Frank would eat it, no matter how bitter the taste. They were both done with the restaurant business.

CHAPTER THIRTY-THREE

TONYA

Tonya pinched the bridge of her mask tighter as she watched the yellow bucket fill with fresh water. The acidic smell of urine still lingered in the air, despite her emptying the mop system's dirty water tank and rinsing it with detergent. Tonya suspected that the scent came from the mop head itself. She unscrewed the microfiber cloth at the end of the pole and pivoted from the basin tucked in a nook near the kitchen entrance to the giant laundry bin where the restaurant tossed its used linens.

Before she pitched it inside, Tonya stopped herself. Without diners, it was doubtful that Philip was paying for laundry service. Most likely the mop head would be left to mold, its funk deepening until someone became aware of it and began to publicly wonder who the idiot was that had abandoned pee-soaked fabric in the kitchen—not to mention where the urine had come from.

She couldn't have anyone wondering that.

Her nose wrinkled, creating a gap between her mask and

mouth through which more of the smell entered. Tonya silently cursed as she brought the mop head back to the basin, holding it far out in front of her. She dropped it in the giant sink surrounding the mop bucket and redirected the spigot on top of it. Rather than dilute the stench, the water seemed to intensify the stink, beating the pee particles from the fabric into the air. She grabbed the bleach and poured it onto the cloth, stopping only when the smell of chlorine burned her sinuses.

Tonya turned off the water. She left the mop head to soak as she lifted the bucket out of the basin to the floor. Cold water splashed over its sides and onto her apron, making her shiver as she added the detergent. She was watching the bubbles form when a door slammed.

Tonya braced an arm against a wall, as if the noise were an earthquake's rumble and the ground might begin shaking. Her heart seemed to explode in her chest. The sound didn't make sense. The chefs had all departed hours ago—including Philip. He'd taken the garbage out and said good-bye twenty minutes earlier.

"Hello?"

She regretted calling out a nanosecond after she'd done so. Whoever had entered had likely been ignorant of her presence before. That was no longer the case.

Tonya grabbed the mop, which was little more than a stick without its cloth head. She stepped down the hall toward the doorway, wielding her weapon with both hands in front of her body, the way she'd seen in kung fu movies.

Philip emerged from the kitchen's washroom. His face was red, as if he'd gone out for a run rather than emptied the trash. Sweat pasted down his hair. He looked at her stance with his head tilted to the side before shrugging and un-buttoning his military-style peacoat. Instead of hanging it on the hallway hooks installed for that very purpose, he folded it over his arm.

"You're still here?" he asked.

"I thought you left," she said.

Philip's nose flared. "Yeah. I'd thought so too. But then I realized there's still work to be done before tomorrow's dinner shift."

He strode past. Tonya listened to his footsteps fade before they disappeared behind a door's clang. Philip had locked himself in his office, she supposed. She couldn't blame him. Who would want anything to do with a jumpy nutcase prac-ticing fake martial arts with a mop stick?

She shook her head as she reassembled the mop with a fresh pad and resumed her duties. A larger-than-usual number of pots and pans had been used during the evening's dinner service. Washing them had taken most of her shift. She still had to mop the floors and wipe down all the food surfaces.

Tonya pushed the bucket into the kitchen and got to work, humming to create some sound besides the slosh of soapy water. She finished half the room before determining that the liquid in the bucket was too gray to continue. Mopping with dirty fluids would ruin everything.

Tonya dragged the bucket back to the basin area and heaved it into the sink. Gray soapy sludge splattered inside and slurped down the drain. She righted the pail and turned on the hose, watching the clear, fresh water pool into the cleaning contraption.

The bucket was near full when a metallic whirring pierced the air. Tonya winced at the noise, assuming that some kitchen device had gone haywire, no doubt because she'd erroneously left it plugged in while wetting its area. She rushed into the main kitchen, praying that her inadvertent damage would be of the inexpensive variety.

As she entered, she realized that she was hearing a blender of sorts, turned up to its highest setting. Philip stood at a counter beside a shiny, metallic device. A chunk of skinless pink flesh lay in his right palm. More pieces were spread on a cutting board in front of him. Tonya could see bands of white fat running through ropy red muscle. Philip dropped a piece into the machine, force-feeding it with the aid of a plunger. Pink and white ribbons spiraled from holes in a round plate at the grinder's end.

Tonya gagged at the sight. Eating the proverbial sausage and knowing how it was made were different things. She wanted to enjoy one without the other.

She retreated to the basin, put a fresh head on the mop, and resumed working. She slapped the soapy water onto the still-dirty part of the floor and then drove it toward the baseboard. After, she swirled the mop in a figure eight, dancing with the dingy tiles, wishing for music. Her wireless headphones were somewhere in her storage closet, at least ninety minutes away by public transit. Tomorrow she'd venture out to Bushwick and try to find them, she told herself. The shift would pass faster with tunes.

At the moment, there was only the screech of the grinder. Philip worked with efficiency, feeding a new meat chunk into the machine before it could finish its prior morsel. As a result, the sound never stopped. It droned on, too loud for white noise yet too consistent to keep her attention.

Tonya was nearly finished with work when it finally stopped. In her peripheral vision, she watched Philip escort the pan of extruded meat to a counter. He covered it with plastic, labeled it with a Sharpie pulled from his jacket pocket, and then placed the pan inside the walk-in fridge.

As he turned from the door, they made eye contact. His unmasked expression was tight, as if he were annoyed that she was still there—or that she'd been watching.

She pointed to the meat grinder. "Do you want me to take that apart and wash it?"

Philip reached toward his ears. He removed two plugs and then brandished them, indicating that he hadn't understood.

Again, she gestured to the machine. "Want me to handle that?"

"I got it," he said, his face relaxing. The redness from earlier had faded into a graying pink, like expired beef. "Caribbean spiced meatballs are on the menu tomorrow. We've got a bunch of leftover flank steak from dinner service. Home diners don't want to eat as decadently as they do when they go out."

He approached the grinder. "I have to adjust my ordering."

"I remember having those meatballs," Tonya said. "Delicious."

"Yeah, Dominic usually put them on the staff menu. They'll be on the main menu now." Philip didn't look at her as he spoke, concentrating instead on twisting off the metal circle from the meat grinder's main body. "As well as whatever dishes I can invent between now and tomorrow morning for the rest of the trimmings. Maybe I'll make Jamaican beef patties. It has so many spices, scotch bonnet, onion, ginger, paprika, allspice. Doesn't really matter what cut of meat's being used."

Philip's lack of eye contact read as guilty to Tonya. He wasn't simply talking; he was confessing how he cut corners and controlled costs, recycling the leftovers into staff meals and upscale street food. Tonya's nose scrunched at the thought that all these years she'd been consuming parts of the cow perhaps better suited for dogs. Shank or tongue. The whole head, maybe.

"This is few-day-old flank steak," Philip said, perhaps reading the expression visible above her mask. "Sometimes we use chuck or even sirloin in the meatballs, depending on what we have." He snorted, returning his attention to disassembling the meat grinder. "Don't worry. The parts that most people throw away end up as pâté. That's where chefs hide all the livers, glands, and other sweetbreads."

Tonya pointed a finger in Philip's direction. "Good to know."

She brought the mop over to where her boss had been working. Any meat left on the floor was sure to attract vermin.

"Hey, I wanted to ask you something."

Tonya nearly dropped the stick in her hands. In her experience, men only wanted to "ask you something" when it was something inappropriate.

"Did you know Nate?"

The name set off her body's alert system. Hairs stood up

on the back of her neck and arms. Her heartbeat quickened. "Nate Walker, the one who was in the papers?"

"Yeah." Philip stared at her, gas burner eyes on their highest setting.

Beneath her mask, Tonya's upper lip grew damp. She could feel the sweat gathering at her ears. "Well, his daughter went to the school, so I knew of him."

Philip's eyes narrowed. He knew she was lying. How did he know?

"Um, why?"

"Imani thought you might know him."

Tonya raised her eyebrows, performing surprise to cover her concern. Perhaps Nate had said something to Melissa over the years, and the woman had chosen not to confront her. Instead of causing a scene in front of the school community, Melissa could have decided to limit her reaction to crying to her best friend. She probably would have seen it as the mature thing to do. Taking the high road. Refusing to address the young tramp who'd tried to steal her husband.

"The school wants to say something nice about him, and she was looking up people he'd helped at St. Catherine's over the years." Philip dismantled another piece of the meat grinder. "She came across the scholarship that he'd endowed and the letter that he wrote in favor of Layla receiving it. Apparently, he said a lot of nice things about her and you. He mentioned you'd auditioned for him."

Philip looked up at her, demanding confirmation.

Tonya wondered what he already knew—or suspected. Had Nate mentioned to Philip that he was seeing one of his waitresses on the side? Had Philip known all this time and kept quiet?

"I didn't really know him." Tonya spoke like she was testing a hot pan. "I went on so many auditions in my youth for directors, producers, casting agents. God knows I was always chatting. Trying to be memorable and get the part, right? The scholarship isn't the Nate Walker scholarship—it's just an academic and need-based thing. I wasn't sure who was endowing it."

Philip continued to stare. Did he know that the last part was a blatant lie? Was she failing this audition, trying too hard to make her story believable, keeping her voice too high to feign surprise? Should she have changed the dialogue to something that fit better?

Tonya lowered her tone, an effort to sound less flippant about a man who, as far as Philip likely knew, had supported her daughter's education and then been murdered. She should sound sadder, she realized. More appreciative. "He was your friend, right?"

Philip's lips pressed into a line on his unmasked face. "More the husband of my wife's friend."

Tonya exhaled, thankful that the mask was there to muffle the sound. If Philip and Nate hadn't actually been close, then chances were that Nate hadn't disclosed anything. Philip hadn't been tactfully avoiding the subject all this time. He really didn't know the deal.

"He came here a lot before the pandemic," Tonya continued, shifting the conversation from her relationship with the director to Philip's clearly complicated one. "I remember waiting on him in Coffre. I guess he really liked the food."

Philip's noncommittal expression morphed into a smirk. "I wish."

"Well, I mean, if he was coming here, he had to like it." She forced a laugh that only managed to sound nervous. "He certainly wasn't scouting for actresses to put in a movie."

Philip pulled the four-pronged blade from the meat grinder. In his hand, it looked like a throwing star. "He thought his presence would help publicize the place," he said, carting the grinders' parts to the sink. "He'd invested behind the scenes. I guess he thought it would give him cachet. De Niro co-owns restaurants, so Nate wanted to get in on the action. And, unfortunately, I couldn't afford to fund Banque's refresh and all Coffre's start-up costs myself."

There was a bitterness in Philip's tone that Tonya hadn't heard before. "It was a great addition," she said, hoping to lighten the conversation.

Philip continued cleaning. "Yeah. But such is life, right? There are no guarantees. Sometimes you open up a restaurant to rave reviews and a pandemic forces its closure. There's nothing to be done. You can't take out the money you put in already. It's gone." Philip shut off the faucet and reached for a towel. "Nate could stomach the loss, though. The man had millions in the bank. And his partners weren't poor."

The reminder of Nate's wealth worked like a match, rekindling all the hate Tonya had for him. The man had possessed money, fame, and power, and he'd abused it all, using his cash and cachet to make the problems that he'd created go away.

And she'd let him do it.

Tonya put away the mop and went for the other cleaning supplies. Karma had ultimately come for Nate Walker, she told herself. Though he might not have paid as much as she'd felt owed, life had turned out fair. He'd definitely paid in the end.

CHAPTER THIRTY-FOUR

IMANI

Imani didn't want to see it. She sat in her office, laptop balanced atop her thighs, staring at the cursor hovering above a link promising to take her to Nate's dead body. Once she clicked, there'd be no going back. No unseeing the exploded brains of a man with whom she'd shared food and drink while chatting about politics, parenting, and myriad other subjects. No forgetting that every individual—even those in possession of unique intelligence, beauty, or strength—was just another animal, an assemblage of muscle, sinew, and fats laced together by an electrical system. A machine that could be instantaneously reduced to parts.

Still, there was a reason why people had open-casket funerals. Without seeing a body, it was easy to treat any death like a dream, to convince the part of oneself responsible for action that none was needed. The dead disappeared from view and could be assumed to be off doing whatever they did when alive and out of sight. There was no need to mourn. No need to fight.

Imani was losing her sense of urgency to find Melissa. It had been nearly a week since she'd spoken to the lawyer who'd suggested that her friend was guilty, days since Imani had reached out to Melissa's suspected boyfriend or learned that Nate had paid for Layla's school—a fact that Philip had apparently followed up on and insisted was nothing more than Nate doing a solid for a struggling actress. At Philip's request, Imani hadn't brought up Nate with Tonya herself. Their renter's acting career was a sore spot, according to her husband. In the interest of everyone living peaceably, Philip thought Imani should forget about it.

But she couldn't forget Melissa. When Imani closed her eyes, she could see Melissa stifling laughter and expressing sympathy, holding her hand or tearily cradling Jay, tipsily pulling her into the center of a living room to dance during a cocktail party or whispering to her on a playground bench about school gossip. She saw a montage of a friendship, regardless of whether Melissa had shared her secrets. She saw a life shared.

So she needed to see how Nate had died. She needed to see what Melissa had faced before running away—or being taken.

Imani clicked the link. A notice appeared asking if she was certain that she wished to leave the *New York Post*'s site and the page featuring a flowery article about Nate's career, peppered with praise from film critics and high-powered producers. Imani selected yes and held her breath.

Her screen flashed white. Rather than a web page, a red message appeared in the center of the screen. "This site contains malware," it warned. "Attackers on your..."

Imani closed the site and opened a web search page. Something like Nate's crime scene photos would go viral. Screenshots were bound to be on someone's page.

True-crime blogs delivered. Imani clicked on the first one and leaned into her screen.

The hunt for the images had made her forget the graphic nature of what she was searching for. As a result, she wasn't prepared for the blood or the body. She gagged as she took in the horrific mess replacing Nate's face. It had been blown off at close range, apparently. Bullets that entered from afar made neat holes—or so she'd gleaned from horror movies.

Without an intact visage, it was almost possible for Imani to convince herself that the body hadn't actually belonged to Melissa's husband. Almost. The room was obviously Nate's den. Imani had hung out there often, especially when the kids had been young. She and Melissa had made a habit of eating together Thursdays or Fridays, sometimes at Philip's restaurant, more often at a cheap pizza joint, and then tucking all the kids to bed—pulling out a trundle in Ava's room for Vivienne and blowing up an air mattress in the playroom for Jay—before sneaking several flights downstairs for adult conversation and cocktails. Nate would join them after returning from his latest networking dinner. Philip would appear as soon as his shift ended, usually with a nice bottle of scotch or wine to thank the Walkers for their frequent hosting.

Imani examined the photo for clues pointing to Melissa's culpability. Scattered books that her friend might have tossed in an uncharacteristic rage. Furniture overturned during a desperate escape from a drunken husband waving a gun in the midst of an unexpected breakdown. A hastily scrawled, faux suicide note in Melissa's loopy handwriting.

Besides the body, all Imani saw was a desk with an open drawer, a bottle of Bushmills, and a heavy scotch glass. Nate, no doubt, had the same quarantine wind-down routine as Philip. Grab a whiskey. Sip while reading or watching television. If still unable to sleep, repeat.

Imani zoomed in. The desk appeared to have a condensation ring. Nate's own glass could have formed the mark before being moved. But it also could have been left by another vessel, the glass of whoever he'd been drinking with. Melissa was not a whiskey fan. "Motor oil by any other name is still motor oil," she'd joked once, bastardizing Shakespeare. "It goes down the same."

Imani saved the photo to her desktop. She then leaned back into her Eames lounger and closed her eyes, trying to insert her friend into the image on her computer. She pictured Melissa and Nate in some drama-worthy lovers' quarrel, perhaps over Melissa's online love affair. She imagined Melissa holding the gun—a gift from a director who'd thought Melissa the rightful owner of the weapon that her character had shot over and over in a blind rage. She imagined Melissa firing at Nate, playing out one of her unhinged roles. And then . . .

Imani could see Melissa calling the cops. She could picture Melissa phoning her with news of a terrible accident and asking that Ava be allowed to stay over. If Imani forced the rational woman whom she knew into a state of absolute state of panic, she could even envision a scenario where Melissa absconded with her daughter. But there was no way that she could fit Melissa into a narrative that had her leaving her kid inside to stumble upon her dad's dead body.

She opened her eyes, switching her view from the laptop to her phone. Her last Instagram message to MickyKline_Drinks still sat at the top of the list. Unanswered. She typed out another message.

"I'm not trying to get you in trouble," she wrote. "I truly believe my friend is in danger and the police aren't looking for her properly because they're busy concentrating on your relationship with her. You not responding makes it appear that either you and Melissa planned something together or you have her."

Imani sent the message and then stared at its appearance in the one-on-one conversation that she was having with herself. He'd never answer back, she thought. Her stomach twisted as she had an even worse realization: knowing the police were on his tail might push him to do something drastic.

Her vision began to blur. Reaching out had been stupid and ill thought out, the act of a desperate friend rather than a methodical detective or even an experienced therapist. She hadn't given enough consideration to how an obsessed kidnapper might respond to knowledge that the police were on his tail. Philip was right. She shouldn't be playing detective. She might have made things so much worse.

A sharp ding caused the tears to freeze. There, on her screen, was a message from MickyKline_Drinks. Imani frantically opened it.

"I had nothing to do with Melissa Walker's disappearance. Her husband was a bad guy. We can meet. I'll tell you what I told her."

All of her earlier caution vanished. Imani started typing. "Just tell me when and where."

CHAPTER THIRTY-FIVE

TONYA

Tonya opened the freezer like she was afraid of its contents. She wanted to avoid the unmistakable pop of the air-seal breaking, the sound that would announce to Imani that her illegal tenant was making a withdrawal from the communal food bank. Tonya had gone grocery shopping earlier, filling a small freezer drawer with items that Layla would recognize: chicken nuggets, frozen mixed veggies, premade peanut butter and jelly sandwich packs that would defrost in her bookbag by lunch. Unfortunately, Imani had been at work when she'd returned with the Gristedes bags. Her landlord wouldn't know that Tonya was taking her own stuff.

She removed one of the sandwiches. Walking through aisles of fresh produce had worked up her appetite. She needed something to tide herself over until her shift started and she could eat whatever one of Banque's cooks whipped up for the staff "family" meal.

Tonya flipped over the package, reading the instructions.

It said to microwave for thirty seconds or wait two hours to thaw. In two hours, she'd be getting ready for work.

Tonya resigned herself to making noise. She ripped open the plastic package and then popped it in the microwave. The machine's buttons beeped with every press before whirring to life.

She glanced over her shoulder to see Imani in the neighboring sitting room, dark curls cascading onto a couch's roll arm. Sneaking around was silly, Tonya told herself. The home's size and her subservient relationship to the man who owned it was unnecessarily intimidating her. If she was going to be living here for any length of time, she'd need to work out the kitchen-share situation with the mistress of the house. What part of the pantry did her off-the-books-work-for-rent agreement entitle her to? Would it change after her first unemployment check came and she was paying them?

The microwave blared that her sandwich was ready. Tonya removed it, batting it between her palms until it cooled enough to easily hold. Steam clouded the plastic covering. Peanut butter oozed from a seam in the sealed bread. The unmistakable smell intensified her hunger. Tonya worked the sandwich up over the lip of the packaging and sank her teeth in.

Hot peanut butter and jam scalded her tongue. Tonya didn't care. There was something so delicious about a PB&J. It was the taste of her youth on the farm. The flavor of childhood.

She took another bite as she headed into the sitting room, swallowing it moments before speaking. "Hi, Imani."

Philip's wife looked up from her cell phone. Her nostrils expanded like she'd whiffed garbage. The expression quickly vanished behind a strained smile. Still, Tonya had clocked it.

"I was hoping to talk to you about the food situation," Tonya said, overenunciating to cover the remnants of backwoods Pennsylvania that occasionally crept into her speech. "I purchased some groceries today and put them in one of the freezer drawers. I stored a few other things in the pantry."

Imani nodded. A noncommittal gesture. *I understand,* it said. Not, *Oh, sure, mi casa es su casa.*

"Obviously, I wouldn't expect you to share anything in your fridge," Tonya continued. "I can label my groceries with a marker if you want so that we don't get the food mixed up. I know I'm renting rooms, not room and board."

Imani's nose wrinkled as she said "rent." The woman pointed at her sandwich. "Is that a peanut butter Hot Pocket?"

Tonya waved her food. "Frozen PB and J. They're great for a quick snack."

Imani's face fell. "I'm sorry. I should have mentioned before. Philip and Jay are highly allergic to peanuts. It's genetic, apparently. We try not to have it in the house."

Tonya's earlier conversation with Philip came back to her. He'd said he was allergic, but he'd also said that he used peanut oil in the fryer. Clearly, his allergy didn't preclude peanuts being in the vicinity. "Oh. Philip had mentioned a sensitivity to them, but I thought it was only dangerous if he ate something containing peanuts."

Imani fingered the neck of her cream cashmere sweater, as if the lush fabric were making her itch. As if she, not Philip, had the allergy. "Unfortunately, even the steam from cooked peanuts or peanut products can cause reactions. When Jay was about four or five, he broke out in hives in school. Peanuts weren't allowed, so I didn't understand. Turned out that a kid in his class had eaten peanut butter and crackers before school and then held his hand with the oil residue on it. Just like that"—Imani snapped her fingers—"hives all over the back of his hand and wrist. Some on his face too. I guess he touched it after the kid's hand."

Tonya forced herself to nod. As a fellow mom, she could understand how scary it was for Imani to pick up a toddler having a full-blown allergic reaction. But Jay was in middle school and older than Layla. Both he and Philip knew not to eat peanuts or go around holding hands with near strangers. Surely she and Layla having a PB&J wasn't a big deal. Moreover, Tonya had just spent eleven dollars on a case for Layla's backpack.

"I'll make sure not to cook this anywhere around him," Tonya said.

Imani's brow pinched, finally adding an age-appropriate wrinkle to her smooth brown skin. "I know allergies are a pain. Philip plays his down because he's in a kitchen. A chef with a food allergy is kind of taboo. But it's serious."

Death and cancer were serious, Tonya thought. Losing a job was serious. Getting thrown out of an apartment during a pandemic after your child support was abruptly cut off was serious. A peanut allergy was an annoyance, easily managed by reading packaging and not eating food that she'd already agreed to label.

"Well, I'll try to avoid buying anything to cook with peanuts. These are all prepackaged in plastic, in the freezer, in a box separated from the other food, which I'll slap my name on. I don't need to microwave them. I usually pop them in Layla's bag for school and let them defrost during the morning session."

Imani's eyes narrowed. She held Tonya's gaze as she placed her phone on the coffee table. "So, Philip tells me you were an actress."

Tonya examined Imani's expression. Was her landlord simply switching the subject or fishing for information about her connection with Nate and the scholarship? Or was she being bitchy because of the peanut butter? Imani had used the past tense concerning her prior career, hammering a nail into the coffin of Tonya's acting profession. Tonya didn't think of her acting in the past tense. Once an actress, always an actress, she thought, even if twelve years of taking orders instead of auditions had long erased any illusions of her being a *working* actress.

"I did a few off-off-Broadway productions. A couple commercials," Tonya said.

Imani's dark eyelashes fluttered. "Anything I'd know?"

Her voice was friendly, but Tonya detected notes of strain. "One of the commercials was to advertise a gym. I was running on a treadmill. In another, I'm stressing about a college loan. I think my line was, 'How am I ever going to pay for this?'"

Tonya delivered the question using the same ingenue

inflections she'd employed during the actual shoot. The reenactment made Imani flinch. Was she surprised how quickly her tenant could get into character? Tonya wondered. Or had the query simply hit a nerve? No doubt Imani was wondering the exact thing: How would a waitress ever pay them for anything?

"Did you ever audition for films?" Imani asked. "Or was it mostly theater?"

Philip's wife asked as though she was making casual conversation, but Tonya knew not to trust the tone. Imani wasn't needling. She was digging.

"Mostly theater," Tonya responded. "I auditioned for Nate Walker once or twice. I didn't know him the way you and Philip did, so I didn't think it worth mentioning. Philip said that you'd found the recommendation that he wrote for Layla, and the scholarship info."

Imani sat back in her chair. For a moment, she reminded Tonya of a kid who'd been caught stealing sweets. "He seemed very impressed by both you and Layla," Imani quipped.

Tonya felt her own polite smile press into a pout. "It's hard not to be impressed by Layla."

"She seems like a bright young lady."

Tonya didn't like the addition of "seems," as if Imani were simply waiting for the curtain to fall, revealing the intellectual dullard she probably expected a woman without a sophisticated career would raise. People like Imani and Philip—the progeny of middle-class if not wealthy parents—didn't understand what it was like to chase a dream living check to check. They didn't get that poor people didn't abandon bad jobs for the possibility of better ones, that they picked up double shifts in dead-end careers rather than took time off for interviews or extra classes or even auditions. Tonya's lack of success wasn't due to some deficiency of brains or talent. She'd suffered a string of bad luck and was still paying for a few poor choices. For people without generational money, a few poor choices were enough to become permanently stuck.

"She *is* a wonderful kid," Tonya corrected.

"Nate definitely thought so. She made quite an impression."

Tonya raised her sandwich in a mock toast, bit a hunk off, and headed to the stairs. She chewed angrily, letting the peanut butter glue her mouth shut so she couldn't whirl around and ask the questions on the tip of her tongue. Why did Imani keep bringing up Nate? What did she know? What information was she really angling for? It was clear that Imani's conversations were not simply polite small talk. Folks did not engage in casual conversation about the recently murdered.

By the time Tonya exited onto her floor, she'd finished the sandwich and fished her phone from her pocket. This arrangement with the Bankses wasn't going to go well if Nate kept coming up. She needed living options.

She needed Layla's money.

Tonya dialed Kelner. As usual, the lawyer's secretary answered in a tone that didn't promise help. Her boss was not available, the woman explained. Tonya could leave a message. "Tell Kelner that I need to see him," Tonya said.

"Mr. Kelner is not conducting in-person consultations at the moment," the secretary said.

"Not Kelner," Tonya shot back. "*Him.*" The secretary

cleared her throat. "Excuse me. Who exactly should I tell Mr. Kelner you'd like to see?"

"It's not 'like to see.' It's need." Tonya spoke directly into the speaker. "As in, if it doesn't happen, I'll *need* to explore my other options. And don't worry about the name," she added. "Kelner will know."

CHAPTER THIRTY-SIX

IMANI

Imani walked toward the promenade, mentally rehashing her conversation with Tonya to avoid considering the craziness of what she was about to do. Philip had been right, she admitted. The minute she'd brought up acting, Tonya had become extra defensive.

Not that she'd ever thought him wrong. As she crossed the street, Imani accepted that she'd wanted to rankle her tenant. The woman's stubborn refusal to respect a reasonable rule in the interest of a twelve-year-old boy's health was beyond insensitive. She'd thought bringing up Tonya's failed career might remind her whose home she was in, perhaps make her a bit more humble and agreeable. Instead, the subtle dig had emboldened their young interloper. Tonya was not a woman who easily backed down.

Imani entered the tree-lined park overlooking the East River and scanned for passersby. An older woman walked a dog in front of the iron fence cordoning off the water-view brownstones. She wouldn't be much help in a fight, Imani thought. But she might be able to call police.

No other people were visible. It was too dark. Too cold. The sun vanished before five o'clock in winter, taking with it the ten-degree temperature difference between tolerable and intolerable. No one wanted to be out once Earth's star dipped below the horizon. Not gangsters. Not burglars. Not drug addicts.

Maybe kidnappers, though. Perhaps murderers.

Imani couldn't be sure that MickyKline_Drinks wasn't one, or both, of the two. Still, she had to meet him. He'd claimed to have information that might explain what Melissa had been thinking or doing before she'd disappeared, which he clearly wasn't willing to share with the cops nor likely with a large husband looming in the background. As a therapist, she was used to getting people talking. He'd be more open with her alone.

Or he'd try to grab her too.

Imani stroked the handle of the blade in her coat pocket. She'd absconded with one of Philip's eight-inch knives. The Shun blade had been her husband's favorite until he'd switched it out for a forged German brand that he'd believed slightly more durable, albeit less attractive. The knife she'd taken was long and pointed like a shark's tooth, and probably sharper. It was constructed of Damascus steel, Philip had once explained, which meant that it had been crafted from layer upon layer of metal, much in the same way samurai swords were fashioned. The result was a lightweight blade around a solid core, ready to stab and slice and carve without breaking. It was only the leather sheath encasing it that prevented the point from making her bleed.

The knife would only be useful to her if she got in trouble while in close contact and managed to pull it out in time. However, she didn't intend for her conversation with Micky to bring her nearer than six feet. She'd promised herself that she'd take off running the second she got a bad vibe.

Imani reached one of the candy-cane streetlights beside the railing separating the promenade from the train tracks below and the highway beyond. She stood in its glow, hoping that someone might notice her in one of the buildings above and pay attention to any screaming. Even if people heard, though, there were no guarantees that folks would care. New Yorkers were adept at ignoring "street noise."

Her breath steamed in front of her face. She'd removed her mask in hopes of creating trust and, more importantly, preserving distance. If Micky wasn't a killer, then he wouldn't want to get within a sneeze-length either.

Imani looked through the cloud of her condensed breath to see a man entering the park. Like her, his face was also uncovered. Again, she sensed that she'd seen him before—not only from his Instagram photos but also in person.

As he drew closer, the fog in front of her face bloomed. Micky didn't appear that big. Several inches smaller than Philip, if she hazarded a guess. Of course, Imani reminded herself, his relatively small stature compared to her husband didn't matter since he was considerably taller than her, and Philip wouldn't be able to get to the park in time if things got physical.

"Mrs. Banks."

Imani stiffened. Somehow he'd learned her surname. Her Instagram profile only had her first name followed by the letter B and a 3. She'd wanted anonymity. It wouldn't do to have patients tracking her life, bringing up special moments during their sessions as if she were their friend.

"Did Melissa tell you my name?"

The question stopped him. "No. I..." An exhale blurred the bottom half of his face. "I'm here to tell you what I told Mrs. Walker before she..."

Imani braced herself for the end of the sentence. *Died.* *Disappeared.*

"Well, before whatever happened, happened," he said.

"What did happen?" Imani tried to keep her voice gentle and inquiring, despite her fear. "I know you want to tell someone."

The man looked up. Even in the streetlight's dim glow, she could detect the hurt in his strained expression. "It's not what you think. I reached out to Mrs. Walker to discuss abusive behavior by her husband."

Imani stiffened. Nate hadn't hit Melissa. She was sure of it. However, she was also certain that an obsessed kidnapper would justify his actions by calling the husband a "bad guy" and "abusive."

"I'm an actor," Micky continued, "so I know a lot of female actresses, some of whom have auditioned for Mr. Walker. He pressures young women to perform sexual acts with him under the guise of getting into character. He promises them parts for their participation and 'bravery.' Their commitment to roles. Then, after he's gotten what he wants, he discards them. No pay. No movie roles. They're left feeling absolutely ashamed."

Imani struggled to reconcile her image of Melissa's husband

with this new information. She'd seen Nate work a room, flirting and cajoling. On the scholarship committee, she'd seen him throw his weight around, albeit always in someone else's interest. He'd never demanded anything for himself. However, Imani supposed that she'd never seen him in a capacity where he would have needed to.

"You personally know women that Nate did this to?"

"Yeah." The cloud in front of Micky's face grew thicker.

"Why haven't any of these women pressed charges?"

It was the wrong question, Imani knew. As a therapist, she realized that the right one would have expressed sympathy for Micky and his victimized friends. It would have suggested that she understood and empathized with their lack of power in relation to Nate and how difficult things must have been for them. But the part of her that had once considered Nate family felt the need to express a little loyalty. For all she knew, Micky was a crazy stalker making up stories.

"It wasn't always like today," Micky said. "Now men are getting canceled or whatever for this behavior. But this happened to my gi—" Micky wiped his hand over his mouth. "This happened to my friend over a decade ago when she was barely out of her teens. She really thought she was auditioning for a risqué role. When it became clear that the part was a pretense, she'd already gone so far." Micky shuddered. "Now she has a kid. She doesn't want to come forward and have her child read horrible things about her mother."

Once she'd got Micky explaining, his words had come out fast and furious. Imani's brain raced to keep up. Micky's friend had a child. Did that mean Nate had an illegitimate kid? Was that what this man was saying? Was that what he'd told Melissa?

Before Imani could ask, a whoosh of air pushed her from behind. A big truck barreled out of its burrow beneath the promenade, its top reaching eye level, its screeching overwhelming any attempt at conversation. Imani's hands were already in her pockets because of the cold. But her thumb went to the knife's smooth handle. Micky didn't seem to want to hurt her. He seemed to be telling the truth. Still, if he planned on doing anything, the time for it would be when traffic could drown out any calls for help.

As quickly as it had arrived, the giant semi vanished into the distance. Micky hadn't stopped talking, despite the noise. "At the very least, this guy should suffer some marital consequences for abusing his power," Micky said, already mid-monologue. "I guess I also thought, if she knew, Mrs. Walker wouldn't ever blame my friend if the news came out. She'd realize that her husband had pressured young women into things using false pretenses of auditions and their desperation to break into the industry. He'd manipulated them. It wasn't my friend's fault."

Micky threw up a hand. "Anyway, maybe you can tell the police that or, I don't know, tell them that I will tell them that and there's no need for any sting operation or whatever they're planning. I don't have Mrs. Walker, and I never thought if I told . . ."

Imani had so many questions. But the way Micky trailed off only lent itself to one. "How did Melissa react when you told her?"

A stream of hot air swirled from Micky's lips like cigar

smoke. "Like you'd expect," he said. "Like she was going to kill him."

The words were hot coals pressed to her chest. "Melissa wouldn't have stood for what you're saying," Imani conceded. "But she also wouldn't have left her child. Even if she killed Nate because he started threatening her or something when she confronted him, she wouldn't have left Ava. She would have made sure that her daughter understood what had happened."

Imani didn't know whether she was saying the words to convince Micky or herself. On some level, she needed to hear them aloud. She needed to see their impression in the air, to know that she'd spoken in her friend's defense, even if she was no longer completely convinced of it.

"She could have panicked," Micky said. "Or she might not have been thinking clearly. If she was drinking . . ."

The last word echoed in Imani's mind, bringing with it an audible sense of déjà vu. She'd heard him say that before. *What are you ladies drinking?* Imani imagined the man before her, visible only from the waist up.

Suddenly, she knew where she'd seen him before. "You work for Philip!"

Micky's cold-reddened face seemed to lose its color. He shook his head.

"You do. You were the bartender at Coffre." Imani could suddenly see him passing her and Melissa two dirty martinis—extra dirty, as per Melissa's request. She could see his hazel-brown eyes. His grin and quip that they were on the house. "Not only because you two are beautiful," he'd explained, "but I hear you know the owners."

Micky backed up.

"Melissa and I went in for drinks all the time when it first opened," Imani called after him. "You were behind the bar."

Abruptly, he turned around and took off toward the park exit. Imani didn't dare follow. Just as she'd been spooked by his knowing her identity, he had to feel similarly scared that she could tell police exactly who he was. She knew better than to chase a frightened man.

Micky's confirmation wasn't necessary. She'd recognized him—and that meant she knew something else. Tonya was the only actress with a kid who'd been working with Philip for years. And she'd already admitted to auditioning for Nate.

Tonya's sensitivity about her acting career wasn't about professional failure, Imani decided. Nor had Nate's scholarship for Layla been out of the goodness of his heart. For eleven years, Tonya had been raising Nate's illegitimate child. She'd wanted Nate to own up to his responsibility. Or she'd wanted revenge.

CHAPTER THIRTY-SEVEN

MELISSA

Imani floated above her, arms outstretched. She was saying something that Melissa couldn't quite make out. *I found you* or *I got you*. Melissa reached for her, but her limbs weren't long enough. The room blurred as if she were crying. Only she wasn't. She was underwater. Sinking. Her voice couldn't break through the surface.

Melissa woke with a gasp. A new light was on. She could see it from her position on the couch, a soft glow from a solitary pendant lamp, illuminating the onyx expanse of a bar.

She scrambled upright. Melissa had always thought of herself as a thinker and a fighter, the kind of person who would MacGyver her way out of a locked room with a safety pin, a rubber band, and some lint, or make a weapon from a paper towel holder and beat an attacker to death. Her time trapped in darkness had forced her to confront a very different reality. She was a fighter—for forty-eight hours. But she became a different sort of person after her anger and shock gave way to sadness and fear. She became someone who cried herself to sleep rather than continued to feel around for weapons or ways out. Someone who started to give up.

"I'll tell them it was an accident."

The words were meant as a salve rather than salvo. She had no way of fighting her way out of the room. It was too strong, and she was far too weak. Days had passed since her last meal. Her torso felt like a stretched accordion, bloated from all the water she'd been slurping from the bathroom sink to fill her empty belly.

"I'll say that I saw the whole thing, and Nate pulled the gun on you."

It stepped from the darkness into the light's glow. "I've thought more about things," It said. "The cops won't believe that you ran off without Ava. You're right."

A chill ran down Melissa's spine. Being right wouldn't get her out of here. "I'll make them believe it," she said. "I'll say how afraid I was and confused. I'll claim that I went into shock."

"It's not going to work."

"It will." Melissa could hear the desperation in her own voice. "I'm a trained actress. Making people believe me is my job."

It leaned forward over the bar, bringing its frowning face into view.

"People already think you're responsible," It said. "You'd have to explain what really happened to exonerate yourself."

There were two implications to what It was saying, Melissa realized, though both indicated the same thing. It would be better off with her dead. She'd take the blame and the truth with her, leaving It to resume life as before.

But life would never be the same after murdering an innocent person. It had to know that. How else to explain why she wasn't already dead?

Melissa stepped closer to the light, hoping the glow highlighted her face. "You don't want to kill me. That's why you haven't already. And you don't need to. What if I was to take the blame? I could confess to killing Nate myself."

"You won't do that."

"I will. Please. Just let me out of here, and I'll say I did everything." Melissa pressed a hand to her head. The force of her begging was making her light-headed.

"You won't be able to let your daughter think that you killed her father," It said. "She'd hate you."

Ava's face flashed in her mind. Melissa pictured her kid's features twisting with revulsion. She heard her crying and screaming about unforgivable betrayal. Her captor was right. The truth was that Melissa would never be able to stomach her only child going through life believing that her mother had taken her father from her.

But the truth wouldn't set her free.

"She won't hate me." Melissa squeezed her eyes shut, forcing Ava's image to disappear. "Not when she knows why I did it. I'll tell her that he was cheating on me with young actresses. He was manipulating these women into sleeping with him by promising movie roles. I'll explain that I was going to leave him. I already started the financial process. When she finds that out, she'll understand how Nate and I could get into a violent argument."

Footsteps punctuated her speech. Melissa opened her eyes to see It coming in and out of the light. Pacing back and forth. It was considering her offer—perhaps weighing whether she'd be able to deliver on her promises.

"I'm an actress," she said again. "I'll make everyone believe it. I'll make Ava sympathize with me. She'll understand."

Melissa choked on the last word. Ava had adored her father. She'd never accept infidelity as an excuse for murder.

The break in her speech stopped Its movement. "It won't work. I'm sorry."

"No!" Melissa wailed. "Please. You don't need to be sorry. Just let me out."

It retreated from the halo of overhead light. "I can't."

Melissa rushed toward the sound of Its voice, before it disappeared for good. "Please, please. Please. I'll make everyone believe. I'm an actress."

An arm shot out, striking the pendant light. The bulb swung over the bar, briefly illuminating the far wall. Melissa caught a glint of something metal. Thick.

"You couldn't even convince me," It whispered. "It's too late."

The same hand that had hit the light landed hard on her shoulder, pushing her back against the bar and out of the way. Footsteps hurried to the main exit. Melissa threw herself in their direction. "You can't leave me here," she screamed.

Again, the hand landed on her body. This time, it grabbed her neck.

Instinctually, Melissa clawed at it. She was choking. Her hands struggled to wrap around her own throat in the universal signal. Another hand joined in. Melissa felt thick fingers digging into her skin. Blood rushed to her head, like mercury rising in a glass thermometer, about to burst.

Suddenly, the pressure released. She doubled over, coughing. Melissa saw the sliver of light like before. She crawled toward it, advancing a foot before she heard the dull thud of the door closing. Again, she was locked in darkness. Only this time, she knew It would never let her leave.

PART THREE

CHAPTER THIRTY-EIGHT

TONYA

She needed a drink. As Tonya squeegeed the exterior of the walk-in fridge, she could think of little else than the taste of tequila, the feel of it sliding down her throat, smoky and sharp with a hint of citrus. She imagined how it would work its magic, relaxing her tired muscles and blurring the image of Imani's disdainful expression as she'd demanded that Tonya throw out her hard-earned groceries and then acted appalled by what Tonya had considered a generous counteroffer *not* to microwave the PB&Js in the house. One little shot of Cuervo would soften everything. Unfortunately, dulling her constant thoughts of Melissa and Mike and everyone else involved in the sordid events of the last several days would require a whole bottle.

Tonya swapped the squeegee for a shammy and began drying the fridge door. She moved her hand in circles. Wax on. Wax off. *The Karate Kid* was before her time, but she'd resurrected the film to watch with Layla because of the iconic lines and high rating on family movie websites. Mr. Miyagi's moral was that mundane tasks could teach valuable lessons. But what lesson was there in *clean the fridge*? Don't sleep with high-powered men who suggest they can leverage their influence to launch careers? Don't fall for the married friends of such men? Don't have the baby thinking that, maybe, it will all work out?

Tonya slapped the towel against her arm before putting it down. Shame on her for thinking that way. It *had* all worked out. Her daughter was worth every indignity. She would scrub a million fridges for Layla. She'd done far worse than that.

Still, she really wanted a drink.

Tonya tiptoed toward the dining room. A metallic rattling stopped her. It was a strange noise for a restaurant, more befitting a ship or a construction site. She whirled around, scanning for an item coming loose from a wall or the ceiling. There was the sound of something spinning followed by a thud.

Tonya strained to hear more. Footsteps were followed by the creak of a door opening and closing. The front door, Tonya assumed. Someone had come into the dining room— and left—through the patrons' entrance.

After hours, that door was typically bolted shut. She wondered who would have the code to the electronic lock. Philip, surely. Perhaps a building maintenance crew. Tonya could also imagine the head chef doling it out to business partners or anyone he trusted to deal with deliveries relating to the bar. Mike had possessed it at some point, hadn't he?

Whoever had been in the dining room was gone, Tonya figured. But the liquor was surely still safe on the bar's illuminated shelves. A lot had happened this past week. She just needed to oil the edges of her memories, make them easier to swallow.

Tonya barged into the room and strode toward a glowing row of reposado tequilas. No one would notice a shot or two gone from an already-open bottle, she figured. When Mike had been bartending, he'd always doled out a couple pours after an extra-long or boring shift, listing them as "spills." Philip hadn't seemed to mind giving the staff a few freebies. One of the unspoken rules to keeping a minimum-wage-earning restaurant crew happy was the discount on food and drink.

Mike wasn't behind the bar now, of course. But the same rules surely applied—though Tonya didn't exactly want to ask Philip outright if that was the case. It was uncomfortable enough that she'd shown up at his door homeless. Begging for booze would pretty much erase the distinction between her and a wino.

Besides, he wasn't even in the restaurant. He'd disappeared shortly after the last cook had taken off. Now that she'd been cleaning for more than a week, he probably didn't think it necessary to babysit her while completing odd jobs in the kitchen.

Tonya slipped behind the front bar and scanned for a bottle with a broken label over the stopper. One "spill" was all she wanted. One shot to ease walking into and waking up in Imani's peanut-free household.

Tonya spied a previously uncorked bottle of Casamigos. She grabbed it, feeling like a thief, even though she assured herself that she wasn't stealing anything that she wasn't entitled to. If Philip were here, he'd probably have a shot and offer her something too. Tonya popped off the bottle's cap and selected a glass from the counter.

Behind her, a door opened. Tonya jammed the stopper back on the bottle's neck, pressing it down with her thumb as she pushed it away. She whirled around. "Hello?"

Philip walked toward her. He seemed to bristle at the sound of her voice. His posture became painfully erect, as though tensed from an unexpected shock. "Why are you in here? Shouldn't you be in the kitchen?"

The light emanating from the back bar wasn't enough to highlight Philip's expression. But Tonya didn't need to see his full face to feel his anger. It was evident in Philip's seething tone. His stiff body language.

"I was thinking maybe the bar needed a dusting."

Philip continued his approach, eyes bright and burning. "I don't see a dust cloth."

Tonya chuckled, partly out of embarrassment, partly to lighten the mood. "You're right. To be honest, I was hoping to take my end-of-shift shot."

Philip stepped within feet of her. He held his arms out from his sides in a way that Tonya found aggressive. As if he might need to come out swinging. "What end-of-shift shot?"

Tonya felt the blood rise to her face. "Sometimes you would give us all a pour of whiskey, remember? Or, sometimes, whoever was working the bar would let us toast at the end of the night."

Philip's peaked brows rose. Molehills becoming mountains. "You're saying Mike gave out free booze on the restaurant's tab?"

Tonya winced. She was going to get Mike fired instead of furloughed. "No. Not usually. Once in a blue moon, probably when he thought the staff needed a pick-me-up."

Philip's hands landed on his hips. "This is why restaurants fail. People take advantage. They take free booze. Free food. They invest so they can seem like big men to their friends and then want to pull all their money at the first sign of trouble. Restaurants fail because everyone is a fucking mooch and no one wants to earn anything."

Tonya stood a little straighter. "I know that I'm living in your home without paying rent. But I am working here every day and—"

"And the job's over."

"What?"

"You cleaned, right? The fact that you're out here means you've finished cleaning?"

"Yes."

"Then go home, Tonya."

Philip slipped behind the bar as he spoke, reducing the impact of distance on his size. Standing directly across from him, Tonya could appreciate what a physically intimidating presence Philip truly was.

"I'm sorry, Chef. I shouldn't have thought to pour myself a shot. I didn't think it would be a big deal, and I would have definitely asked you if I'd known that you were still here. You weren't in the kitchen, and I didn't think to check anywhere else—"

"Where else is there?" Philip cut her off. "There's nothing in the dining room anymore."

Something about Philip's voice drove Tonya several steps

back. He wasn't yelling. But there was a seethe in his tone. He sounded like water in a pot, right before reaching a rolling boil.

"I'm sorry. I won't come back in here."

Philip's cold blue eyes seemed to register the tremble in her voice. They softened along with his body language. "Sorry. It's just that the kitchen is the only place we're really maintaining at the moment. We don't want anyone leaving food or spilled liquor in the other rooms. The pandemic is driving the rats insane. If anyone gets bitten, or news gets out of an infestation, that will be the end of everything."

Though Philip's voice was back to normal, the memory of his prior tone kept Tonya timid as she slid from behind the bar. "I understand."

Philip looked at her like he was profoundly disappointed, either at her or at himself. "Do you want a ride back?"

His enraged speech against moochers still reverberated between her ears. There was no way she was going to accept another favor. "It's fine. I have to pick up some things. I'll grab the subway."

"Take the ride, Tonya."

He wasn't asking. Tonya found herself nodding. "Of course. Yes, Chef. Thank you."

CHAPTER THIRTY-NINE

IMANI

A door slam woke Imani. The view outside the window was a deep gray expanse that could have belonged to any hour save for those between midnight and 4:00 a.m. Beside her, Philip's breath clawed its way from his throat, a bear emerging from hibernation. Her husband snored whenever he drank or went to sleep overtired. Lately, that was every night.

Imani rolled toward her bedside table and grabbed her cell to check the time. Seven a.m. The door slam hadn't been the kids. Teenagers squeezed every second of sleep out of Saturday mornings. Most likely Tonya had gone out for a morning jog, maybe to buy some Skippy on toast for breakfast.

Imani pulled back the duvet and rose from the mattress. Peanuts were the least of her problems with her "renter." The bigger issue was that she was living with the kind of woman not only shameless enough to have an affair with a married man in hopes of furthering her career, but also sufficiently bold to send the resulting child to the same school as the kid's half sister—no doubt as some sort of power move to blackmail Nate into giving her more money. Keeping an affair silent was worth considerable cash to anyone, let alone a celebrity couple. Avoiding scandalizing one's child was worth even more. Nate would have paid nearly anything to keep Layla's parentage under wraps, Imani was sure of it. Tonya must have gotten really greedy for things to end in murder.

Imani headed to the bathroom, even though what she really wanted was to wake Philip and relay everything that she'd learned. He'd returned home past midnight the prior evening, too late to discuss a treasured employee. Philip's natural response to confrontation was to become defensive— a consequence, Imani speculated, of his father being verbally abusive and physically domineering during his childhood. If she didn't want her husband immediately launching into an argument about Tonya's work ethic, Imani needed to wait until he was well rested and had let down his guard.

She was nearly finished showering by the time Philip rolled in. Imani saw him through the steam-covered glass door, a blurred male figure that she would recognize half blind. After nearly eighteen years of marriage, Imani knew her husband. She knew him by his walk and his voice. She could tell when he'd had a bad day by the way he entered a room. She knew what set him off and what excited him, what he was passionate about and what would never reach his radar.

Her love was built on this knowledge. Adoring particular characteristics of an individual was for newlyweds and hopeless romantics, Imani thought. Long-term spouses loved each other simply because they'd decided to, because they'd done so for long enough that not doing so was to become a different person entirely.

Philip sauntered over to the toilet bowl. Imani finished rinsing the conditioner from her hair as he relieved himself. She shut off the faucet, wrung out her curls like a washcloth, and then pulled back the shower door, expecting to see Philip with a towel in hand. He knew that she always forgot to bring one within arm's reach.

Her husband stood before the vanity, examining his face in the mirror. Philip wasn't vain, but even he had to see the impact of the past year on his visage, the way his skin seemed to pull on his facial muscles. Imani was suddenly struck by a deep sadness, different from the dull ache that she'd felt since Melissa's disappearance. Her husband was struggling.

She exited the shower, wrapped a towel around herself, and kissed him on the back of his shoulder. "Hey, honey."

"Hey, baby." He turned around, smiling for her benefit. She could tell the difference between a brave grin and a natural one when it came to her spouse.

"I need to talk to you about something."

The smile vanished. Imani touched Philip's arm to indicate that the coming complaint wouldn't be about him. "Actually, it's probably better if I show you."

She beckoned for Philip to follow her into the neighboring room. He did so reluctantly, taking one step to every two of her strides. "I don't like surprises," he said.

Imani had no desire to keep him in suspense. She quickly unlocked her phone and opened Instagram. "You recognize this guy?"

Philip took the cell from her. "Yeah." He squinted at the screen. "That's Mike. One of my bartenders. I guess he goes by Micky online."

"He reached out to Melissa before she disappeared to tell her some things."

"What things?"

"That's what I wanted to know, so I met with him in the park last night."

Philip gripped her phone tighter, a pitcher with a baseball. "You met with a strange man, at night, in the park. Are you crazy?"

"The police said he'd been talking to Melissa. They implied an affair."

Philip glared at her. "I thought you were going to stop playing detective. We agreed. It's not your job. You're supposed to be here taking care of our kids and helping—"

"He said that he contacted Melissa to tell her about Nate pressuring young actresses to sleep with him," Imani said. "It happened to his girlfriend, and she got pregnant."

Philip rubbed his forehead with his free hand, his signature processing gesture. "So you think Nate had an affair and Melissa killed him—"

"No. I—"

A crash cut her off. Her phone hit the wall with a dull thud thanks to the screen protector. She rushed over to the device and collected it from the floor. "Philip, why would—"

"Who did it, Detective Banks?" Philip shouted. "What theory have you developed running around, unarmed, after strange men who for all you know are murderers? What have you learned that's worth our kids missing a parent, huh?"

Philip's volume wrested Imani's attention from the cracked plastic atop her cell screen. "It was nothing to worry about. I went to see a guy who worked for you."

"You didn't know that then, though. Or you would have told me."

"I wanted to. But you've been so stressed—"

"I'm stressed because, instead of focusing on our family, all you care about is Melissa!"

Philip had never hit her. But Imani saw the desire in his stare. She'd seen that same focus and fury on the faces of other men who had later been revealed to be abusive.

Imani raised her hands in surrender. "Hear me out, okay? Tonya works at your restaurant and knows Micky or Mike or whatever. He said Nate pressured his friend when she was in her twenties. The friend got pregnant. Layla would be the right age."

Philip drove both hands into his hair. "What are you getting at? Do you even hear yourself? Why does any of this matter?"

"Because." Imani realized she was shouting to match Philip's volume. She lowered her voice. "Because I think Tonya might have been blackmailing Nate for money to keep quiet about Layla. I think that's why she lied about knowing him and why he paid for Layla's schooling."

Philip's chest was rising and falling rapidly, as if he were running a marathon standing still. "So what if Nate was paying her tuition?"

Imani patted the air. Even if Tonya had left, Layla might be in the house. "Please keep your voice down and listen one second." She took a deep breath, modeling the behavior she wanted from Philip. "Clearly Nate stopped giving her money at some point for child support. Otherwise, she'd still be in her apartment."

Philip crossed his arms over his chest. "And . . ."

"And I think, maybe, she confronted him about it and things got ugly." Imani took a deep breath. "I think it's possible that Tonya killed Nate."

For a moment, Imani thought that Philip was going to scream again about her being ridiculous or needing to let the police do their jobs. As her words sank in, however, some of the blood receded from his face. He finally copied Imani's exhale.

"What do you want to do?"

CHAPTER FORTY

TONYA

Feelings were the world's best photo filter. How else could Tonya explain the difference between how she'd once seen the man across from her and how she viewed him now? He was older, of course. The near-dozen years that had passed since she'd been with him were visible in the once-faint lines that now bled into his cheeks. But a few more wrinkles couldn't account for all the physical attributes that she'd once found attractive now appearing offensive. The perma-tanned skin that she'd considered a mark of success—of a career that followed the sun—now looked fake and vain. His army-style haircut was an effort to stave off balding rather than evidence of a man too masculine and practical to primp. The button-down shirt, unbuttoned one notch too many, wasn't sexy but trying too hard.

"So, as we were saying, the new account needs to operate differently."

Glen Kelner adjusted his face mask, perhaps to draw Tonya's attention from Layla's father to the matter at hand. In person, Kelner was far less intimidating than on the phone. He had receding mousy brown hair and a weak chin that faded into his neck. His rumpled suit only added to the feeble impression. Looks weren't everything, of course. Still, seeing him, Tonya was annoyed that she'd let herself be bullied by a guy who didn't look the part of power player.

"It should be a custodial account in Layla's name operated by a fiduciary, namely myself. Mr. Redsell will fund the account in a similar manner. And the rent will be paid through direct withdrawals to . . ."

Kelner's words melded together into an unintelligible drone. The lawyer might as well have been reading a manual on how to assemble a blender or the fine print of a lengthy phone service contract. Tonya couldn't pay attention to the speech—not when she was finally in a room with the man she'd hated for so long who, ironically, also possessed features of the person she loved most in life. Layla had inherited her biological father's smoky blue eyes. Her nose, too, was a paternal hand-me-down with its upturned tip that called for kisses. Tonya had pecked that nose so often when Layla was a child. So strange to want to break it on the thinly masked face across from her.

"You're getting divorced." Tonya's interruption was the equivalent of pulling a power cord, cutting off the background buzz of Kelner's voice.

Rick Redsell finally met her gaze. He'd been staring at Kelner, pretending to scrutinize the attorney's every word. Without his lawyer speaking, there was no choice but for Rick to face the girl he'd seduced after she'd been rejected by his famous director client for an unconvincing sexual simulation that they'd all known had, later, gone far beyond "acting." He'd consoled and complimented her the evening following that fateful night. He'd even told off Nate for letting things go too far. Rick had won her over by acting as her knight in shining armor.

She should have known that no man could be honorable and still entertain a friend who so easily used his position to take advantage of women. But she'd let her ego be soothed by Rick's attention and flattered by his success. And, as much as she was ashamed to admit it, the fact that he'd been a big-time agent and, therefore, capable of boosting her career hadn't exactly hurt.

"That's why your wife hired the forensic accountant, right?" Tonya asked. "You're getting divorced."

Rick grabbed his right side, as if he had a cramp by his ribs. He took a shallow breath. "Does it matter?"

"Did she catch you having an affair?" Tonya asked.

Rick glanced at his attorney. Kelner averted his eyes to the papers in front of him, perhaps embarrassed by his client. Though the guy was being paid to cover up Rick's transgressions, he had to pity Mrs. Redsell. In retrospect, even Tonya felt bad for Rick's wife, though she'd conveniently ignored any such sympathies when she'd been falling for her husband.

"We're going our separate ways." Rick leaned back into the plush chair in front of his attorney's heavy desk. "The kids are grown, so there's little point pretending anymore."

Tonya dug her fingernails into the fabric arms of her own chair. If there was no point in lying, then why had he allowed his wife to close the account? Why hadn't he immediately wired money so that she and Layla could remain in their apartment?

Rick seemed to sense her questions before she asked them. He gestured to Kelner. "Earlier, I was under the impression that my relationship with my wife, though not really much of a marriage, was salvageable. But as I now understand it, she'd hired a private investigator and was already looking into the finances. She had pictures of me . . ." Rick trailed off with a shrug. "Anyway. It doesn't matter. I have a girlfriend. She knows. I'm moving on."

His wife had learned of his affair and was leaving him. Tonya couldn't help but wonder if things would have turned out differently had she refused to keep Layla a secret. Perhaps Rick would have had no choice but to divorce his wife and be a father to her daughter. He would never have been a faithful husband to her, of course. Tonya was not so naïve as to think that she would have fared any better than his spouse. But Rick might have filled a position that, given Layla's reaction to his existence, she'd been wanting.

Tonya forced herself to focus. She was here for Layla's money, and Rick still hadn't explained why he'd stopped paying, nor when he would start to do so. "In the interest of moving on, when can I expect child support payments to be restored?"

The attorney cleared his throat. "The issue, unfortunately, is that all significant expenditures must be submitted to Mrs. Redsell's attorneys, and as per my client's prior prenuptial agreement, certain actions carry a cost. In the interest of avoiding unnecessary expenses—"

"You mean that he gets charged every time he has an

affair, so he still needs to keep Layla's existence quiet." Tonya fought a smirk. "How much does he get charged?"

"The terms of Mr. Redsell's prenuptial agreement are really none of your concern," Kelner said.

"On the contrary, they are my concern, as they're why I'm not currently receiving my legally required child support. If he was paying, I wouldn't be here. And as I've made clear, I see no reason to keep Layla's parentage secret now that you, Mr. Kelner, revealed that she wasn't the result of a sperm donation."

Kelner winced. "Well, as I explained, I—"

"The divorce will probably take a year." Rick looked at her like she disgusted him. "How much more do you want to shut up for twelve months or so?"

"Three hundred grand."

The figure rolled off her tongue, even though Tonya hadn't realized she'd come into the office with an amount in mind. Since being booted from her apartment, she'd been thinking about the cost of getting Layla into a more stable environment, and she also wanted a bit added for pain and suffering—compensation for Layla's pain and a bit of financial suffering for Rick. Her subconscious had apparently been running the numbers.

Rick started to stand from his chair. Before he got up, he gripped his side and slumped back into the seat. "That's nuts." He gestured aggressively at his attorney. "That's way more than I'd have to pay in child support."

"Crazy, huh?" Tonya tightened her grip on her chair arms, fighting the urge to rise and meet Rick's volume. "Imagine what these past few weeks have been like for Layla.

Here she is, an eleven-year-old girl going to school in the midst of a pandemic, wearing masks on the subway as she commutes to and from classes, worried about contracting a deadly virus. Yet, in spite of everything, she feels somewhat safe because she's lived in the same nice apartment for a decade. She's always had food on the table and clothes on her back. She feels secure and loved. Then, overnight, all that safety is taken away. She learns that there is a father out there who knows of her existence but wants nothing to do with her, and she's thrown out of her apartment because you abruptly stopped paying child support without any warning. Large guys barge in while I'm at work, taking all her stuff, tossing it on the street, breaking photo frames, and ripping up her artwork."

Tonya's voice caught on the memory. As she composed herself, she realized that Kelner must be a father. The man's eyes looked sad.

Rick folded his hands like a hammer. He beat the air once before letting his hands drop onto the chair arms.

Tonya transferred her stare to his slumped figure across from her. "I want a down payment on a home to make sure that Layla never deals with anything like that again. And I don't think that's *crazy*, especially given that she knows she has a dad out there, desperately wants to reach out to you, and you're asking me to deny telling her your identity for a whole year and support her on a waitress's salary alone. There won't be any extras for her. No new clothes. No shoes if she grows out of them. We are staying in a room in my boss's home at the moment. Layla has to go to school with their kids, feeling like a homeless charity case. You don't think she deserves to maybe have some stability after all she's going through—all you've put her through."

Rick's eyes dropped to his lap. "I didn't know. I...uh...I'm sorry...I understand."

"Do you?"

Rick pressed his eyelids shut with his thumb and forefinger. "It will take time. But once the divorce is finalized, I'll make sure you get the down payment and the back child support. I'll sign something to that effect."

Tonya felt her lashes flutter. She hadn't expected Rick to give up so easily. The man she'd once known had been full of fight. But the guy across from her had been beaten down—figuratively but, perhaps, also literally. Clutching his side was clearly not for show.

Tonya barred her arms across her chest. "Good. Then we can proceed."

———

Tonya exited Kelner's office not feeling much better than when she'd first walked in. Though she would be nearly four hundred thousand dollars richer in a year, she was near destitute at the moment. Supposedly, her unemployment check was in the mail, but it wouldn't be much when it arrived, and she had little prospect of padding it with extra work. Her industry had been decimated, and it was doubtful that Philip would shell out for her cleaning services once she could pay rent. Most likely, he'd ask the line cooks to wipe down their individual stations and mop the floor on rotation.

Tonya strode through the law firm lobby, leaving Rick and Kelner to discuss other matters likely related to Rick's misdeeds. She walked as if someone was following her. Her new sensitivity to germs added to the vulnerability she already felt being in Rick's lawyer's office. She needed to get outside.

Tonya exited through etched glass doors into an elevator bank. She pressed the call button and then scrolled through her missed messages, checking to see if any were from Layla. Her daughter hadn't left a voice mail, she realized. However, there was a text from an unknown number.

Tonya clicked on it. "Hello, it's Imani," she read. "Please let me know when you return. I would like to discuss something with you."

The message was the sort left by principals for the parents of misbehaving students or, perhaps, therapists unhappy with a patient's progress. Maybe landlords wanting to know why the rent was overdue or what the funny smell was in the laundry machine. There was little chance Imani wanted to "discuss" something pleasant.

Before she could type her ETA, the arriving elevator dinged. "Hey, Tonya. Hold it for me?"

Tonya wanted to pretend she hadn't heard the man behind her. Unfortunately, Rick was at her side before the doors fully retracted. He entered as she passed through the doors.

Immediately, Tonya retreated to the far corner of the elevator. To Rick, it probably seemed that she was socially distancing in the tight space. Really, she was moving out of striking range. Acquiescing to giving her money didn't mean that Rick was happy about it. Tonya didn't think he'd hit her.

But she couldn't put anything past a man she already knew to be a liar, a cheat, and deadbeat dad.

"Does she really want to meet me?"

There was a whiny quality to Rick's tone. What did he care? Tonya wondered. He'd made clear enough that he had no interest. Was it an ego thing? Did he like the thought of his daughter out there, pining for him?

"She's an eleven-year-old girl coming into her own and learning about herself," Tonya said. "She wants to understand her background. That's all. It's not about you specifically."

Though she said it, Tonya knew that Layla's desire to meet her father ran way deeper than knowing her genetic history. But she wasn't going to give Rick the satisfaction of acknowledging that he meant something to a person he'd so adamantly refused to let mean anything to him.

"I heard she's a great student."

Tonya hadn't told Kelner that, had she? "Where did you hear that?"

"It's not true?"

"She's an excellent student," Tonya snapped. "But I asked where you heard that."

Rick unhooked his mask to scratch at his stubble, revealing his full face. Objectively, it was as handsome as Tonya remembered, though the five-o'clock shadow looked dirty rather than sexy given her loathing. "Nate told me before." Rick sighed, selfishly releasing a ton of unidentifiable particles into the air. "He was teaching a writing elective or something for kids after school. She'd taken it."

An invisible fist squeezed her heart. Somehow, Layla's absentee father knew something about her daughter that she didn't. Layla had never mentioned taking Nate's class. Why wouldn't she have told her? Why wouldn't she have shown her any of her work?

"He said her stuff was really good. Told me I might have a screenwriter in the family."

Tonya pressed a hand to the elevator wall. It was descending too fast, a free-fall carnival ride. She felt her stomach rising into her throat. "You talked about her?"

"Not really. Nate wasn't working much, so we didn't talk all that often. I called him a week before he died about the status of a mutual business investment. In the interest of full disclosure, he told me that he was teaching my kid."

"She's not your kid," Tonya spat. "You have to raise a child to call them that."

"Fair enough." Rick cracked a smile. "Nate told me that Layla's very pretty. Looks a bit like me, he said."

Tonya shuddered at the thought that Nate had been checking out her child. The man hadn't been a pedophile— at least, not to her knowledge. But he had been a predator. She doubted he could look at her beautiful daughter and not recall what he'd done to her mother. Had the memory made him feel guilty, she wondered, or aroused?

Or had it made him angry?

When Layla's preschool teachers had recommended that her "gifted" daughter apply to St. Catherine's and try for a scholarship, she'd reached out to Nate. Her auditions regrettably hadn't landed her any parts, she'd said, but news of how they'd gone wouldn't do much for his career given millennial attitudes toward men who abused their power. She'd agreed to remain silent in exchange for Nate putting in a good word and endowing a scholarship. At the time, it had seemed the least he could do.

"After the dust settles with the divorce, I'd like to see her," Rick said.

The elevator shuddered as it reached their floor. Tonya's own body shook, less from the impact than from Rick's sudden interest. She didn't want her daughter's self-esteem at all reliant on gaining his approval. Her kid had been happy not knowing her father. Surely, she could be happy again without him.

Tonya watched the doors open in silence.

"Tell her I only need to work out a few more things and it's complicated," Rick continued. "Tell her I'm trying not to unnecessarily upset people because of circumstances, you know, but once everything is out in the open, there won't be anyone more to hurt. We can meet then."

Tonya headed into the hallway, ignoring Rick calling her name. The way he'd phrased his request warned against responding. Rick didn't think there was anyone to hurt after his divorce finalized. But that was only because his consideration didn't extend beyond his immediate family. There was still someone who could very much be hurt by him. There was still Layla.

Fingers suddenly pressed into her shoulder. "I said wait!"

Tonya wrested from Rick's grasp as she whirled around. "Don't touch me."

He held his hands up in mock surrender. "You wouldn't stop. And I wanted to ask you..." Rick winced. He leaned forward and gripped his ribs. His breaths became short and shallow.

"Are you okay?" Tonya asked. She didn't really care, she told herself, but she needed him alive and working to pay his child support.

"I had an accident. It's given me some perspective." He straightened with difficulty. "Are you really staying with your boss? Philip Banks?"

Tonya bristled. Had she known about Rick's interest in seeing Layla, she wouldn't have mentioned where she was staying. "What does it matter?"

"He's not a good guy."

Tonya tilted her head to the side, amazed at Rick's capacity for selfishness. Rick had never been friends with Philip, so she doubted that he knew anything about the man. He simply didn't want Layla around anyone remotely connected to his social circle. "You've nothing to worry about. I won't tell him you're Layla's father, and Nate won't either, obviously."

Rick sneered. "Philip's a thief. He stole from me, Nate, and another investor in Coffre. Guy totally misappropriated funds. You can't trust him."

"You think I should take your word for it?"

Rick gripped his side tighter. He looked like he needed to sit. "In this case, yeah. I know what he's capable of. He's a violent guy."

Tonya crossed her arms over her chest. "Takes one to know one, huh?"

Rick's eyes narrowed. "What are you talking about?"

"You and your act. You pretend to be all macho and moral with guys that overstep with women. You threatened Nate, right? Got in his face after what happened with me? Told him what he did was wrong? You told me that you wouldn't *let* him touch me ever again. But really, you protect men like that. They're your friends. You just like being a bully."

"And you—" Rick dragged a hand over his mouth, wiping away whatever insult had been moments from his lips. "Look. Keep Layla away from him. That's all I ask."

"I know what's best for my daughter. Not you."

Rick held up both hands in surrender again. The act seemed to pain him as one hand quickly returned to his side. He kept it there, holding his ribs. "Don't say I didn't warn you," he said before limping toward the exit. "Remember, I warned you plenty."

CHAPTER FORTY-ONE

IMANI

Working from home was slowing her down. Had Imani been in her office, the billing would have been finished already. Instead, she was filling out her third insurance claim out of the dozen or so she had pending. Everything was distracting her. The lingering scent of coconut curry from the dinner that Philip had whipped up. The dishes that she knew were sitting in the kitchen sink. The sound of the occasional passing car. The front door that had yet to open.

Tonya hadn't replied to her message. But her renter wouldn't avoid the coming conversation by ignoring a text. Imani was determined to sit at the dining room table all day if that's what it took. The woman had to return sometime. She lived there, after all.

Though not for long. Hopefully.

For the umpteenth time since Philip had left, Imani wished that he was home. He'd argued that his role as Tonya's boss put him in a precarious position with regard to kicking her out of the house. If he were present, Tonya could twist the conversation into a business issue, perhaps claiming that he was leveraging his position to make her acquiesce to something unfair. He didn't want to give her grounds for a lawsuit.

Imani couldn't imagine how Tonya would sue Philip for asking her to leave his family residence. But she also knew that even frivolous lawsuits cost money to defend against. She'd ultimately relented, letting him hide out at the restaurant, leaving her to deal with the problem he'd created.

Imani returned her attention to the insurance claim on her screen. Her ten-o'clock appointment on Tuesdays was a twelve-year-old boy with hyperactivity and extreme anxiety. His insurance had yet to reimburse her for the past five sessions. She was becoming nervous that the health care provider intended to dispute the diagnosis.

As she filled out the form, there was a sound at the door. Imani looked over her laptop at the entrance, back stiff and heart racing. Confrontation wasn't her strong suit. She was good at asking questions, drawing people out, making them feel secure. Philip was the one who could throw a person out or fire them.

The door swung back revealing Tonya, wrapped in a peacoat. A floppy red hat covered her head. It had a fuzzy ball plopped on top, reminding Imani of the woolen beanies that she'd stuck the kids in as toddlers. It made Tonya appear a teenager rather than thirty-something.

Imani felt a pang of guilt. She would be putting out this young, single mother in the middle of winter, during a pandemic. But what else could she do? Continue to house a woman who'd been sleeping with her best friend's husband

and had his child? Who, for all she knew, had been involved in the confrontation leading to his murder? Who might be the reason that her friend was hiding out, trapped, or, worse, dead?

Thinking of Melissa solidified Imani's resolve. She stood from her chair. "Tonya, did you get my message?"

Tonya entered the main room without removing her outerwear, as if she sensed that she wouldn't be staying long. "Yes. Sorry. I meant to reply and got caught up. What did you want to discuss? Is it the peanut butter again?" Tonya began fidgeting with her coat buttons. "I realize that we had a bit of a misunderstanding there. Philip told me that his allergy is really only triggered by eating peanuts. He uses peanut oil in the restaurant to fry chicken, so I didn't think my bringing it in would be a big deal."

"His father died from ingesting peanuts." Imani said it without thinking. She didn't want to argue about legumes or allergies, but she hated that Tonya was making her seem unreasonable.

Tonya continued unbuttoning. "Really? I thought his father died in a car crash because he'd been drinking or something."

Imani felt her jaw drop. Tonya was wrong. Michael Banks had perished after suffering a heart attack behind the wheel brought about by anaphylaxis. The story had run in the *New York Times*. But Philip had always said that his father had been a drinker. Tonya hadn't gotten her news from nowhere. Clearly, her husband had discussed his personal tragedy and his dad's behavior with his employee. How intimate had things gotten between them all those late work nights?

"No." Imani heard the snippiness in her tone. "Philip's father ate chicken liver pâté, which I guess the chef had mixed with some peanut butter to make it creamier or something. His throat swelled, preventing him from breathing. The lack of oxygen led to a heart attack while he was driving. He wasn't even fifty."

Tonya's mouth opened, no doubt breathing out microscopic peanut particles from her breakfast. "How do you know?"

She couldn't possibly care, Imani thought. No one could be this invested in eating PB&J—or winning an argument. "Philip worked at the restaurant at the time."

"What post?"

Was she testing her? Imani wondered. "I don't know. A low one. He wasn't even really cooking yet."

"Garde-manger?" Tonya asked.

Imani waved a hand, dismissing Tonya's comment. She'd had enough of this tangent. Clearly, her renter had sensed that she'd wanted to talk about something serious—something warranting her immediate departure from the house. Tonya was attempting to distract her, buying time until the kids returned from school, no doubt in hopes that Imani wouldn't kick her out in front of Layla.

"I didn't want to talk about peanuts," Imani said. "What I'd like to discuss is Nate. I met with your friend Micky. He explained the situation."

Tonya's big blue eyes grew impossibly larger. "What situation?"

Asking questions was Tonya's arguing tactic, Imani thought. Don't admit or deny anything, just keep playing the wide-eyed ingenue. "Nate sleeping with you—"

"He used my name? He wouldn't—"

"He said his friend. I figured out that it was you after I recognized him from the restaurant." Imani grabbed her purse off the back of her chair and rounded the table. She didn't like the large piece of furniture between them, trapping her in a corner while giving Tonya rein to run upstairs or into the kitchen to grab God only knew what. Earlier, Imani had moved the big butcher knife from her meeting with Micky into her handbag.

"As I'm sure you can understand, I can't live with someone who was having an affair with my friend's husband." Imani moved her hand closer to the bag's mouth, in case Tonya got violent.

The woman chewed her bottom lip, shaving another few years from her already youthful face with the uncertain fidget.

"I didn't have an affair with him." Tonya's voice was quiet. "That's not true. Mike wouldn't have said that."

"He made clear that you two had a sexual relationship."

"We didn't."

Imani had expected Tonya to excuse her behavior, rather than outright deny it. Surely, Tonya had to assume that Imani had guessed Layla's parentage and put together the reason why her child support, had suddenly run out.

"Come on, Tonya. You can't deny it. I get that it's embarrassing to carry on with a married man and that it wasn't all your fault. Mike said that Nate pushed you into performing sex acts with him during auditions by dangling the prospect of getting a role in his movies. But the evidence is Layla."

Tonya trembled in front of her. Imani didn't know whether

the motion was fear of what would happen now that she'd been found out or rage. She dipped her hand into her purse, checking on the blade.

"Layla is not Nate's," Tonya said.

"Well, whose kid is she?"

"Mine." Tonya's lips twisted into a sneer.

Anger surged through Imani, electricity returning to a long-dead outlet. Tonya was mincing words, implying her lies rather than speaking them. Layla was hers alone because Nate wouldn't publicly acknowledge her, not because he wasn't her biological parent. Did she think Imani too stupid to understand the nuance?

"Why all the secrecy if Nate's not the father?" Imani rubbed her thumb against the knife's smooth handle. "First, you deny knowing him at all. Then, after I stumble upon his scholarship for Layla, you admit to having met him but characterize the relationship as strictly professional, which it obviously wasn't, according to your own friend."

Tonya shot her a murderous look. "It's none of your damn business."

Imani wrapped her fingers around the handle. "As long as you're in my house, it's my business. This is the safety of my family at stake."

"How's that?" Tonya shook, a tied string under too much tension. "How does my daughter's father have anything to do with your safety? I told you he's not in our lives."

"Because he's dead, right?" Imani gripped the knife tighter. "What happened? You went to confront him about not paying child support, and he got drunk and belligerent? He ordered you out of the house at gunpoint?"

Tonya's hands dove under her hat. "Oh my God. Are you kidding me? You think I shot Nate? Why would I even do that if he was funding my life, as you so clearly believe?"

The knife vibrated in Imani's palm. "Where is Melissa?"

"How would I know? South America? Russia? Anywhere without an extradition treaty is my guess."

"She had nothing—"

"As long as we're making up murder theories, let's look at you and Philip," Tonya shouted. "You two were the ones with all these fraught ties to them. Nate had invested in Coffre. Obviously, that didn't work out well for him."

"What are you talking about?" Imani's shock loosened her grip on the weapon. Philip had never said anything about taking money from the Walkers. Was this another of his business transactions that he'd thought she hadn't needed to know about?

"You really didn't know?"

The question was a slap across Imani's face, both a wake-up call and an act of aggression. Tonya was underscoring that Philip had been more candid about his dealings with her than with his own wife. Imani felt like a woman accosted in the ladies' bathroom by a younger girl claiming to know where her man had been last night.

She steeled herself, determined not to give Tonya any more satisfaction by showcasing her ignorance. "Are you really accusing Philip of murdering Nate?"

Tonya's pupils moved counterclockwise to the twelve o'clock position. "I'm only saying that pointing the finger at me is as ridiculous as suggesting it was your husband." Tonya clapped, a nursery teacher trying to draw the class's attention. "You are so desperate to avoid the obvious conclusion that you've invented this whole bullshit scenario. You can't accept the truth. Your best friend was married to a complete and utter philanderer who used his position as a big-shot director to pressure women into sex acts and, I'm sure, extramarital affairs. She found out, grabbed their gun out of a safe or wherever they kept it, and shot him. Afterward, she ran off to avoid spending the rest of her life in jail and is now probably pretending to be a full-time barista in Montenegro or Saudi Arabia. End of story."

Imani wanted to shut Tonya up, to put an end to her haughty and cruel commentary. The woman had no right to treat her this way in her home. To talk down to her. She raised the knife closer to the lip of her bag. "You're spewing lies to cover up your involvement," Imani said.

"I'm telling you the truth that you refuse to see," Tonya retorted.

"I want you gone." Imani nearly pulled the weapon from her purse as she spoke. "That's the truth. I want you out of my house."

Tonya crossed her arms. "Well, then, you're going to need a lawyer. There's a moratorium on evictions, and we have an agreement."

"There's no contract. We took you in out of the goodness—"

"Spare me. I've been paying rent in the form of labor," Tonya said. "And it doesn't matter. You need a sheriff to evict me. So, if you want to tell the police how you brokered an off-the-books work-for-rent situation, feel free." Tonya started toward the stairs. "I need to get ready for my job."

The knife seemed to pulse in Imani's hand. "I want you to leave."

"I don't care," Tonya shouted behind her.

Imani stepped in her direction. It was now or never, she thought. If she was going to order her tenant out at knifepoint, now was the time, before Tonya had the higher ground.

Imani released her grip on the weapon. She was a healer, not a fighter. "I'll call the police!" Her threat didn't even sound credible to her own ears. She didn't want the cops in her house, possibly writing citations for them taking in Tonya in the first place.

"You do that!" Tonya yelled.

Imani heard more footsteps, followed by a door slam. She'd accused the woman of murder and still Tonya wouldn't leave her house. That meant one of two things, Imani decided. Either her tenant was innocent, or she was even more dangerous than Imani had ever imagined.

CHAPTER FORTY-TWO

TONYA

Tonya pressed her back to the closed bedroom door and slid to the floor. Her hands were still shaking from the confrontation with Imani. If Philip's wife made good on her promises, everything Tonya had feared and more would come to pass. The world would know that she'd slept with Nate in hopes of landing parts in his movies. At best, Layla's classmates and parents would think her mom a sort of escort, willing to trade her body for opportunity and fame rather than money. At worst, they'd believe her a homewrecker who'd murdered a man after she'd grown sick of him denying her child.

She grabbed her suitcase from the closet, tossed it atop the bed, and pulled the zipper. The top flopped open. Frantically, she turned her attention to the dresser, yanking drawers free and gathering the contents in her arms. If she left, maybe Imani would keep quiet. Deep down, Philip's wife had to realize that her theory of Nate's murder was baseless. She had to know that the worst Tonya had done was have sex with a married man.

Tonya dumped a load of clothes into the bag and then stopped. The truth didn't matter to Imani, she realized. The woman was trying to create reasonable doubt for her friend. Whether Tonya left or not wouldn't stop her from offering police another explanation of the crime to explore. The truth wasn't the point. Imani only cared about providing cover for Melissa.

Tonya rubbed her hands quickly over her face, using the friction to force herself to focus. If leaving wouldn't help, perhaps appealing to Philip would. He couldn't believe his wife's crazy hypothesis. He knew her. Respected her, even. He would listen to reason.

Or bargaining.

Philip had killed his father. Tonya was nearly sure of it. In fancy restaurants, the garde-manger oversaw all the cold food: chilled soups, caviars, salads, smoked fish, and pâtés. He would have known if his father's chicken liver had been fattened with peanut butter. He would have been the one to introduce the secret ingredient.

As much as Tonya liked Philip, she knew that he was prone to bursts of anger. She'd witnessed several in the time that she'd known him. And he'd indicated that his father had been physically abusive. Perhaps he'd added a bit of his dad's allergen in hopes of making the man too sick and tired to start an argument later. Or maybe he'd decided that he'd had enough and wanted to inflict similar pain.

Tonya grabbed her coat off the bed where she'd thrown it earlier. She slipped an arm into a sleeve. With luck, she could catch Philip before the chefs started arriving to prep for the dinner service. As Imani would say, they could have a discussion.

————————

The staff entrance was dark. Tonya passed through anyway, sliding her hands along the brick made oleaginous by aerosolized cooking oils. There would be a light switch somewhere within the first few feet. Chefs did not want to stumble into a dark kitchen on a daily basis.

As Tonya felt her way along the wall, she heard metallic taps coming from somewhere overhead. The pings sounded every few seconds, too steady to be random, not timed perfectly enough to be mechanical. Melting snow, maybe. Tonya supposed water could be seeping through the building's roof and striking the ceiling pipes.

Finally, the tip of her finger snagged a different surface, smoother and more worn than the brick. Plastic, if she hazarded a guess. She pressed the bottom of the tab and braced herself.

Pot lights flickered on. Some of them were missing, Tonya realized. Several of the ceiling bulbs, including the one directly above her head, remained dark despite the fluorescent glow of their neighbors. It was dangerous to have burned-out bulbs in a kitchen. Chefs could cut themselves. She should tell Philip.

Thinking about her boss brought the reason that she'd come to the forefront of her mind. She would ask Philip to talk Imani down, explain that his wife's grief over her friend's actions had led her to develop insane theories. She'd ask him to let her remain in his home until her unemployment checks arrived and it became possible to rent elsewhere. If he said no, she'd bring up her own suspicions about his parents and subtly suggest that no one need know about ancient family history, providing that he help her for a few months.

He'd take the deal, she figured. Every other man in her life had been willing to pay for her silence. And she wasn't even asking for money in this instance. She was simply buying time.

Tonya passed the mop basin and stepped into the kitchen. The stainless-steel countertops gleamed under the lights, a cloud-covered ocean waiting for the storm to come, the frenzy of blades and bodies, flames and animal flesh.

"Philip?"

Her own voice echoed back to her. He had to be here, Tonya thought. The world was shut down. There was nowhere to go but home, and Philip truly lived inside Banque Gauche's kitchen.

She removed her coat and hung it on one of the hooks for staff garments. "Philip," she called out again, advancing farther into the space. "It's Tonya. Can we talk?"

The dull thud of a heavy door closing answered. The clicking of metal gears responded to it, a conversation between machines. Similar sounds had emanated from the dining room the prior day. They hadn't come from the restaurant's front entrance, Tonya realized. That was secured by an electronic dead bolt that slammed into place.

The only other door in the dining room was Coffre's closed vault. But there was no reason for anyone to open it. The short-lived restaurant had been gutted months ago. Would Philip go inside simply for nostalgia's sake?

Footsteps followed the noises. Tonya sidled up to the butcher block with the house knives. She didn't plan on needing them. But blocking access to sharp objects was never a bad idea when confronting someone with an unpleasant proposition.

Philip strode into the room. His uncovered face was flushed as if he'd done something that required some amount of physical exertion. Tonya pulled down her own mask.

He frowned as he saw her face. "Tonya." The name sounded like an epithet followed by a "you."

"Hi. I know I'm early. Can I talk to you for a moment?"

Philip resumed his advance into the kitchen. "I have to prep for dinner service."

Tonya wanted to quip that Philip had people for that. Chefs who earned far less than he did made sure that all the ingredients for the following night's meals were chopped and stored in airtight Tupperware before the major cooking even began. But she stopped herself from disagreeing. He was trying to avoid speaking to her, probably because he'd known of Imani's theories before she'd voiced them. Picking a fight over a silly excuse would only push him to further side with his wife.

"Imani spoke with me a few hours ago regarding her concerns about me and Layla temporarily living with you all. She seems to be under the impression that Nate and I had an affair and that letting me stay there would be a betrayal of her friendship with Melissa."

Philip stopped mere feet from her, too close for comfort

during a pandemic. She interpreted the proximity as a signal to continue.

"As I told Imani, I didn't have a relationship with Nate." She sighed. "I know you two are friends, and I don't want to speak ill of the dead, but because there's clearly some misinformation going around, I feel the need to tell you what happened."

Philip's blue eyes zeroed in on her face, lasers trying to read the information off of a disc. The direct stare wasn't simply giving her permission to continue, Tonya realized. It was challenging her to prove that she didn't deserve forcible removal from his home.

"I auditioned for Nate Walker. He asked me to do things that made me very uncomfortable." Tonya looked away from Philip's clinical gaze. "I did many of these things anyway because I wanted a chance at being in one of his films. I guess I figured, in for a penny, in for a pound, you know?"

She forced a chuckle. The sound came out strangled, a desperate gasp rather than a guffaw.

"Anyway, what happened would have been embarrassing to both of us if it came out, but especially to Nate since he was married. As a kind of consolation prize, he wrote Layla a recommendation for school and agreed to put money toward her tuition."

Philip's stare turned cold. "Is Nate Layla's father?"

Part of Tonya wanted to answer, to let the room reverberate with Layla's dad's real name like charged air after a thunderclap. But she couldn't. The man's identity was worth three hundred thousand dollars and then some.

"It's not important," she said.

"Does anyone know who he is?"

Tonya shook her head. "No."

"Who does Layla think he is?"

Tonya shrugged. "Until recently, she thought he was a sperm donor."

"What does she think now?"

A bitter snort escaped her as Tonya considered the question and realized the horrible, likely answer. "I haven't told her the truth. However, I recently learned that she was taking Nate's writing class and didn't tell me. Given that he was paying for her schooling and other folks know about it, she probably thinks it's him."

Philip was on top of her before Tonya could react. He grabbed an arm and spun her around. She tried to reach for the knife block with her free hand. But he pinned both her arms behind her shoulder blades before she could do anything but scratch air.

"What are you doing?" Tonya screeched. "You can't think that I killed Nate too."

"No. But I think the police might."

Tonya pulled forward. "What are you saying?"

Philip yanked her arms, jerking her backward. Something sharp pressed against her spine. She felt a wetness trickle toward her behind. "Walk," Philip instructed.

Tonya did as told. If she stopped, the sharp point against her lumbar section might sink deeper into her skin, preventing her from ever walking again. "I don't understand," she said, continuing to march in a straight line as Philip steered her with rough pulls of her held hands. "Why are you doing this?"

"You had an affair with Nate for years, Tonya. You had a child with him. You'd hoped he'd leave his wife."

"That's not true."

The knifepoint slid down her spine. She felt her long-sleeved top part in the back, chicken skin separating from the meat. "When he didn't, you two got into an argument. You shot him."

"I didn't."

The knife pricked her back. He pulled her pinned arms to the left, guiding her out of the kitchen and into the main dining room. She slowed her walk as she realized where they were heading—Coffre.

"Philip, please." The knifepoint pierced her flesh, hushing her pleas. She gasped for air.

"Don't stop walking," Philip whispered in her ear.

She picked up her pace. "I didn't do what Imani said. You have to believe me."

"Then his wife came down," Philip continued. "And you know what you did then?"

The tone in which he posed the question turned it into a joke. He wasn't asking. He was setting up a punch line. Philip didn't believe she'd killed Nate, Tonya realized. In fact, he knew she hadn't.

Because he had.

"You won't be able to pin this on me," Tonya yelled. "The police will realize that Nate invested in your restaurant."

Philip yanked her in front of Coffre's closed vault door. The grip on her hands relaxed. "Turn the wheel and open it."

Tonya stepped to the side, opting to make a run for it instead. A slash to her oblique changed her mind. Instinctively, her hand went to hold together her severed flesh. Hot blood poured through her fingers.

"Do it!" Philip roared.

Tonya turned the wheel. She knew that he intended to lock her inside, but she'd at least be alive in there. If she tried to run, he'd cut her into pieces.

Tonya's hands shook as she gripped the wheel. She slowly rotated it. "The cops won't believe I'm responsible." Her voice was small and squeaky. Fear had wrapped around her throat like a boa constrictor. "They'll realize what happened to your parents—that special pâté that you made for your father. They'll figure out you killed him."

If Philip reacted to her accusation, Tonya didn't hear it. Metal pins popped from their locks. She felt the blade at the base of her back. "Open it," he said.

Tonya closed her eyes and pulled on the wheel. The door inched back. As it did, a rush of hot liquid dribbled onto her thigh. Her exertion was speeding up the bleeding.

Philip pressed the blade into her back as he grabbed the wheel and pulled. The door retracted another foot. A new force slammed into both her shoulder blades. She stumbled forward, tripping over the lip of the vault door.

Her knees crashed into the hardwood floor. "Philip, please!"

The dull thud of the door answered her cry. She flung herself at it, releasing a fresh wave of blood down her side. "Don't do this!" she screamed into the void enveloping her. "Philip. No! Please!"

A scratching noise sounded behind her. Something moved in this darkness, Tonya realized. She was not alone.

CHAPTER FORTY-THREE

IMANI

Imani hovered over the sink, wiping remnants of tomato sauce off Layla's plate. She'd whipped up spaghetti for Tonya's daughter, even though Vivienne and Jay had willingly eaten the curried chicken that Philip had prepared as a late-lunch, after-school snack before heading to the restaurant. Imani had witnessed Layla's nose wrinkle as she'd picked at the meat in its yellow soup of sauce and told her not to worry if she didn't like it.

"Your mother left you food," she'd said, putting on a pot of water to boil. In truth, Tonya hadn't stocked her side of the pantry with pasta. The only items Tonya had purchased aside from her precious PB&J sandwiches were canned soups, a few sad vegetables, and some frozen meals that looked about as healthy and appetizing as congealed beef stew.

Imani would never let a child go hungry in her house. But the extra effort to make Layla a homecooked meal had been fueled, in part, by her own guilt over the conversation with the girl's mother. She still thought Tonya was lying about

Layla's parentage and her relationship with Nate. Imani wanted her gone. But she'd begun to doubt that Tonya could have had anything to do with Nate's murder.

Anger and fear were emotional tempests, Imani knew, destroying carefully constructed higher functions like the abilities to reason and restrain. She'd nearly let her lesser feelings get the better of her. Nearly allowed anger to transmogrify her mind into an animal brain that only knew power and control, that had been inches away from telling her body to pull a knife on a young woman who'd somehow maintained her composure despite being accused of murder.

Imani put the dish into the washing machine and then got to work on the pasta pot. As she squeezed soap into the bottom, she couldn't help but wonder if Tonya was in Philip's kitchen doing something similar—scrubbing cookware while scrutinizing their conversation. Wondering what had been said solely to win a debate point. What had possessed deeper meaning?

According to Tonya, Nate had invested in Philip's restaurant. Imani doubted the woman had simply made that up. Along with what Tonya had said about Philip's father, there had to be a grain of truth to her claim, likely coming from Philip himself. Either Philip had confessed something about Nate's involvement or Tonya had seen Nate at Coffre and figured out that his interest had to extend beyond grabbing a good whiskey and slider.

Imani could see a certain logic to Philip seeking Nate's investment. The fact that he'd taken out a home equity loan indicated that the banks had considered Coffre's projected revenues and opted not to offer her husband an attractive business line of credit. Melissa had always complained of Nate's poor investment acumen. She'd said that he picked projects because he was attracted to them creatively or because they fueled his ego. Over the years, Philip had even heard her tease Nate over his business ideas. After being rejected by the number crunchers, her husband might have seen Nate as a natural lender of last resort.

Imani pulled the faucet head to the soapy pot and began spraying. Philip seeking Nate's money didn't mean that he'd had anything to do with the man's death, she told herself. But then why did she feel so uneasy? Why was there a hollow sensation in her bones like someone had cleaned out the marrow?

Imani left the pot to soak and went to her laptop, pushed onto the dining room hutch. She logged on, opened the unnamed folder, and accessed the saved image inside. There was the den that she knew so well transformed into a scene straight out of a splatter film. Blood coated the floor and speckled the walls. Nate's body lay in the foreground, his face disintegrating into flesh and bone. Atop his desk was a thick tumbler with a diamond pattern carved into the base, a swallow of scotch reflected in the prisms. There was a circular mark next to the glass, perhaps the condensation from another drink. Between the two sat a bottle of Bushmills.

Imani's heart seemed to dislodge itself from behind her rib cage and push into her throat. She could feel it throbbing in the center of her neck, feel it sending the blood to her head with every beat. Melissa didn't drink whiskey. But Philip did.

And Bushmills was his favorite.

CHAPTER FORTY-FOUR

TONYA

"Who are you?" A raspy voice emerged from the blackness. It was weak and quiet, almost distorted, as if coming through on a frequency between stations.

"Who are you?" Shouting sent a stabbing pain through Tonya's torso. The knife's sharpness had confused her nerves, delaying her reaction to it severing her flesh. But she felt everything now. A phantom blade dug into her right side, causing the underlying muscle to throb and gush. Her fingers stuck to the wet fabric atop the gash.

"I'm Melissa." The ghostly voice seemed to emanate from another part of the room. "Melissa Walker."

Tonya felt her stomach drop somewhere between her knees. Philip had killed Nate and locked the man's wife in this room. She'd been trapped inside here for more than a week, no doubt trying to escape—and failing.

"We're going to get out of here, Melissa." Tonya turned toward the area where she'd heard the door close. She ran her hands over it like she was smoothing wallpaper, seeking a seam where the door connected to the wall or some sort of unlocking mechanism. "You and I are going to get out of here."

"Who are you?" The voice echoed from a new location. For a moment, Tonya wondered if Melissa was even in the room. Perhaps the woman's ghost was visiting her, demanding that she own up to what had happened before meeting their maker.

"Tonya Sayre," she answered, praying that her name meant nothing to the other woman, that Philip hadn't engineered some sort of blind cage match between the jilted wife and naïve paramour. "I'm one of Philip's waitresses."

A long exhale ended in a coughing fit. "He plans to pin it on you, then."

The voice sounded right behind her. Tonya whirled around, one hand in front of her body, the other protecting the gash on her side. "What?"

"He left me here to die, thinking that the police would assume I'd done it and gone missing. But I kept telling him that they'd never believe I'd leave my daughter without either of her parents." Tonya flinched as something warm and fleshy brushed against her arm. "I'm sorry. I thought he would let me go. I guess he found another solution: blame the other woman."

Tonya wanted to defend herself, to explain that she'd never carried on an affair with Nate, that the relationship had been struck under false pretenses and quickly abandoned. But every sentence uttered seemed to expel more blood from her side. She needed to conserve her energy.

Tonya returned her attention to the cool metal expanse

of the door, feeling along its grooves for a handle or knob. Fingers wrapped around her bicep. Tonya heard a wheezing, a death rattle inches from her face. Speaking was difficult for Melissa, Tonya realized. Had she been fed at all during her captivity? Or had Philip shut the door and forgotten about her?

"This room was a bank vault," Melissa whispered. "The door only opens from the outside."

Tonya hastened her pat-down of the walls. "It was a restaurant. There must be a way out. A fire exit, maybe?"

"I've felt along every surface and haven't found one," Melissa said. "I think because it's a restaurant inside another one that it got some sort of exemption."

"A window?"

Melissa's hand traveled up and down Tonya's arm. She must have meant the touch to be comforting but being stroked by a stranger's bony fingers in the darkness felt like being caressed by a skeleton. "It was a vault. We're stuck."

Tonya shrugged off Melissa's hand. "If he wanted us to die, he would have killed us. There must be something he wants. Something we can negotiate with."

Footsteps padded against the hardwood. Tonya sensed a figure backing away. "He won't let us out. He's waiting for the right time to do it, maybe after he's pointed the police in your direction. Or he intends to leave us to starve."

Tears pressed against Tonya's lower lids. If she died, what would happen to her daughter? Her parents weren't equipped to care for a child, let alone a city kid accustomed to spending her days riding a subway to a school that had classes in playwriting, Mandarin, and set design. And even if Rick was willing to support Layla, his money wouldn't come for a while. Without Tonya pressuring him, maybe he wouldn't pay child support at all.

"We'll get out of here." Tonya said it even though part of her was already accepting that she wouldn't. Part of her was imagining Layla on her parents' farm, milking cows and shoveling horseshit, watching her dreams shrivel like crops in a drought.

"Do you think Imani knows?" Melissa's voice cracked on her friend's name.

Imani's prior accusations played in Tonya's mind. Philip's wife might have been grasping at straws to clear her best friend, but she hadn't been doing it to exonerate her husband. Imani's surprise at learning of Nate's investment in Philip's restaurant had been too genuine. Too raw. "Not unless she deserves an Oscar," Tonya quipped.

A sharp gasp was the reply, followed by the distinct sound of sobbing. "She'll come for us, then." Melissa's voice sounded like it was being carried away, fading before the words were fully intelligible.

"She doesn't know that Philip had anything to do with Nate," Tonya countered. "People are speculating that you did it and are on the run."

Melissa coughed. "She's my best friend. She knows me." A staccato gasp punctuated each phrase. "She's smart. She'll come."

Tonya leaned against the wall, grabbing her side. She didn't know Imani like Melissa did. Still, she thought her co-captive's faith misplaced. All things being equal, of course Imani would want to find and save her friend. But the man who wanted them dead was Imani's husband. Even if Imani began to suspect Philip—even if Tonya's diatribe had raised doubts—it would be easier for Imani to turn a blind eye, to buy into the fiction that her friend had done something terrible rather than face the fact that her husband and the father of her children wasn't who she'd thought.

"She'll come." Melissa repeated the words like a prayer. "I've been signaling for her. Tapping the pipes."

Tonya recalled the sound that she'd dismissed as a ceiling leak. It had been inaudible when the kitchen was bustling or Philip was using a meat grinder, but perhaps that was because Melissa had lacked the strength to make a real racket. There were two of them now.

"Show me."

Melissa didn't seem to understand her question. Tonya heard her murmur. Her voice was growing more distant. She was walking away. Or maybe falling asleep.

"Melissa," Tonya shouted. "Don't leave."

Something creaked in the darkness. A sliver of light snuck into the room. "It's the toilet," Melissa said. "I'll show you how to make the noise."

CHAPTER FORTY-FIVE

IMANI

The alleyway behind the restaurant was always dark, permanently shaded by the tall buildings flanking its sides. However, the blackness Imani walked into was of a different character. The lights that would typically shine from the neighboring buildings had been extinguished, a consequence of office cleaning crews no longer needing to toil into the inky morning hours to prepare for daylight's computer workers. A solitary streetlamp posted outside Banque Gauche provided the only light. It cast a swirling beam into the space that faded out several feet before the restaurant's side door. This was a noir scene, Imani thought, and she wasn't a detective or a femme fatale. She didn't belong.

Imani pulled the door handle, half expecting it to be locked. She'd tried to time her arrival for after the cooks departed, but before Philip typically left. The coming conversation about her husband seeking Nate's investment—and hiding it from her—was bound to get heated. Imani didn't want Philip's colleagues hearing them shout at each other, nor did she want the kids listening in. In fact, she didn't even want them to know she and their father were having a serious discussion. She'd waited until they'd all retired to their rooms before leaving. With luck, they might not even realize that she'd gone.

The door gave way, revealing a fluorescent blaze that was too bright for what her eyes had already adjusted to. She shielded them with her hand as she stepped onto the restaurant's tile floor. "Philip?" she yelled, announcing herself. "It's me."

Imani passed the cleaning closet with its sink and mop. Beside it, Tonya's coat hung from a wall hook. Imani felt her stomach sink. She'd known that Tonya might be with Philip. When she'd heard the front door slam hours earlier, Imani had suspected that Tonya had gone to the restaurant to work and plead her case. Still, Imani had hoped that Tonya would have left by now and been en route to her house.

Imani removed her own coat and hung it beside Tonya's before advancing deeper into the restaurant. "Hello?"

Her voice and footsteps reverberated in the empty kitchen. The sound emphasized the space's barrenness, adding to the bleak atmosphere. Without the bustle of chefs chopping vibrant ingredients and lighting things on fire, the restaurant seemed cold and clinical. The stainless-steel surfaces resembled morgue tables. The containers for knives morphed into carts for medical instruments.

"Philip!" Imani shouted. "Philip."

A door opened. Philip emerged from a small office on the side of the kitchen. He wore his chef's jacket. Imani had always found the uniform attractive in the way that military and police dress were sexy. They implied a certain discipline and drive, a willingness to reach an objective regardless of the obstacles. Is that why Philip hadn't told her about the restaurant's struggles? Had he thought securing financing his task to complete no matter what?

"Imani?" Philip's voice rose at the end, asking why she'd come without verbalizing the question.

"I spoke to Tonya," Imani said. "She insists that she never had an affair with Nate."

Philip scratched at his jaw. Blond stubble lined the edges of it. In the overhead light, the bristle resembled needles on a prickly pear, the ones that would dig under the skin, causing days of swelling and itching.

"You don't believe her." His tone told more than asked.

"I don't know what to believe."

Philip drew closer. Imani spotted a swath of red at the hip of his jacket. Stains were a sign of a bad day in the kitchen. On a good one, all the food and by-products remained confined to cookware. Stains meant spills, mistakes, and lost revenue.

"Tonya came here, and I spoke to her. I told her that her connection to Nate, and the fact that she hadn't mentioned anything, rubbed us the wrong way. I—"

A metallic banging cut him off. Philip's eyes rolled toward the ceiling and the unseen source of the noise. He raised his voice to be heard over the clatter. "I told her that she needed to find someplace else to live."

Imani patted the air, encouraging Philip to lower his voice. "Isn't she here now?"

The racket continued, like hail hitting a metal gutter or

the sound of pots and pans striking a fire escape. Imani had heard plenty of the latter in the pandemic's early days when New Yorkers had made a nightly ruckus to show appreciation for frontline health care workers.

"No." Philip's volume ticked up another notch. "I assumed she'd gone back to the house to get her daughter and leave." He put his hands on his hips and scowled at the overhead tiles, admonishing whatever lay behind them to be quiet. "Damn pipes. There must be a leak somewhere—or rats got into it."

The thought of vermin scurrying above made Imani shudder. "You need an exterminator."

"It's on the list." Philip returned his attention to her face. "Speaking of, I need to go down to Pennsylvania tomorrow."

The mention of the Keystone State came out of left field. She and Philip rarely left the city, and when they did, it was to visit Westchester or see the leaves change color in New England. Occasionally, they went to the airport. What was in Pennsylvania for Philip? Produce?

"Why? Farmer's market or something?"

Philip rubbed his forehead. "More and more places are being broken into, and I'm leaving late every night." His hand dropped to his side, a surrendering gesture. "A friend gave me a gun, but I need bullets."

Imani examined Philip's expression for a sign of sarcasm. Her liberal, anti–Second Amendment, embittered ex-marine husband did not do firearms. "You said that the last thing you ever wanted to do after a tour in Afghanistan was clean or hold a handgun. Firearms belong on battlefields, not in cities full of civilians. That's your mantra."

Philip's blue eyes fixed upon her face. She'd begun to associate their color with water because they'd so often possessed a glassy quality. However, seeing them now, she pictured a different image: two blue dwarf stars, each its own nuclear explosion.

"Circumstances change, Imani. The pandemic made every moron run out and buy a gun, and now they're all waving them around like we're in a spaghetti western. They've got no training whatsoever, but with a gun, they can kill someone. They can kill me or you. The kids. I need to protect us."

As Philip spoke, the banging picked up. Its rhythm had been consistent, like the ping of a steady drizzle, the kind of noise that could be relegated to the background despite its volume. But it was now rising to a crescendo, rain reaching the heaviest part of a downpour. If rats were behind this, they'd been worked into a frenzy.

"We should get out of here." Philip glanced at the ceiling. "It's not good for the kids to be sleeping alone in the house."

Though Imani agreed, she hadn't left them in the first place only to avoid asking what she had to know. "I actually came because I wanted to talk to you about something Tonya said to me. She mentioned that Nate had invested in Coffre."

Philip shook his head dramatically, a toddler pretending that he had no idea where the crayon on the wall had come from. "Where'd she get that idea?"

"I'm guessing from you."

Philip stared at her, as if he wanted to burrow into her brain and dig out the memory of Tonya's revelation. She met his look. Imani was not about to be intimidated by the man she'd slept with and leaned on and laughed with for nearly twenty years. Philip owed her an explanation.

He averted his eyes, conceding the staring match. "Yeah. Okay. When I started Coffre, I asked him if he wanted to come in as a silent partner. The home equity line of credit that I took out couldn't cover all the investments in the new place plus Banque's refresh, so I needed money, and Nate and his friends were all hot to be restauranteurs like De Niro. I guess they thought it would add cachet to their images."

"Why didn't you tell me?"

"Am I supposed to tell you every business decision that I make? Do you tell me the circumstances of every patient that you see?"

"This is different."

"Nate invested. So what? It's not like he was the only one. He brought in some business associates as well, who, I might add, have proven to be nothing but pains in my ass. But I don't tell you all that nonsense because you don't need to hear me griping after a long day of work. I know that you get enough of that from your patients. When we're together, it's about enjoying each other and our kids. Not rehashing all the shit."

"That shit is part of our lives, Philip. That's what you do in a marriage, share the good and bad. It's a line in the standard vows."

Philip snorted. "Well maybe it shouldn't be, Imani. You know what you learn in the marines other than how to shoot a gun or maybe disarm some idiot waving around a pistol?"

Imani glared at her husband, waiting for him to answer his clearly rhetorical question.

"Compartmentalization." Philip nodded, agreeing with himself. "You learn to leave your childhood in the past because you can't be thinking about how Daddy hit Mommy when you've got to shove a gun in some guy's face in front of his kid. You learn to channel all the anger and hurt and whatever other crappy emotions you've felt and direct it squarely at the enemy.

"And then you know what you learn? You learn to walk away, to leave the battlefield back there so you're not coming home screaming at your kids or slapping your own wife. You learn to be home when you're at home and at work when you're working, and that business is not at home. It has nothing to do with it. The kids have nothing to do with it. You have nothing to do with it."

Philip's body language grew increasingly agitated as he delivered his monologue. His arms flailed. His jaw worked back and forth.

Again, Imani refused to be intimidated by her husband. "Of course I have something to do with it when it involves our livelihood and our home and our friends!" She was shouting, both to be heard over the banging and to match Philip's aggression. "You didn't think it could impact our family's relationship with the Walkers to go into business with Nate? I mean, Melissa always said he wasn't known for investing well. How did he handle it when the place went under? I have a hard time thinking he shrugged and said, 'Welp, that's business.'"

Philip stepped toward her. His shoulders were square.

His arms were held out from his body. A chill ran up Imani's spine.

"Nate's a dolt. He invests in Coffre, right? Gives me money to set the place up and market it, run it for a while until it takes off. Then, when the place has to close because of a damn pandemic, he tries to argue that he should get his money back, completely ignoring the fact that we had to pay the rent for the entire restaurant space, including Banque, during the shutdown. It's not like we could keep Coffre functioning while letting the main restaurant fail. What's Coffre going to operate inside? An ABC Carpet? A Google headquarters?"

Philip gestured wildly as he spoke, his fingers coming within inches of Imani's face. She stepped back. "When did you have this conversation with him?" She lowered her voice, afraid of her follow-up. "Was it the night he died?"

Philip abruptly stopped moving, a freight train slamming into a wall. Imani could almost feel his body buzzing across from her, reverberating from the impact.

"No."

"I saw the crime scene photos, Philip. There was a bottle of Bushmills on his desk. Black label."

Philip's hands went to his hips. "It's a good whiskey." His eyes shrank to slivers. "What are you getting at, Imani?"

Hairs stood up on the back of her neck, not only from the cold tone of his question but also because she knew exactly what she was suggesting. Her husband had gotten into an argument with Nate. Things had become heated. Nate had grown intimidated by Philip, perhaps even scared. He'd grabbed Melissa's gun, and Philip had gone into war mode.

He'd compartmentalized, forgetting that Nate was a friend, focusing only on neutralizing the enemy. The only question was what he'd done with Melissa.

And what he might have done with the woman whose coat still hung in the kitchen.

"Where is Tonya, Philip?"

He shook his head. "Huh?"

"Her coat is on the hanger. It's freezing outside. She wouldn't have left without it."

Philip shrugged. "I guess I got a bit adamant when telling her that she had to leave. She must have run out without it."

He was lying. Imani could see it in his eyes, the way his gaze grew more intent as if scanning her face for signs that she believed him. She remembered what Melissa had told her all those years ago about controlling her own micro-expressions and forced herself to picture a blank wall, to stare at Philip but see something else entirely, an expanse of fresh cement, smoothed like the surface of an undisturbed lake.

"It's on the hook by the mop, next to my coat," Imani said, keeping her tone casual. "Go get it for her? Layla was asleep, so she'll still be at our house by the time we come back."

Philip's pupils flitted from her to the knife block that Imani knew was behind her and then the walk-in fridge. He was a combatant weighing his options, she realized, figuring out how to neutralize the threat that she posed.

"We can get it on the way out," he said.

"All your talk about rats makes me not want to be in that alley. Go get Tonya's coat while I grab some aspirin, and then we can head out the front door." Imani added a bit extra breath into her voice to simulate exhaustion. She touched her forehead, mirroring Philip's common stress response. "The drama of today has given me the worst headache."

Before he could respond, Imani strode to the far side of the kitchen and the cavernous entryway that she knew led to the pantry. "The medicine's in here, right?" she yelled over her shoulder as she passed into the adjacent room, navigating by the light from the kitchen outside. Wire shelves were filled with dry goods. Rice. Flour. Clear Tupperware bins of spices labeled with tape and markers.

What she was looking for lined an entire bottom shelf. Giant tins of frying oil were arrayed like glistening sardines in a can. Olive. Sunflower. Peanut.

Imani heard Philip's footsteps, walking away, doing as she asked. She uncapped the peanut oil, lifted the jug to her lips, and took a large gulp. It tasted unctuous, like pouring liquid soap on her tongue. She forced herself not to spit it out— or swallow.

Philip's footsteps drew closer. Imani could feel the heat of his presence behind her. She turned around, confirming that he stood in the space between the pantry and kitchen, blocking her exit. Heavy black wool was draped over his forearm. He pulled one of the coats free and held it out to her.

Imani couldn't speak. She walked over, smiling her thank-you, and wrapped her arms around Philip's waist. She put her head on his chest. Tears filled her eyes as his arm went around her back. She concentrated on the warmth of his hand running up and down her spine, trying to commit the feeling to memory, knowing that she might not feel it again.

She loved Philip, but she'd only ever known one side of him. The other side was a monster.

She lifted her chin and stared at him with all the love that she could muster, forcing thoughts of Melissa and what he'd done to her out of her mind. For a moment, she needed to remember that her husband was also the man who'd given her Vivienne and Jay, who'd lifted her over the threshold of his carriage house, who'd danced and laughed and cooked and made love with her. She needed to remember the twenty years of mostly happy moments that they'd shared on the occasions that he'd been able to wrest himself from his restaurant.

Philip leaned down. His lips pressed against hers.

Imani was sure he'd taste it immediately. She grabbed the back of his head, holding it steady as she forced his lips open with her tongue. She pushed the oily liquid held in her cheeks into his mouth, a mother bird feeding a chick. He tried to back away, but she held on, kissing him harder, determined that every drop end up down his throat.

Philip shoved both hands into her chest. She stumbled back, grabbing on to a shelving unit to stop herself from falling. Her husband's face was red. He headed toward her, fist raised, ready to knock her lights out.

Before he could act, his hands went around his throat. His mouth moved, trying to say something, to accuse her, perhaps. To ask why. No sound emerged. His throat was closing.

"I love you," she shouted. "And I'll call nine-one-one. But I need to find Tonya."

She ran past Philip's doubled-over body and into the

kitchen. The banging was still audible, though fainter than before. Imani followed the steady pings, aware that they were a signal. Rats had not gotten into the ceiling. Someone was jostling the pipes.

The sound seemed to grow louder as she exited the kitchen into the main dining room. It was nearly empty, just stacked chairs and tables, a large bar, and a big open floor. No one was in here. Imani turned to the metal expanse at the room's end.

The vault door was massive, a stainless-steel eye with a multi-pronged iris at its center. She ran toward it, removing her telephone from her pocket as she did. Emergency was three simple numbers.

The phone was ringing before her hand hit the wheel in the middle of the door. She wedged the cell between her shoulder and ear as she began to turn.

"Nine-one-one. What's your emergency?"

"My husband is having a severe allergic reaction. He's in his restaurant, Banque Gauche, and he must have eaten peanuts. You have to come. I don't have an EpiPen."

"Does he keep an EpiPen anywhere nearby, or Benadryl?"

Imani suspected that both were somewhere in the kitchen, but she couldn't give either to him. She pushed the wheel left with all her might. "Please come."

Metal pins slammed into place, unlocking the door. Imani pulled it toward her. Her arms vibrated from the weight of it. The phone fell from her ear. She leaned back, employing all her strength to retract the wall of an entrance.

It cracked open. She moved to the fissure and pushed the door back, peering inside. The space beyond was pitch-black, the kind of darkness that seemed to make objects magically disappear. "Hello, Tonya? Are you in there? It's Imani."

A scratching, shuffling noise answered. For a moment, Imani was tempted to shut the door. Maybe she'd gone crazy from grief and isolation. Perhaps all that was really inside Coffre were starving, cannibalistic rats.

"Hello?" Imani screamed again.

A strange form stumbled toward the doorway. She could just make it out in the slight shift of darkness. Imani stepped back.

The woman who emerged was severely dehydrated and malnourished. Her skin was taut against her bones, like the plastic of a drum against steel. Her blond hair lay oily and tangled against her shoulders. Imani had never known her to look like this. Still, she'd know her best friend anywhere.

"Melissa," she shouted.

Her friend limped from the room. She started to fall forward, exhausted by the weight of the other woman leaning heavily against her side. Imani pulled both Tonya and Melissa into her arms. As she did, her side grew damp. She touched the spot and raised her hands to her face.

It was blood.

"I knew you'd come," Melissa whispered. "I knew it."

It was the last thing she said before collapsing into Imani's chest.

CHAPTER FORTY-SIX

MELISSA

The nurse couldn't find a vein. Dehydration caused them to constrict, she explained while jabbing the inner fold of Melissa's arm. It was the second attempt in the right arm after failing to insert the cannula between the bones on the back of her left hand. Melissa could only nod in response. The days of silence and darkness had rendered the outside world intolerable. Everything was too loud. Too bright. Her senses needed time to adjust.

She wouldn't receive any respite, though. Through the door to her private room, Melissa could see two people hovering. Though they wore hospital masks, Melissa pegged them as cops. Her circumstances and the dour looks that she'd seen imitated on too many *Law & Order* episodes seemed to confirm it. They were watching the nurse's attempts to fit the needle beneath her flaky, near-translucent skin, waiting for her to take in the liquid required for her brain to function.

During her captivity, she had drunk handfuls of water from the bathroom sink. But she hadn't gorged after her belly had become more and more bloated from lack of food. Melissa wondered if, secretly, some part of herself had made the decision that quickly dying of thirst was better than slowly starving in darkness. She hadn't worked that hard to keep herself alive during the last days of her confinement. Once she'd realized that Philip couldn't be negotiated with, she'd unconsciously begun preparing for the end.

But she was alive. Melissa wasn't sure if that was true of the other woman. By the time they'd limped out of Coffre, Tonya's shirt had been soaked in blood.

"Is she okay?" Melissa shouted toward the door as the needle pierced her skin.

The nurse looked at her as if she'd expressed pain in a foreign language.

"Tonya," Melissa said. "Did she make it?"

She wanted to know. Perhaps just as much, she wanted to get the police interview over with. The sooner she spoke to the detectives, the sooner she could see Imani. They wouldn't let them talk until she'd given a statement, Melissa figured. Otherwise, her friend would be here. Unless, of course, there was some crazy COVID protocol preventing patients who'd narrowly escaped being killed from quarantining in the same room.

The nurse glanced over her shoulder at the detectives, providing tacit approval for them to enter.

"Hello, Mrs. Walker," the female said. She extended a hand and then, seeming to remember that no one shook hands anymore, patted the slick side of her tight bun. "I'm Detective Linette Calvente, and this is my partner Detective Roger Powell."

"Is she all right?" Melissa tried again. "Tonya, the woman who was stabbed."

"She's in surgery," Linette said.

"We're hoping for the best," her partner added.

Melissa had barely seen Tonya's state, having collapsed shortly after escaping. But she'd felt the woman's blood, hot and wet against her side as she'd helped her limp from the room. They'd both been banging the pipes with all their might, despite Melissa's dehydration and Tonya's wounds. Before Imani had rescued them, Tonya had nearly collapsed. It had taken the last of Melissa's energy to drag her out the door.

"Melissa"—the female detective said her name with a certain amount of awe, as if Melissa had been resurrected—"we need to know what happened."

She told them everything from the moment that Philip had ordered her into his car at gunpoint and demanded that she drive to what she now knew was his restaurant— though, at the time, she hadn't been sure of anything. It had been a dark night, and the city had looked so strange with all its empty streets, bereft of the markers by which she'd usually navigated—the recognizable restaurants and storefronts. She'd only known that Philip had forced her out of the car into an alley and then dragged her through a door into a darkened space leading to the pitch-black abyss where she'd spent her captivity. Melissa also explained the impetus for Nate inviting Philip over to discuss business. Hours earlier, she told the detectives, she'd asked for a divorce. She'd learned from Tonya's friend Micky that her husband had been sleeping with female actresses, and she'd decided to leave him.

"I'd always known that Nate was a flirt, but I'd never thought he was cheating."

Melissa was surprised at how easily the news rolled off her tongue. Before her kidnapping, she would have guarded the information. She'd resolved to tell the paparazzi that her marriage was ending because of the standard "irreconcilable differences." But being held in darkness had added value to bringing things into the light.

"The prospect of dividing our wealth in half spurred Nate to reexamine his financial dealings," she explained. "He thought Philip owed him the unused part of his investment. I don't know if he did or not, but that's clearly what they'd been arguing over. Nate had been drinking since I'd told him my intention to leave. My guess is that he'd invited Philip over for more booze, things got heated, and he pulled this stupid gun I'd gotten in a drunken machismo power play." Melissa shrugged. "He pulled it on the wrong guy. Philip took it and shot him. After, he panicked and kidnapped me."

Detective Powell wrote furiously in a notepad as she spoke. Meanwhile, Detective Calvente kept her hand around the play button of a tape recorder.

"So you think it wasn't premeditated?" Powell asked.

"I think he only wanted to talk—at first," Melissa cautioned. "But after you guys seemed to be pointing the finger at me, he thought maybe it would be best to let the search die down. He couldn't bring himself to kill me, so he was allowing me to starve to death. I assume he thought he'd ultimately get rid of my body and pin the murder on me."

Detective Calvente exchanged a guilty look with her

partner. Their quickness to *blame the spouse* had contributed to her entrapment. "So, why bring Tonya into things?" Calvente asked.

A sharp pang in her temple kept Melissa from answering. She rubbed the side of her head with the hand unattached to a suspended plastic bag and glanced at the needle that the nurse had placed in her arm before slipping from the room.

"I gather that Tonya had been involved with my husband at some point." Melissa cleared her throat. "Perhaps under duress."

Detective Calvente's eyebrow rose.

"You would have to speak to her or her bartender friend Micky, who informed me of my husband's indiscretions. Apparently, Nate had been using his position to influence young actresses to begin romantic relationships." Melissa smirked at the last part. *Romantic* was such a poor euphemism for fornication.

"So he thought Tonya..." Detective Powell trailed off. He knew what she was getting at, Melissa thought, but he wanted her to say it.

"My guess is he thought Tonya could be blamed for the murder. She was a pissed, abandoned lover, or something. I don't know. I gather that he thought the police might not believe that I'd left my child."

Detective Powell looked up from his notes, clearly wanting some sort of justification. Why would Philip believe that the police wouldn't accept Nate's wife had killed him?

"Imani never thought I was guilty," Melissa said. "He knew she'd keep harassing you about my innocence until you looked deeper. He wanted an excuse that his wife would accept."

As she finished her answer, Melissa spied a shadow in the doorjamb. Imani stood in the hallway. Melissa saw her hair first, curls turned frizzy by the events of the past twenty-four hours. A flash of bronze skin followed. Imani's expression registered moments later.

If Melissa had researched an image for bittersweet, she would have found her friend's face. Imani wore a smile, happy to see her alive and well. But there was so much pain behind it.

Melissa raised her good arm and motioned for Imani to come closer. Tentatively, her friend crossed the threshold. Detective Calvente glared at Imani over her shoulder. Detective Powell raised his pen over his notepad.

"Do you think she ever suspected what Philip did?" he asked.

Melissa stared at the door and Imani's big brown eyes, filling with tears. "No," she said, more certain than ever. "My best friend saved me as soon as she figured it out."

The detectives seemed satisfied by the answer. They retreated toward the exit, giving room for Imani to enter. She tentatively approached the side of Melissa's bed, perhaps unsure whether it was too early for visitors.

"How are you?" she asked.

Melissa raised the hand with the IV. "Better now that I'm drinking."

Imani smiled. The situation was too serious to laugh. "I'm so sorry. I swear I didn't know."

Melissa reached out with her good hand and grabbed her friend's palm. "I know you didn't."

Imani's eyes welled. Melissa watched her tears fall for a moment before Imani wiped them away and turned her attention to the hovering detectives. "What will happen now?"

Detective Calvente awkwardly smoothed the button-down covering her chest. "Philip will have to answer for what he's done."

Imani pressed her hand to her heart, as if she could stop it from shattering by holding it tight enough. Her bottom lip quivered. But as she made eye contact with Melissa, it stopped. "I'm so sorry," she said again.

Melissa caught Detective Calvente's sideways glance at her friend, as if she was expecting her to admit to something. "You didn't know," Melissa emphasized.

"I should have figured it out sooner." Imani looked at the ceiling, blinking away tears. "I guess I've only ever seen one part of Philip, or maybe I only allowed myself to see one part of him. It was like he was this ink blot on a folded paper, and I assumed that the side out of view matched what was in front of me. But it didn't. And I never opened it up, you know?"

As Nate's wife, Melissa knew exactly what her friend meant. Love wasn't blind, but it involved blinders. She'd seen Nate as the debonair director whom all women wanted long after his appeal had faded, and he'd begun using his influence to force himself on unwilling girls. She'd kept courting his attention as if he'd still been the artistic genius she'd married.

A sob escaped Imani's pressed lips. Melissa continued clutching her hand. They'd both been in the dark about their husbands. Now their spouses were gone—one dead, one destined for prison. But they were alive. Together, they would find the light.

CHAPTER FORTY-SEVEN

TONYA

SIX MONTHS LATER

No more secrets. Tonya mentally repeated her new motto as she watched Layla twist the fine threads of the friendship bracelet on her wrist. Her daughter's nervous fidget was the only sign of the momentousness of what they were about to do—what Tonya was poised to give up.

She reached out to Layla's head and tucked a clump of wavy hair behind her ear. Sunlight glinted on the copper strands in Layla's blond mane, reminding Tonya of the sea at dawn when water took on the sky's red and gold hues. In the past couple of months, the sun had also added freckles to her kid's nose, which was finally unmasked thanks to Layla's twelfth birthday and the vaccines that were now widely available for anyone of middle-school age and up.

A glance around the park revealed how the world was transitioning out of the worst of the pandemic. Adults and older children were reveling in their maskless freedom. They turned their faces to the sky and seemed to fill their chests with river-scented air. They sat on the grass beneath the

Brooklyn Bridge within arm's reach of one another, confident that the shots for which they'd all scoured the internet and waited in lines spanning city blocks would prevent them from contracting anything deadly or debilitating, if not from contracting the virus completely.

Young children could not yet enjoy such liberties. Tonya watched a pair of elementary schoolers sprint through the park, the bottom halves of their faces covered in rainbow paper masks. Despite the gear, there seemed to be a new lightness about these kids. They grasped the handles of playground equipment without looking over their shoulders for parents with a waiting bottle of hand sanitizer. New Yorkers, always a devil-may-care bunch, had returned to their former state, accepting the danger that accompanied regularly interacting with strangers.

The hopeful atmosphere made Tonya feel even more certain about her decision to come clean. Though she was by no means well-off, she'd managed to keep a roof over her and Layla's heads using her unemployment checks—though that roof had been in a basement Bushwick apartment nearly an hour away from Layla's school. Her new restaurant job and the salary bump she'd negotiated due to the shortage of returning hospitality workers would give her a cushion as she and her daughter—hopefully—moved into a place closer to Brooklyn Heights.

Tonya felt her daughter stiffen beside her. She followed Layla's gaze to see Rick entering the park. He appeared tan and handsome, which Tonya was surprisingly thankful for. Layla looked like her father's side of the family. It was better for her daughter not to fear what that meant.

"Is that him?" Layla whispered.

"Get behind me," Tonya answered.

Once Layla was hidden, Tonya raised her hand to wave Rick over. The movement stretched the deep scar on her side, making the wound itch and throb. Still, she kept her hand up. The Rick Redsell she knew was a liar and a coward; she needed him to come to her before he spied Layla and ran down the street.

Rick's brow rose as he noticed her signaling. He strode over, all swagger and expensive clothing, no doubt ready to bully her about remaining silent a bit longer for the apartment down payment. Tonya braced herself for his reaction when he realized that she couldn't be bought anymore. Blackmailing Nate to fund a scholarship for Layla had provided the tie to his murder that had nearly gotten her killed. She was done selling her silence.

As Rick drew within a foot's distance, Tonya stepped to the side, revealing her daughter. Her ex's dropped jaw advertised that he knew exactly who he was looking at. Layla had the hair color that he'd probably possessed as a child. She had his eyes. Even the shape of their faces was similar, though Layla had the younger, feminine version.

"Rick Redsell, please meet Layla Sayre, your daughter," Tonya said.

His focus shifted from Layla's to Tonya's face. Though he didn't speak, Tonya could read his thoughts from the intensity of his stare. Did she know how much he stood to lose by her revealing his identity? Did she know what she'd lose?

"Nearly dying helped me gain perspective on my life, and who I was helping and hurting with my secrets," she explained. "Layla deserves to know who her father is, and you should pay child support—on the books. Everything needs to be aboveboard."

"I—"

Tonya held up a hand, not wanting him to say anything that could potentially devastate her child. "I understand how this changes things, and it's fine. We only want what you're legally required to provide. I won't keep quiet anymore. It's not fair to Layla or your ex. It's not even fair to you because you're missing out on this wonderful person standing right in front of you. And I think, if you give her a chance, you'll find that knowing her is worth so much more than keeping any secret."

She met Rick's hard stare with one of her own, one filled with what Tonya had come to understand about herself. She was more than a victim who manipulated men after the fact to regain some sort of equal footing. She was a fighter. Though she'd been gravely injured, she'd fought to be heard in that dark room banging on the pipes. She'd battled to rebuild her and Layla's life in a different neighborhood on very little money while struggling to physically recover. She'd pushed and shoved her way into a new job that would pay enough to support her and her daughter. And she would fight Rick for what he owed her. More than that, she would win.

Rick seemed to sense her new resolve. He nodded solemnly and turned his attention to Layla. Her body was trembling with anticipation. Tonya could see the emotions in the shaking hand that Layla extended in front of her.

"Nice to meet you," she said.

Rick smiled. "Hi, Layla. I'm sorry it's taken me so long."

CHAPTER FORTY-EIGHT

OKSANA

The guilty verdict was a foregone conclusion. Oksana knew from snippets of conversation overheard while gathering empty wineglasses in sitting rooms or wiping down kitchen counters as homeowners chatted on the phone. Brooklyn Heights' potential jury pool had already decided what word to scrawl on their ballots. Philip Banks had misappropriated Nate Walker's investment in his spinoff restaurant by directing it toward the rent for the larger establishment. Confronted with that fact—and an inevitable lawsuit—he'd freaked out and killed his famous director friend, robbing the world of the movies that the man might one day create.

Oksana hadn't known the killer's motive when she'd moved that empty bottle of Black Bushmills onto Nate's desk, but she'd suspected the man involved. As she sat in her favorite chair in the living room of her Sheepshead Bay apartment, the *New York Post* open to the metro section folded on her lap, she thought about all the bottles of

Black Bushmills that she'd taken to the recycling bin over the years while working for the Banks family.

Philip's excuse for letting her go at the beginning of the pandemic never made sense to Oksana. A guy who worked in a restaurant kitchen, interacting with a full staff and the occasional patron, wouldn't worry about catching anything from the masked cleaning lady who tidied up while everyone was at school or in the office. She'd reasoned that Philip couldn't afford her anymore.

Just like she'd guessed that he'd been drinking with Nate and something had gone south. In all the time that she'd cleaned for both families, she'd only ever seen Philip's favorite whiskey at the Walkers' residence after a visit from the Banks brood, which she'd inevitably hear about from either Imani's or Melissa's attempts at casual conversation the following day. *Oh, you were at the Walkers' place this morning? We were there the prior night. Hope we didn't make too much of a mess.* Or *sorry for all the glasses downstairs. We had the Bankses over for a nightcap.*

As Oksana looked at the paper in her lap, she felt some pride in the role she'd played in solving the case. She could never have accused Philip publicly without risking all her clients in the neighborhood. But she'd made sure to include the liquor in the photograph, figuring that some mutual friend of the Bankses and Walkers might make the connection. According to the article, seeing the whiskey had led Imani to accuse her husband. So Oksana had ultimately done her part.

She felt a little bad about that too. Philip had testified that Nate had drunkenly waved a gun at him. Oksana knew from living through battles that there were only two acceptable responses when a firearm was aimed at your chest: raise your arms and hope for the best or fight like hell to kill the other guy before he got you. The chef had been a marine. He was never going to choose the first option.

Oksana put the paper on her bedside table and stood from the chair. Sunlight poured through her window, advertising the ninety-degree temperatures melting new parts of the pavement. Kids were biking down the street in tank tops, letting their full faces tan. She thought of the chef's wife and his children. Did that woman wish she'd let him choke on the peanut oil? Oksana wondered. Was Imani regretting having directed the paramedics to where he'd fallen or pointing them to his EpiPen in the kitchen?

Now Philip's wife would have to deal with the fact that he still existed—but in prison. Even if by some miracle the man got off on self-defense for Nate's murder, he would still serve time for kidnapping the guy's wife and attempting to kill both her and the waitress. From the coverage, Oksana was guessing he'd serve at least twenty years. Perhaps more.

If it were her, she'd have left him to die. But the chef's wife had been a therapist. Probably, she was the forgiving type. The kind of person who would rationalize and make excuses, who'd avoid confronting who she'd really married.

Oksana chuckled to herself. People incapable of deep darkness didn't recognize it in others. They were like deer befriending wolves, unable to spot the difference in the teeth. Fortunately, she didn't have that problem. Life had taught her exactly where to look.

ACKNOWLEDGMENTS

I chose to include the present pandemic as the backdrop of this book because I think it is forever intertwined with our future. Even after the worst passes, going through this time will have fundamentally changed the calculus about what is important for many of us. COVID-19 has forced a reevaluation of our responsibilities to ourselves, our families, and one another. It has required a reckoning about what support systems societies require and what jobs are grossly undervalued. For some of us, it has heightened our appreciation for family and friendships. For others, it has crystallized how compatible, or incompatible, we are with those closest to us.

This book is set in the pandemic because our lives have been set in a pandemic. And it would not have been possible without the efforts of so many who are fighting to keep us healthy and safe while simultaneously struggling to preserve our way of life. Thank you to all the medical personnel on the front lines. Thank you to medical researchers, like my brother, James Holahan, who help study and test vaccines with the goal of saving lives and getting us back to life as we knew it. Thank you to the scientists who have dedicated their lives to discovering cures. Thank you to those who fund that research. Thank you, as well, to all the essential workers who risked their lives so that society could continue to function. Thank you to the technology workers who changed corporate operations in short order to keep so many of us employed.

A great big thank-you to my family: my wonderful husband, Brett Honneus, and my daughters, Elleanor and Olivia. I love you all so much. Being quarantined with you, and the somewhat guilty joy that I've felt having this time with you three, is a testament to what amazing people you all are.

Thank you to my mom, Angela Holahan, and my father, Jay Holahan, for their love and support. Thank you to my sister, Tara Williams, her husband, Trey Williams, and my nephews, Miles and Hudson, for being such a big part of our lives and always there for us.

Thank you to my friends and extended family for your love and support. Missing you guys during the worst of the pandemic reminded me how much I rely on your wit, counsel, conversation, and company. I love you all!

Thank you to my wonderful editor, Alex Logan, who always makes my books better—not to mention regularly saves me from embarrassing myself with silly errors or quips that aren't as clever on the page as they seem in my head. Thank you to my lovely agent, Paula Munier, who keeps me working.

Thanks be to God, who I see in so many acts of human kindness, compassion, and love.

Last, thank you to all the loved ones lost during this time, from coronavirus and otherwise. We may not have had the ceremonies that you deserved, but you will remain forever in our hearts.

ABOUT THE AUTHOR

Cate Holahan is a *USA Today* bestselling author of psychological and domestic suspense novels. Her books have been an alternate selection of the *Good Morning America* Book Club (*Her Three Lives*), a *Kirkus* Best Book of the Year (*The Widower's Wife*), an official selection for the Book of the Month Club (*Lies She Told*), and have received multiple starred reviews. A biracial Jamaican and Irish American writer, she is a member of Crime Writers of Color, Sisters in Crime, and the Authors Guild. She lives in New Jersey with her husband, two daughters, and food-obsessed dog.

You can learn more at:
   CateHolahan.com
   Twitter @CateHolahan
   Facebook.com/CateHolahan